NO INTUITION

The Fiona McCullum Story

LYNDA IHENACHO

Britain's Next
BESTSELLER

First published in 2021 by:
Britain's Next Bestseller
An imprint of
Live It Ventures LTD

126 Kirkleatham Lane, Redcar. Cleveland.
TS10 5DD

www.bnbsbooks.co.uk
@BNBSbooks
Cover design: Lynda Ihenacho

Printed in the U.K

'Finding yourself' is not really how it works.

You aren't a ten dollar bill in last winter's coat pocket.

You are also not lost: Your true self is right there, buried under cultural conditioning, other people's opinions, and inaccurate conclusions you drew as a kid that became your beliefs about who you are.

'Finding yourself' is actually returning to yourself.

An unlearning, an excavation, a remembering who you were before the world got its hands on you."

~ Emily McDowell~

Prologue

W inters in England were always freezing and crisp, a time when the sun would only grace us with its presence for a few hours of the day.

Today was no exception.

A bitterly icy overcast of cold air had enveloped the sky, as I sat in the business lounge at Heathrow international Airport, eagerly waiting for an update on my flight. It hardly ever snowed in London, but of course, the heavens had decided to open up the weekend I was due to fly to Chicago. I was embarking on a new start and a new life. I looked at the announcement board and saw my flight was one of many being delayed due to bad weather. Just my luck, I thought to myself.

In hindsight, perhaps I should have taken that as a sign not to leave, to walk straight out of the airport and go back to my family in Fulham, South West London, England. But on that very day, I decided nothing was going to stop my thirst for adventure. I was young, free, and single, and there was no better time than the present to take risks, to see the world, and to make new choices. The decision to move to Chicago wasn't one I had taken lightly, as I had toyed with the idea of perhaps moving to somewhere a little more exotic.

Southeast Asia was always on top of my list, a bucket list objective that was the new fad amongst my peers. The idea of travelling to the far south sounded rather fearless, but the logistics were much too difficult for an inexperienced traveler, such as myself. Moving somewhere like Asia would mean that I would have to obtain a work visa to stay in the country. And there was the difficulty I could face - trying to get a job without at least some basic understanding of the language.

After some research and advice from friends, the least challenging choice for me was to go to America. I had been born in Wisconsin, in the United States of America by mere chance, while my mother was on a work trip. She was seven months pregnant at the time. She was attending an accounting conference as a guest speaker when she suddenly took ill. As a result of this, she was put on bed rest and classed as a flight risk, spending two months in America until I was born. We returned back to England soon after my birth, but being an American citizen by birth, meant that I could live and work there freely if I chose to.

This was a perk that would always make my older sister, Sarah, a little envious. I stood almost a foot taller than her, at five foot eight, something which I despised while I was growing up, towering over everyone in my class wasn't always seen as a good thing. But now, having come of age, it made me stand out for all the right reasons. To some, I was the tall, slender brunette with brown eyes, and the not quite Kate Moss model looks. Still, for me, all I ever saw when I looked in the mirror was an ivory-toned pallid and skinny girl, not yet grown into herself, lacking the curves of womanhood and the maturity to call one's self a woman.

So, at 25, having finished my MBA and wanting to hit the ground running concerning future career prospects, I decided to pack up and find my true calling in life. Working in the financial world seemed so enticing to me, the buzz, the adrenaline, and the allure. I had seen my older sister finish her MBA, get married, and become a housewife. Some life! That wasn't going to be me. I wanted to break free from the monotony of London life. The inertia of my life was starting to stifle me, and I needed a fresh start. I craved for a little something to jolt me out of the monotony that had become my daily routine. The never-ending lunches, parties, and events, all seemed like an endless performance; a sensationalised version of life, which would inevitably lead to a dull existence if I stayed.

London was a great city to grow up in, especially coming from a very English middle-class background, with parents who were both born and raised there. The city had its charm, but it was tainted with the sullying of the disillusioned go-getting daydreamers looking for a quick buck. It was a metropolitan city full of culture, a fast-paced mixture of energy and diversity. One could acquire opportunities at one path and be faced with pitfalls at the other end that could make or break you in a flash. I called it the 'Hollywood' of England, and it attracted both the lonely and lovers combined. A place where love existed not in the realms of reality, but in the palms of the technologically elite, who could do nothing else but swipe left or right to acquire a sense of belonging.

Somehow, I felt at odds in this place of diversity; even

with all it had to offer, I still strived for more, more challenge, more opportunities, more love, just more.

My parents had spent most of their youth working in the city for big financial firms and had built a good living from it. My mother was a very independent woman who had made a career for herself in accountancy and had met my father during an office Christmas party. In her day, she was a force to be reckoned with. Her ambition was to climb up the career ladder, as high as possible, to break through the invisible glass ceiling, which kept men and women apart on the career scale.

My father had worked for a rival firm as an Investment Manager. He was the youngest Investment Manager his firm had ever hired. At twenty-six, he was leading a team of twelve senior analysts. He was on his way to becoming one of the youngest CFOs in London's financial hub. They had dated for a few months and, like something out of a modern-day fairytale, were married within seven months of meeting.

To this day, I always think that the story of how they met, fell in love, and got married was too ambitious to be true. They stuck to this version and regaled both myself and my sister, Sarah, over and over again. Whether the story holds is not one I can confirm nor refute. This is what motivated my sister and me to achieve the same level of longing concerning matters of the heart.

For as long as I can remember, I always wanted to be successful in life, to have a stable career, fall in love with an amazing man and pretty much follow in the footsteps of my parents; so when my older sister informed us that she was not going to pursue a career at all and that she just wanted to start a family with her husband and pretty much become a housewife, I was somewhat disappointed in her lack of ambition. Her idea of happiness was to have a family and nurture her children. Although she had studied hard, she somehow had decided somewhere along the way that having an esteemed career wasn't necessarily the path to happiness. She couldn't imagine herself working a twelve-hour day, just to come home and repeat it all over again. To her, that was a charade, a distraction from what life had to offer. She craved the family life, and that's what mattered the most.

I, on the other hand, didn't subscribe to this philosophy. My parents worked hard, juggling their careers, and a happy household. They highlighted there was no need to choose between ambition and family life when you could have both.

Looking back now, I was so ignorant and ill-advised. I had so much to learn, and who knew that a few years down the line I would be yearning for what my sister had and that I would long for life just like hers; a happy home, loving husband and beautiful children. Something in me wanted to fly the nest, to seek adventures far afield, to see pastures much greener than those on my side of the fence.

I looked at my watch, my flight was supposed to be scheduled for departure at 3 pm, it was now 6.30 pm, and I had no idea how long I would have to wait. I searched through my handbag, looking for something to amuse me, or at least something to pass the time with and finally settled for my cell phone.

I pulled it out and started to scroll through my phone book. Who should I call? Who would entertain me for a few minutes? "Hello Mom, you never guess where I am" there was a slight pause, and I could hear my mother cooking in the background. She always made a big meal at the weekends, and we would all come together as a family to share the events of our week with some good food and good wine.

"Um- you couldn't have reached Chicago already? I hope you're not calling me from the flight? You know how dangerous the signals can be to the engine and the pilot's radio and the…" She was rattling on as usual.

"Mother," I interrupted. "Jeez, give me a minute to answer," I scolded.

This was our usual routine. I would tell her something, and she would always cling on to something negative that could potentially happen. I once tried to surprise her with a weekend trip to Scotland and had suggested that we fly there. After about fifteen minutes of her incessant dissection of how the engine could fail if a flock of birds flew directly into the engine, I retreated and settled for the train journey instead.

"No, I'm still at Heathrow, the stupid snow is causing a delay. I didn't realise a little bit of snow, and we get this much drama."

I could hear her laughing in the background, and I knew what she was going to say.

"This is the UK, Fiona, a little snow, and everything gets grounded. You know, it's not too late to come back, my darling. We will welcome you back with open arms. Why do you have to go all the way to America? Couldn't you have just settled for Manchester or something close? You know I hear that Leicester is a good city and very modern, you would like it there. Isn't it freezing in Chicago anyway, and don't they all carry guns?"

My mother was a very rational woman, but she did worry a lot. In hindsight, I wish I had taken her up on her offer to go back home. At least I would be close to the people who genuinely loved me. I had no idea what would befall me almost four thousand miles away. I couldn't have believed it if someone had told me how the next part of my life would pan out.

It is a well-known saying that foresight is better than hindsight; if I had paid attention, perhaps I would have saved myself from the pain and anguish to come.

Part I

Chapter One

I put on my red leather gloves as I shut the front door to the apartment I was staying in.

It was Friday afternoon in February, and I had decided to go for a walk, to break from the monotony of the day. I had been in Chicago for almost two months. I had found an affordable apartment near the 'Loop,' the city's official downtown area, on West Harrison Street. I wanted to be near the financial district, so I could be available for interviews if and when they materialised.

It was a cold crisp afternoon, and although I was from London, the weather in Chicago was a different kind of cold... or perhaps I felt it more, being so far away from home, and unsheltered from the shadow of isolation.

As I walked through La Salle Street, best known as Chicago's Wall Street, I was impressed by its grand infrastructure and architecture. I walked past The Chicago Board of Trade, the old Continental Bank Building, and the Federal Reserve, in awe of all that was before me. I had walked this loop weekly for the past two months, and every time, I had imagined myself as a top executive, working in one of those impressive buildings.

I had been applying for jobs online since arriving in town and combined with my father's professional contacts in London, I was of the mindset that my job search would be fruitful, yet, nothing had come to fruition. I needed to be patient. It would happen. There was no plan B.

I could always go back home, there was still that, but that would almost feel like defeat.

As I walked through downtown for what seemed like the hundredth time, I noticed how people busied their way through life, bumping into each other, yet maintaining a courtesy that was implied. I envied them, those lucky people, people with lucrative jobs, and the high executives in their big fancy excessively furnished offices. I craved what they had, and I was starting to become tired of wandering around town with no clear direction. This was my melting point, I had to break the cycle of unproductively before it broke me, and I had to achieve success in its fullest.

The laws of attraction state that, what you desire, attract, and focus on will eventually come to pass. This was my daily mantra. I would sit for hours on end and imagine where I wanted to be in life. A timeline of events would see me as a successful businesswoman, matched with a dashing, successful man, who would sweep me off my feet. The setting would always be somewhere picturesque, alongside a grandiose house with a white picket fence, beautiful rare pedigree dogs, and of course, the two beautiful children.

This was my version of the American/British dream; a manifestation of unrealistic ideals; set by the cinematic experiences of a young teenage girl and thinking that the world was a safe and beautiful place.

The problem now was that, fast forward a decade or

so, this romanticised version of reality wasn't always attainable. For me to become more attuned with the real world, the paradigm should have shifted within me; to one which didn't see the female as somewhat reliant on the man. However, instead of a shift in my ideology, those fairy tales, and delusions, devoid of pragmatism, had become ever more so magnified and normalised by my own parents' real-life fairy tale.

That night, disappointed by the universe's lack of alignment and conformity to my plans, I returned to my apartment to map out an idea on how I would improve my job search. I decided that I needed to refocus on networking to try and meet people who could help me achieve my goals. I had seen many of my friends back home find jobs quickly, through job networking websites and career events. As such, if they could do it, so could I.

Nothing was holding me back from achieving all aspects of my plan.

STEP ONE: FIND A LUCRATIVE JOB.

STEP TWO: GRAB A KNIGHT IN SHINING ARMOUR.

⊏⊐

The very next day, I was revved up and full of determination.

I registered on every job website, signed up to every career networking event within a fifty-mile radius, and to make things interesting, even signed up to dating sites for financially minded people. I figured I might as well kill two birds with one stone and appease my mother's need to match me with what she deemed as eligible bachelors.

My very first networking event occurred a couple of weeks later. It was a business start-up group at a trendy bar in Chinatown, only about a fifteen-minute cab ride from where I was staying. I am not sure why I attended. I wasn't looking to start my own business, not right anyway, but I figured I would meet some like-minded people who could lead me in the right direction. It turns out that a lot of people who attend these Start-up seminars are people also looking to catch a break.

Disappointed, and with no leads, I left the seminar with nothing to show for it but a free lunch. Over the next few weeks, I attended at least a couple more dozen seminars, events, lunches, entrepreneurial socials, as they were called. Still, not a lot came from my efforts.

I was heartbroken and was running out of reserves. I didn't want to call home asking for financial support, as this would taint the whole' finding myself experience.' I tried to make it on my own and prove to my sister that you really could have it all. On my way home from another soul-destroying networking event, I decided to go to one of the bookshops dotted around downtown to see if I could pick up one of those self-help books.

As I stood in the self-help section, I recognised a guy from one of the networking events I had been to previously. He was standing in the geography section, which was just a few yards from where I was. I wasn't sure if he had seen me yet, and I wasn't about to make myself seen, but as I tried to make my way out of the store discreetly, his eyes met mine. He immediately glinted recognition and started to wave. I hesitated, and I deliberated whether to stay or flee the scene. Still, before I even had time to make a move, he walked right straight up to me and stuck his hand out, gesturing to shake my hand.

"Hi… erm…" He searched for my name, but his memory failed him.

I hadn't introduced myself at the networking event; which made our exchange a little uncomfortable. We stood face to face, grinning at each other, searching for words that would help to evade a momentary awkwardness. I shook his hand and decided to put him out of his misery.

"Fiona," I interjected, much to his relief.

"Yes… Fiona, Hi. I thought I recognised you from way over there. I was trying to place you. Didn't we meet at the investor's event a few weeks back?"

He looked at me curiously, waiting for my response.

I smiled, indicating that I knew him.

"It was such a good event, wasn't it? I think I can perhaps now go out and invest in something, you know, make myself some millions," I replied sarcastically.

He laughed, noting the sarcasm. He had a warm and friendly face, and as he laughed, I noticed his piercing blue eyes, which sparkled in the light, giving him an almost angelic appearance. Although he had an unobtrusive demeanour about him, I just really wasn't really in the mood to chat, and perhaps at first, my body language gave this away. I had been dealt with so much rejection lately that small talk was just not on the list, especially with someone who I had met at a boring conference. But, something about his aura, his smile perhaps, made me stay and engage in pleasantries, much to my surprise.

"Yes, I don't think we were properly introduced, though, so forgive me, but…" I said with a slight awkwardness, knowing that I had no idea what his name was.

He laughed again, recognising my obliviousness. "It's Christian; my name is Christian Gayle."

I smiled, subconsciously mirroring his movements.

"So, Fiona, are you an avid reader? I do love a good book myself; in fact, I wanted to pick something up about Mexico. They have such a rich and diverse culture there, and I want to know more about its history."

He rambled on for quite some time about Mexican

people and Mexican culture, their history, and their plight. When he finally paused, I was aware I had stopped listening and hadn't quite caught the end of his sentence. I looked at him and smiled, and I think he was waiting for a response to his comment, so I continued to smile and nod.

There was a brief silence, and I guessed it was my cue to speak, but I said nothing. I had already been swept away by my habit of daydreaming, a pattern deeply rooted in my anxiety and fuelled by my inability to make progress on any of my plans.

He shuffled his feet nervously and cleared his throat, a charming trait, I thought.

"So, Fiona, I better pay for this, but here's my card. If you're attending anymore networking events, do give me a call, it may be something I would also like to attend. I am currently trying to venture out into a new career, or perhaps get in on some investments, and I need ideas on what's next. Here's all this talk of disruptive technology being the thing to watch out for, you know. Crypto this, crypto that."

This part of the conversation drew in my interest, and I wished I had paid more attention. He was looking for a new career, I was looking to start one, so maybe he could be of some use.

I smiled and finally broke my silence. "Erm, I am just looking for a job in Investment banking, and figured it was a good idea to attend some events and meet like-minded people."

I went on to tell him about the move from London and how I had envisioned things would be, but of course, finding a job was proving to be fruitless. We talked some more and exchanged stories about other events we had been to, and after a few minutes, he looked at his watch and scrunched up his face.

"Oh, shoot! Well, Fiona, it's been a pleasure, I would love to stay and chat, but I do have to go. The wife will send out a search party for me if I don't hurry back. Ever since we started trying for a baby again, she's had me under lock and key. Hey, but give me your details, and I will have a look around my firm and see if we have any openings for you. It's a slow month with the stock market being so volatile, so everyone is on panic mode, but, for sure, I will see what I can do."

That was like music to my ears.

I handed him a business card. On it, were my contact details. It was essential to have a business card when attending networking events, as it made one seem some-what, more professional, or so I thought. So, a few weeks back, I had about a thousand cards printed out and had been handing them out arbitrarily at the networking events. It hadn't listed a job title on it, but on it was printed, along with my contact details - *MBA Graduate, CFA, ACCA-Professional seeking new opportunities.*

He grabbed the business card from me swiftly, and before I had a chance to speak again, he was gone in a flash. As he bolted for the exit, I noticed that he did not take the time to look at the business card, but instead, it looked as though he crumbled it up and stuffed it in the back pocket of his jeans. That small minuscule gesture squashed any hopes I had. It now appeared that the entire conversation had been pointless.

He was just a stranger, exchanging pleasantries, for the sake of passing the time.

Any illusions I had garnered from the ten-minute conversation that he might somehow provide some useful leads, were just grand delusions, fuelled by his need to appear harmonious.

In other words, he wasn't going to 'see what he could

do.' He was just friendly. I decided I wasn't going to buy a book after all; no self-help advice was going to soothe and inspire me. I decided a better option would be going back to the apartment and hiding under the duvet with a glass of wine.

I would try to drink my sorrows away and reflect on the past few weeks and how askew things had gone.

▭

M y cell phone rang, just as soon as I started to run a hot bath. Just my luck!

"Hello my love, how are you, is it a good time?"

I loved the familiar voice of my mother. She always had this gift for calling when I was feeling low. It was almost as though she knew that I needed a pick me up. No matter how low I was feeling, I could always rely on my mother to perks things up. I didn't reply, and I think she could tell by my lack of response, that something was not quite right.

"No job yet love?" she said, empathetically, waiting for my response. I wanted to lie and tell her that I had been offered a job, for fear that she would be devastated that after months, I still was no closer to realising my dream. She had always been the one who would patiently sit with me and listen in on my plans for world domination, albeit on a smaller scale, of course.

"Hey, Ma. Nah- still trying." I tried to sound nonchalant. "I went to another seminar today. It was interesting. I got some more business cards from a few hiring managers, so I'll be firing away some emails tonight."

I could almost hear the desperation in my voice and hoped she would be none the wiser. A little white lie, I thought.

"Oh, don't worry, dear, any day now, any day. Are you sure you don't want your father to see if he can ask around, might ease things for you, or you could just come home, we miss you so much?"

Those words should have been comforting for me, but instead of noticing the kindness in her gesture, it irritated me slightly.

"Mom, I got this. I'm good. I'm pretty sure I'll get something soon-I have a good lead on a position at a firm near downtown, so any day now really. A businessman I met at a conference is sending me some openings and contacts for me to take my pick."

I was embellishing the truth. I didn't have a lead. I had zilch, and yet, I couldn't face the disappointment that would weigh heavily on my mother. It would be too burdensome for me to carry. I was supposed to be the success story, the high flyer, the tycoon of the McCullum family, the one who wouldn't settle for domestic life, and so, I just couldn't tell the truth.

Focus on your mantra, Fiona. What you focus on will eventually materialise.

"Ok my dear, well, give us a call next week and update us on everything, let us know how you're getting on, we do worry, and you're all alone out there, no boyfriend, no job…"

As if I didn't already know this, like a dagger to the heart, her kind words struck profoundly.

"Okeydokey, mom, no worries. Will do."

We spoke for a few minutes more, and mother filled me on the goings-on back home in London. The usual stuff, Sarah and her husband had started to try for a baby, mother and father had started another house project - rebuilding the conservatory or something alike. All the normalcy of home life, which stirred up my emotions and made me feel slightly homesick.

That night, I cried myself to sleep. I wanted my life in Chicago to begin. I wanted to feel some sort of control over my future, which I had so eagerly elected to leave behind, all but two months ago. I couldn't bear the loneliness, the not knowing, the isolation of being so far from anyone I knew or loved.

I went to bed, having decided that if I hadn't found a job by the end of the month, I would return home and hope for no lasting repercussions for my failure.

More so, I hoped no one would mock me for having flown the nest, only to return with nothing to show for it.

Chapter Two

As it turns out, fate has a way of pulling you back up when you have just about reached your lowest point.

What we focus on will eventually become a reality.

It was a Thursday afternoon, towards the end of April. I'd just about lost hope of finding a job and had started to get my things ready to return to London when my cell phone rang.

"Eh, good afternoon. Is this Ms Fiona?"

I didn't recognise the voice. It was a woman with a Spanish accent. I trawled through my brain to see if I could figure out who it was, but I didn't know any Spanish people, so I drew a blank.

"Yes, this is Fiona," I replied.

"Good afternoon Ms Fiona, please hold the line."

I thought to myself, who in god's name could this be? There were a few seconds pause, and then a man came on the line.

"Good Afternoon, Fiona, this is James. James Foyler."

I didn't say anything and waited for him to continue with his introductions.

"I got your number from an ex-colleague and friend of mine, Christian Gayle. We used to work at Abtint Investments," he continued.

My mind was a complete blank, as I tried to place the name, Christian Gayle. Still, my lack of enthusiasm had reached its lowest and had sapped any rational, cerebral intellect.

"Hello, are you there?" He cleared this throat, waiting for my response.

I searched my mind, willing for a spark, and then it came to me. Christian Gayle from the bookshop! The same person who had provoked me into going home to consume an entire bottle of red wine on an empty stomach.

"He says you're in the market and looking for a new job…" There was a brief silence, and it hit me that I hadn't yet spoken.

I was shocked, more so that the guy had kept my business card.

Admittedly, it had to be a prank call. My sister, Sarah, was surely up to this. I'd told my mother about the chance encounter with Christian at the bookshop, or 'conference' as I had put it to her. Of course, mother had spilled to Sarah.

"Fiona?"

I was jolted back into reality at the sound of my name. I cleared my throat, wiped the beads of sweat from my brow, and finally spoke.

"Hi. Good afternoon, Mr Foyler. Sorry, yes, I know Christian. We met, not too long ago. Yes, I am looking, I mean, I am exploring avenues."

I couldn't structure an intelligible sentence. I was ruining it; I was letting my nerves get the better of me.

"I'm looking for a role, something in Investment banking. Thank you for calling. Did you say you worked with Christian?" I replied in the most elegant voice I could summon to try to hide my nerves and excitement.

"Yes, we used to, I work at Du Greys Investments now, downtown and please call me James. I would very much like to get you in and talk a bit more about your profile. I can see you have an MBA, CFA. All quite impressive, so come in and let's get acquainted and see if we have a role for you. I mean, it depends on your level of experience, of course, but let's meet up first, and then we can take it from there."

I wanted to scream. I could pinch myself. Who was this guy? He sounded significant and influential. Could this be my chance? Could that chance encounter with a stranger in a bookstore lead to my lucky break?

"Of course, I would be ever so delighted to come and meet you. I can email over my resume in the meantime, and we can discuss it when I come down."

I was still using my most beautiful middle-class voice, so I too could sound important. I didn't want to come across as desperate – even though I was.

"Ok great, email that over and why don't you come over to my office on Monday morning, and we can take this further."

He gave me his contact details and office location and then wished me a good afternoon. I pressed the end button on my cell phone and sat in silence for a few minutes. I wanted to digest what had just happened.

Although it wasn't an actual job offer, it sounded very promising.

I couldn't believe I had dismissed Christian. People do

surprise you, and perhaps I shouldn't have judged his actions so definitively. I didn't know whether to call home and tell my mother the news. What would be the point? She would already assume I had secured a job offer, and if nothing transpired out of this in the end, she would be so disappointed.

I decided to leave it until I knew more.

F or the next two days, I did nothing other than work on perking up my resume.

My business experience was lacking. Other than the couple of placements I had done during my degree and MBA, and some part-time work with my father's associates, there was nothing. It was challenging to fill out the mandatory two pages that one is expected to have on a resume. As this was my only real opportunity to showcase myself, I was going to be damned if I was to let it go to waste.

Once I had drafted a nicely worded bio on my laptop, I attached the newly perked up resume. I hit the send key on my computer, and in an instant, my resume was gone. Mr Foyler would get to work on Monday, power up his laptop, and there it would be, lying in his mailbox. I couldn't wait for the weekend to be over. It would be tortuous, not knowing whether my resume would be good enough for his firm.

As I turned around to walk over to the kitchen to make myself a coffee, I suddenly heard a ping on my laptop. I moved in closer to the screen and lo and behold, there in bold black font, was an email from James Foyler. He had replied instantly. I pressed the open button on the email and read the words out loud.

"Hi Fiona, great. Thanks for sending this over. Looks

promising. I'll have a thorough look at it. See you at 9 a.m. on Monday. Have a good one."

The words' looks promising' literally made my stomach do summersaults.

This had to be my break.

———

S unday crawled as I waited for the day to pass.
    I shopped at Walmart for the basics - bread, milk, eggs, and veggies. I couldn't get the email response out of my mind. 'Looks promising.'

Mr. Foyler had given me some much-needed hope. I went home early and cooked myself a hearty meal, a mini celebratory token of my looming success. As I sat down to eat, the phone rang. I looked at the screen, but I didn't recognise the number. I hardly knew anyone in town, so it was a rarity to receive a local phone call. I clicked the answer button hesitantly, half expecting it to be a cold caller.

"Hi Fiona, it's Christian, from the bookstore. How's it going?

"Hi Christian," I chuckled, excitedly. "I'm so glad you called. You'll never guess what?"

He could sense the excitement in my voice and immediately cut me off.

"I think I can. Did James give you a call? Ha-ha, he did, didn't he?"

I smiled. "Yes! Indeed. You pulled some strings, didn't you?"

He laughed. "Not at all. He is an old friend and owes me a favour anyway, plus I told him you were beautiful, keen, and enthusiastic."

I didn't respond. I was quite taken aback by his choice

of words. What did being attractive have to do with any of this?

"Hey, don't get me wrong, Fiona, your business card says it all - you're highly educated, but James will help you, and if he gets to look at a pretty face as well, isn't that a bonus? Besides, I knew that if I told him you were attractive, he would for sure give you a chance for a meeting."

I eased up, urging myself to relax. Men will be men, right?

"Ha-ha, thanks for the compliment... I think. I AM excited to meet with him. Do you know what type of work he has potentially? For me?"

James hadn't promised me anything, yet, I was jumping ahead.

"I just told him you were a high flyer, attending all these seminars, highly qualified, beautiful young woman, very keen and ambitious. Enough said, right? The full package. Don't get me wrong, I'm not hitting on you, I'm happily married. James will see your talent, I'm sure. Just do your best when you meet him. He is a very straight-talking guy. Very professional, so just be yourself, and I'm sure you will be fine. I saw you speak at the seminar. You were eloquent, so as long as you do the same again, I can honestly say I can see no reason he wouldn't offer you something. It all depends on what position you are willing to start from."

I was utterly elated. I'd made a great impression on Christian and was potentially being invited for an interview.

"I'm so grateful Christian. I will surely do my best. Let's just see how it goes first. I don't want to count my chickens."

He laughed.

We spoke for another ten minutes or so about other

seminars he had been to. It turned out he wasn't getting much luck with his new business ideas. He wasn't desperate as he had a good job, but I guess he wanted more. He asked me about my aspirations and even veered towards family life and plans. I think I probably said too much, but it was nice to have somebody to talk to, other than family.

That night, I ate, practiced for my interview, and laid out my freshly dry-cleaned pinstriped navy skirt suit on the sofa, which I had brought from London. I picked out a pair of black court shoes, to go with it, skin coloured stockings, and a white silk shirt. I deliberated whether to go for black stockings but decided it would make me look too frumpy.

For the most part, I still wanted to look nice, as well as corporate, besides my skirt was the obligatory mid-length, which was required to indicate a level of class and professionalism. I was sure I read that somewhere before. I wanted to look the part so that James could perhaps picture me like the investment executive I wanted to be.

After getting my outfit ready, I crawled into bed, excited, but with an uneasiness building in the pit of my stomach. It was as though I was about to embark on something ominous. To distract me from this, I decided to re-read my resume over and over again, and before I knew it, I was fast asleep.

I stirred in bed and suddenly jolted. I searched for my cell phone, which was usually under my pillow or placed on the bedside table, but it was nowhere to be seen. I jumped out of bed and switched on the Television. The news reporter was saying something about the opening of the stock market - it was either up or down, or perhaps sideways; none of it made sense to me anyway. To me, the stock market was illogical by design, but for the sake of being part of this exclusive club, I indulged in keeping au fait of all things business-like.

I looked at the clock at the bottom of the reporter's storyboard. 8:02 a.m.!

I had overslept, and my alarm had failed to go off.

An omen, I thought, but quickly dismissed it. I scrambled into the bathroom, splashed some cold water on my face, brushed my teeth, and pulled my hair back into a tight bun.

With only a few minutes to spare, I quickly slapped on some makeup, got dressed, and headed straight for the door.

It was raining outside, of course, omen number two. I hailed a taxi, and luckily one stopped straight away. There was some early morning traffic, so I arrived at the James building at 8:56 a.m. I over tipped the cab driver, who had, on my instruction, driven speedily, to make sure that I wasn't late. I was so frantic, and I am sure I looked a mess, but I didn't let that thought distract me.

Usually, before a meeting or interview, I would always go into the bathroom and reapply my makeup, making sure everything was in place, but not today. I would turn up in front of James, rosy-cheeked, and a mess. Everything about that morning had been in disarray, so far. It was as if the planets had aligned themselves in such a way to stop me from making it into the Du Greys offices for the meeting.

I didn't believe in signs, or omens, though I spent a lot of time thinking about them. I did, however, believe in serendipity and destiny. I wasn't going to let a broken alarm clock dictate my future.

"Good Morning, I have a 9 o'clock with James Foyler?" I said to the receptionist on the 16th floor, in an almost curious manner.

She looked at me and paused. "Take a seat, he hasn't arrived yet, but I will let you know when he comes in."

I knew the accent. It belonged to the Spanish lady who had phoned me from James' office a few days ago.

"Ok thanks, do you… could… can you please tell me where the washroom is?"

I was a rambling mess, nervous and petrified that I would somehow mess this up. I hadn't had a good night's sleep; vivid dreams had taken over my subconscious, filling my dreamlike state with nightmares that the interview would go awry. How would I face James if I couldn't even manage to hold a sentence with his receptionist?

The receptionist smiled. I think she could tell I was nervous. "It's ok, James is not that scary," she said. "Down the hall to the right."

I thanked her and walked off in the direction of the washroom to straighten myself up and get some perspective. I lowered the toilet lid and sat down and took a deep breath.

Fiona, pull yourself together.

I searched in my bag. Maybe I could call my mother but realised I didn't have my cell phone. I couldn't find it that morning and had decided to leave home without it, perhaps another bad omen, as I had never once left the house without it. My mother always said it was as though I was stuck to it like glue. I wished I had spent a couple of extra seconds looking for it, as I needed to hear the calming voice of my mother.

I sighed and stood up, straightened up my skirt, and walked over to the washbasin. At least I had some time to re-do my makeup. Every cloud has a silver lining, as they say. I looked at my watch, 9:12 a.m. Time for some action!

I walked back to the reception, and the receptionist gave me a nod to signal that James had arrived.

"You can go in now, Ms McCullum. He is ready for you."

I smiled and walked over to the big wooden ornate door that was the door to his office. I stood in front of it for a few seconds, intimidated by its grandness, and taking a deep breath, I stepped forward, reaching out to knock on the door.

I was immediately stunned, as the door flung open, leaving me standing there, fist clenched mid-air, in an almost soldier-like stance.

In front of me, in all his glory, was James Foyler in the flesh.

"Good morning Ms Fiona, I hope I can call you that… Come, come on in. You'll have to excuse my tardiness, but I was stuck in some early morning traffic, you know, the usual."

I wasn't expecting an apology for his lateness; after all, he was doing me a favour. He gestured for me to take a seat, and as I walked over to sit, I couldn't help forming an impression straightaway. He wasn't exactly what I had pictured. The James on the phone sounded very tall, exotic, dark-skinned, and handsome, possibly early thirties.

The man in front of me couldn't have been any more than 5 foot 10, dark brownish hair, Caucasian, late thirties, possibly early forties, with a hint of grey in his hair. He had a pleasant-looking face and looked as though he was in good shape, but nothing like I had imagined.

Note to self; this wasn't important, I was here for a job, what he looked like, should not have even been on the agenda.

His office was grandiose and was almost the size of the apartment I had rented on West Harrison Street. He had a huge modern style glass desk, covered in all kinds of important-looking documents. It was big enough for four people to lay flat, comfortably. Next to it, in the corner, was an L-shaped cream sofa and a black coffee table, complemented nicely with a costly looking espresso machine.

This whole place wreaked of affluence. The floors had a marble effect, and there was a greyish rug placed strategically in the centre of the room. It was all very ultra-modern and state-of-the-art.

"Thank you, Mr Foyler, thank you for taking the time out to see me, it's ever so…" but before I could finish expressing my gratitude, he cut me off.

"No, no, call me James, Mr Foyler is my late father, and no need to thank me, it's my pleasure. Nothing pleases me more than seeing and helping fresh young talent, much like yourself, so you see, the pleasure is all mine."

I walked over to his desk, sat down, and crossed my legs, and as I did this, I noticed his gaze shift quickly to my legs and then away again. He walked back over to his desk and sat down.

"So, Fiona, I see you've got an MBA and a little bit of work experience in banking, that's all very impressive."

In all earnest, I had embellished a little on my resume. A little white lie never hurt, and I technically wasn't lying. I had completed some work experience, albeit unpaid and compulsory.

"I can also see you're a qualified accountant, and you have completed the CFA, you bookworm! So, which is it then, do you want to be an Investment banker or an Accountant?" He smirked. "I mean, I have spaces for both, you just need to tell me which direction this meeting should go in."

He hadn't yet let me speak, and unless I interrupted, he seemed quite happy to go on talking at me.

"To be honest, I set my sights on investment banking,

but I did the ACCA as a fall-back in case I couldn't find anything decent in investment banking."

He rolled his eyes and slammed his hands on the desk, animatedly. "Fiona! There is nothing better than being an Investment banker. Get that accounting bull out of your mind. Let's work on getting you into banking, if you want a dynamic career with the possibility to make millions, then stop all the nonsense. I can't stand it when people come in here, with no vision. Come on. You only have one shot in life. I'm dangling a low hanging fruit here."

His curtness dumbfounded me. On some level, I guessed his position gave him a free warrant to be as overbearing as he liked. Or maybe he was just arrogant. It was hard to tell. Either way, he didn't hold back.

"So, go on, tell me about yourself, hopes, dreams, achievement, the whole lot. Let's get acquainted."

Odd choice of words, 'acquainted.' It wasn't the sort of language one would expect to be tossed around at a business meeting, or perhaps I was reading too much into it. As I spoke, responding to his numerous questions, he seemed to hold his gaze on me, as though he was lost in thought. I wasn't even sure he was still listening to what I was saying, his face, lacking any expression.

He lowered his gaze to my lips, which of course, made me a little self-conscious, and by default, I licked them, only then realising that this perhaps, wasn't the right thing to do in that situation.

He sensed my unease and immediately adjusted his gaze. Still, soon after, his eyes were wandering again, falling to the lower half of my body. I convinced myself this was part of my imagination; that he might have just been scrutinising my outfit to assess whether I had dressed professionally.

When he finally spoke again, he went on to ask questions about what I did in my spare time, and if I was married or had any family or dependents, all very odd questions to have in an interview. I chose to assume that these divergences, in his interview technique, were all but cultural differences. The English don't tend to pry too much into other people's business in such a way and often shy away from less conservative topics. Still, perhaps in America, this was just the norm. His manner of speaking was quite captivating, and about half an hour into it, I, too, found myself asking him questions about his personal life.

The conversation flowed, and although much of it was centred on our personal lives, I seemed to feel at ease with him. He was charming and curious. His confidence was captivating. He drew me in with his words, and after about forty-five minutes, the conversation finally veered back towards business. He told me that he had a mid-level position opening for an Investment Associate.

I would have to work very hard to become technically proficient. He thought a junior position would be too unexciting for someone of my caliber, albeit that I did not have any investment banking experience.

He seemed to have some belief in my abilities, notwithstanding that he had no practical evidence to substantiate my aptitude. Perhaps, he did so, out of charity, compassion, or intrigue.

We talked about compensation and benefits; all topics that should have probably been discussed with Human Resources. I had the feeling that he was reluctant to end the meeting. He finally described how the role would pan out, and that I would be required to take some exams, which didn't scare me but excited me. At the end of the meeting, he shook my hand, and perhaps it was my imagination, but it felt as though the handshake lingered for a few seconds longer than it should have. Nevertheless, I left his office in high spirits, securing a lucrative job that was scheduled to start in two weeks.

I was going to be an investment associate. It sounded so professional, so incredible. I hadn't even been asked for a second interview - he had made up his mind on the first meeting.

I couldn't believe my luck. Just when everything seemed to be about to fall apart, I was finally getting a chance. I phoned home that night and told mother the good news. I could hear the relief in her voice. It was important to me that my family was proud of me.

It had all worked out in the end, and most of all, this meant that I could stay in Chicago!

As happy as I was, my stomach failed to settle, and with it, lingered that ominous feeling that had presented itself the night before.

Perhaps it was all the excitement. Maybe it was fear, or probably my body was trying to tell me something, but for now, I wanted to hang on to the happy feeling.

Anything else would just have to wait.

Chapter Three

A ll week long, I shopped for work outfits, an attempt to ensure that I looked good in the office and maintain a mixture of corporate and chic.

I wanted to be taken seriously, to be part of the new club, an elite group of Investment bankers, destined for world domination, splendour, and power. I wanted to amplify my chances of, one day, meeting the love of my life randomly in a coffee shop or perhaps while out on my lunch break.

On Friday, before I was due to start my new job at Du Greys Investments, I decided to have just one more shot at the shops, any excuse to get out of the apartment. I walked around the stores and purchased several matching skirts and trouser suits. I wanted to cover all the basics. I decided since I was already out, I would call Christian and tell him the good news.

He probably already knew, but I figured I would be courteous enough to call him and thank him nonetheless. After all, he was the one who recommended me to James Foyler.

I dialled his number, and he picked up immediately after the first ring.

"Hello, Fiona!" He sounded excited. "Good to hear from you. I figured I would hear from you sooner or later."

I laughed, realising he already knew about my job offer.

"Hi, Christian. Yup, I guess you already know then?" I replied. "Yup, I do. James called me last week. He said you blew him away, some stuff about how eloquent you were. I think it's the British accent. It gets to us Americans, you know."

I laughed again.

"He also mentioned that he liked your charisma, and he hoped you would be all you promised to be."

It felt great to get some good feedback. I was now in the mood for a celebration.

"Where are you now, Christian? Do you want to grab a quick coffee? If you can take a quick break, I can get a cab downtown to you, it's on my way home anyway."

I wanted to make more of an effort with Christian, given that he had done me such great favour. I could buy him a coffee, and he could tell me more about my new boss to be.

"I have a few meetings, but why don't you come to the Chet and Cher and join me for a few drinks. I am meeting a few friends there after work, so come along, and you can buy me a drink – 6.30 p.m.?"

I agreed. "Ok, sure, why not. I am shopping now, so I will meet you there.

Looking forward to it, Christian, see ya later."

I was making a new friend, getting a new job, all in the space of a few weeks. Life was good. I walked around town for a little longer to pass the time, and I bought a few more items, but once my feet started to ache, I decided to grab a cab and head for Chet and Cher. It was a new hip bar downtown, and from the outside, it looked like one of those trendy bars you would find back home in Soho, London. I'd walked past it occasionally during my many strolls downtown and had always wanted to go in but could never build up the courage to walk into a bar on my own.

I looked at my watch, and it was only 6.02 p.m., so I hailed down a taxi and told the driver I wasn't in any rush so he could take his time. I sat in the taxi, and as we drove off, I realised I wasn't dressed for a trendy bar, with an ensemble of white jeans, red sneakers, and a black cardigan, I looked more country than stylish. I rummaged through my handbag and found a hairbrush and some red lipstick. I layered on the lipstick, using it as a rouge for my cheeks, and unfastened a couple of buttons on my cardigan, transforming my look from country girl to an understated, naughty and nice look.

The taxi pulled in front of Chet and Cher at 6.25 p.m., and I was reluctant to jump out. I was a bit early, as I feared. I walked into the bar and had a quick look around, not expecting to see anyone I knew, of course, but lo and behold, a friendly face waving frantically at me.

Although I was a few minutes early, Christian and his friends had beat me to the bar. I was ever so relieved, as the thought of sitting at the bar on my own frightened me.

"Hey pretty! You came, you look lovely. Come, come and meet everyone."

He moved in closer to me and kissed me on the cheek.

"Hi Christian, I'm so glad you're early. I was worried I would turn up, and there would be no shows."

He smiled and gestured me over to his table, where I was met by a few of his friends. They all seemed lovely and friendly and introduced themselves. I suddenly felt a light tap on my shoulder, and as I turned around, there he was, James in the flesh… again.

"Hey Fiona, fancy seeing you here, work doesn't start until Monday, and you're already out schmoozing with some of the competition."

He smiled, and I could tell he was pleased to see me. There was something about the way that he looked at me that excited me, but also made me a little weary. I couldn't quite put my finger on it. Perhaps it was his unapologetic gaze combined with self-importance that created a concoction of masculinity and mystery. On some level, he didn't seem like the atypical boss, albeit he bore all the typical traits of one. There was just another level to him, which I could sense, even though we had only had the two brief encounters so far.

"Ooh, my god. Hi James, lovely to see you… no, no, Christian took pity on me and invited me out to have a drink with his friends that's all. What are you doing here?"

I looked at him quizzically, as though I too was wondering why he was out with Christian at 6.30 p.m., on a Friday evening. Didn't managers work all hours until dawn? Weren't they always tied to their desks, or some last-minute meeting or something?

"Ha-ha, no chance, it's the weekend now. I believe in working hard and playing hard, something you will soon come to find out once you get going at the firm."

I liked the sound of this. I was determined and possessed a good work ethic, but I also loved the fact that he thought that having a work-life balance was important. I had seen both my parents work so hard, not always remembering to factor in the play part, albeit that they did their best. James's work hard/play hard philosophy negated my sister's antiquated views that one could not hold down a job and have time for other things in life.

Everything I was discovering about James seemed to point to the fact that, as a boss, we would have no problem getting on.

<hr>

T he evening flew by quickly as I immersed myself into this new lifestyle.

Christian and James's friends were easy enough to talk to. Some were professional friends of theirs, while others where just part of their social circle of the elite, the rich, and a wealthy selection of Chicago's venture capitalists. I exchanged numbers with some of the women intending to meet up during the week for coffee. They all seemed very chic, with an air of confidence that money couldn't buy, or perhaps could. I envied them. I wanted to emulate their every move, their fashion sense, and their sense of well-being. They were perfect in every way - the epitome of high class with an aristocratic quality. They seemed to converse so effortlessly, with such ease and fluidity, as though they had no insecurities or hardships.

I tried my best to fit in, to imitate their pattern of speech, their body language, and to keep up the rhythm of the conversation. This was perhaps was lesson one, in how to discourse with intellect and grace.

For most of the evening, I had hardly spent much time talking to James, albeit that this was a concerted effort on my part. I'd tried to avoid too much one-to-one time with him, as I thought it best to maintain a professional stance with him. By 10 p.m., I was ready to head home when James walked over to me and asked if I wanted a refill. I looked at my glass, which was empty and pointed at my watch, signalling to him that I was already on my way out.

"Nonsense, I have barely even gotten the chance to speak to you tonight, Fiona. Is this how it is going to be in the office? Come on, loosen up, it's after hours."

I looked at him and smiled. I didn't want to offend him by refusing his offer to buy me a drink. Still, I had already had four glasses, and my limit was usually three. I bit my lip and then titled my head to the side as if to say that I had given in and that he had won. He smiled and winked at me, then signalled to the waitress for a repeat order of drinks.

"So, Fiona, Monday, eh! Are you excited? Scared? Have you done some reading on the company? I mean, no pressure, but you're going to have to hit the ground rolling."

I frowned, a little irritated to be getting a grilling, so late at night, but before I could speak, he grabbed my shoulder with both hands, smiling.

"I'm pulling your legs. This is a work-free zone. No talk of work, or anything remotely stressful." I felt relieved at this; he had a sense of humour; this was good.

"You got me there, but jokes aside, I'm excited to start and can't wait to meet the team and get some work done. I've been so idle for too long now, and my brain is starting to frazzle. I almost lost hope of finding anything. I almost had to go back to England. If not for you, James... I dunno, you're my saviour."

I had said too much. The alcohol had loosened my tongue. It had made me allude to the fact that I was desperate for this job, and worst of all, I had commended him as being my saviour. He looked at me with slight smugness, but beneath that, there was empathy and sincerity in his eyes.

I had never really noticed the blueness of his eyes, piercing with specs of grey and hazel. They reminded me of the spherical glass marbles that I played with as a child.

James's eyes were just as beautiful as the insides of these marbles, so captivating that I found myself gazing helplessly into them, lost in them, unable to rouse from their hypnotism.

"Fiona!" A loud voice shouted across the room. "You need a top-up? We are doing shots, whoop whoop."

I was bolted right back to reality at the sound of Christian's voice.

"Shots... you want one?"

I had overstretched my alcohol tolerance, but the peer pressure was kicking in, which meant that I needed to be cool, to be someone who could keep up with the guys.

"Hey man, can't you see I'm having a conversation with the young lady, for crying out loud, what the hell?"

James yelled over to Christian. James looked annoyed, the blueness in his eyes suddenly a little colder.

He turned to Christian again. "What's your problem, Chris?"

Christian looked a little stunned, as though he had just been told off by his older brother. I had never been in a room with both James and Christian before. From that small exchange between both, I could tell that Christian had respect for James, or perhaps it was fear. Either way, James oozed confidence. This confidence was quite attractive, something which I guess he used to his advantage. He was no Adonis, but it was apparent that he kept in good shape, and I couldn't help notice his biceps through his shirt as he removed his jacket.

"Sorry, Fiona, as we were saying," James continued. "I'm so sorry you have been having a hard time. I guess things will change now, going forward. There are lots of people at the firm who you will get to meet, and you'll soon forget the first difficult few months here in town. Believe me; there is no way you can be bored in Chicago, no way!"

We talked for a few more minutes, and although the alcohol was intoxicating, he remained courteous and well-mannered. Once I had finished my drink, I announced that I was leaving and that I would grab a cab, as my apartment was only a few blocks away. He seemed almost offended that I was going and insisted that he take me home.

"Chicago may be a friendly place, but sometimes, it's too friendly for a lady, especially one who is new in town, if you know what I mean. Not at this time of night anyway," he said.

Acknowledging his advice and realising that I was probably a little tipsy, I gladly accepted. We said our good-byes to everyone and grabbed a taxi outside the bar. James gave instructions to the driver that there would be two stops, and off we went.

———

The drive back to mine was made in complete silence, which was quite a contrast to how talkative he had been at the bar.

As we pulled up to my street, he turned and looked at me. He didn't say anything, and for a slight second, I was convinced there was something there. He just smiled and stuck his hand out, and as I shook it, I felt a little bit of magnetism towards him, not something I wanted to admit to myself.

"Have a good night, Fiona, and be at work 9 a.m. sharpish."

I smiled awkwardly "Yes, of course, you can count on it." As I got out of the taxi and walked over to my door, I could feel his eyes on me. I opened the front door and turned around and waved.

He winked at me, and the taxi drove off.

Chapter Four

First day jitters are usual, I kept on saying to myself, as I made my way to my desk.

The Du Greys offices had been much grander than I had noticed on my first visit to see James. I had only really seen the reception area and his office, so on my first day at work, when he had offered to take me on the tour of the whole floor, I was quite taken aback by its size. Although the whole office was situated on just one floor, there were sections, sub-sections, nooks and crannies, elevations and lowering, all spread generously across what would be about twelve thousand square feet of open plan office space.

Each team was divided into sub units, with a team leader or a division head, who often sat amidst his or her team. No one had a separate office, apart for James of course, and one other senior partner.

My desk was positioned next to a window, which was perfect, as I had the pleasure of being encompassed by Chicago's amazing views, in its finest, right from the 16th floor. Everything on my desk was ultra-modern, verging on futuristic, even down to my desktop and workstation, high spec and money well spent. James introduced me to my team, which consisted of six people. I had no direct reports and everyone in the team reported to James, who doubled as a division head and Chief Investment officer. There were three females in my team, myself included, and three men, a good balance, I thought. Each person in my team, took turns to introduce themselves, describing what they did on a day to day basis.

I instantly took a liking to two of my colleagues, Julia, and Demetri, basically because they were the only two who made constant eye contact and who seemed down to earth and not too snooty. Julia was an attractive twenty-some-thing year old blond, possibly bleached, five foot nine, with green eyes. She carried herself with such grace and elegance but on some level, it seemed as though she was on the spectrum of being an extroverted-introverted person, which made her seem a little unhinged.

Demetri on the other hand, was the typical geek, slightly overweight, with oversized brown glasses, and hair sleeked back with so much product, that it made his head shine whenever he stood under a light. On balance, everyone seemed friendly enough, albeit that they also looked tremendously busy, and didn't really stop for too long to get acquainted with me. After the introductions, Julia and Demetri walked with me to the break-out area for a coffee, where we had a good long chat about the who's who and who to avoid.

They both seemed eager to get to know me and the feeling was mutual, although I would later find out that James had instructed them to look after me, more like mentors for newbies, or day-care as they would later refer to it as.

Nonetheless, I needed new companions to show me the ropes and get me up to scratch with all things Chicago, as the only people I knew in town at that point were Christian and James.

———

The day flew by so quickly, from endless meet and greets, to meetings and inductions. All very fast paced for day one and by the end of the day, I was truly spent. The office hours seemed quite flexible, some people seemed to stick to the nine to five schedules fervently, while others chose to burn the midnight oil. I was glad that James wasn't the type of boss who cared about clock watching and checking up on our daily movements. He gave his team the freedom and flexibility to manage their work how best they saw fit, if the work was done, then he had no reason to step in.

By my second week at Du Greys, I was already very much immersed into the work life and my surroundings and during those first two weeks, I really hadn't had much contact with James, which I thought was quite odd. The team had a major investment deal which was about to come to fruition, so everyone was extremely busy, and James was constantly in meetings or out of the office.

Most of my training was done with my colleagues, Julia, and Demetri, and I seemed to pick things up fast. My job mainly consisted of booking market trades and placing funds in different investment portals. All very exciting stuff. By week four, I had pretty much had the hang of things and needed very little supervision.

During those first few weeks, I had spent most of my lunch breaks with Julia and Demetri in the break-out area and sometimes we went downstairs to the little café on the corner for lunch. It was nice to have this. It felt like my life was now on track. Occasionally, other team members would join us, but to me, the others seemed a little less friendly, hardly even making conversation with me, constantly making 'In jokes,' and referring to events which I knew nothing of. I would sometimes sense some hostility with other team members, and Julia soon alluded to the fact that there was a running joke going around the floor, that I had been offered the job for my looks and my connections which James.

Of course, the revelation that I was on some level, the office joke, stung a little, but the truth of the matter was that there was some validity to this, but that didn't mean I wasn't working just as hard as anyone else. James had offered me the job knowing full well that I had no prior experience, and perhaps he should have put me at a junior level, but all that didn't matter now, I was here and eager and ready to work, I certainly wasn't going to let their attitude bring me down from cloud nine. As far as I was concerned, I had made it, I had worked hard for it.

O n a Friday morning, a month after I had started working at the firm, James sent round an email to the team for a quick 11 a.m. team meeting, which made everyone on edge.

No one knew what the meeting was about, and there was much speculation in the air, so that by the time the clock struck 11, everyone started to shuffle into the meeting room. James walked into the meeting room, confident looking as ever. He wore a dark blue pinstriped Prada suit, with a crisp white shirt, which had two buttons unfastened, exposing a hint of his tanned and perfectly formed muscular physique. He was effortlessly immaculate, down to his silver Cartier cufflinks and tan Berluti oxford brogues, which probably cost more than my monthly salary. I guess this was the male interpretation of the corporate and chic look.

"Good Morning guys, don't panic, I just wanted to call a meeting to give you some good news on the McDougal deal. They liked our pitch so much that it seems they are willing to let us handle the remaining portfolio, the whole lot, so… well done team. This is really great work."

He continued to speak about the details of the deal and the people who would handle each section. Demetri would be sub team leader, Julia would handle the funds side, John, who was the quietest in the team, and was one of the guys who hadn't yet warmed to me, would oversee the fund valuations. James didn't allocate any specific item to me or the others, but I could tell that it was implied that we would assist whenever it was required.

There was a sudden buzz in the meeting room, as people started to high five each other and mutter amongst themselves. I remained quiet, as I really didn't have much input in the deal, but it was good to see that James showed recognition of hard work to his team.

"On another note," he continued, "I am sure you guys have now got very acquainted with the new starter- Fiona."

I heard someone let out a sigh, clearly in annoyance at James's comment.

"So, let's all go downstairs for team drinks at the end of the day to give her a good welcome to the Du Greys family, and to celebrate the new deal of course, how's that sound? - My treat of course."

I was impressed by his camaraderie with the team, as well as his generosity. He seemed quite the package and displayed a likability that made the team respect him. He was assertive when he needed to be, but also seemed to enjoy picking up the tab without any restraint, which of course helped to boost his appeal.

———

A t about 4.45pm, people in my team began to shuffle out of the office and started to head to the bar downstairs. James walked over to my desk.

"You ready?" he asked as I straightened up my desk.

"Erm, I was just finishing up and I was going to wait until 5 p.m."

James laughed. I could already see that I had said something wrong.

"Fiona, it's the weekend, pack up, let's go, it's your welcome drinks. No point you being late for it."

I smiled and thought to myself, I could certainly get used to this.

"Ok I'll be there in a sec, let me just go and freshen up."

James lowered his eyes to my feet and then back up to my face. "You already look great Fiona, trust me. I don't say that to everyone."

By 5.15pm the whole team was down at the bar. The downstairs bar was a usual hangout spot for end of week drinks, and it helped that the drinks were fairly priced too, as employees of Du Greys got a special promotion on drinks. The bar was full tonight with people from the offices below us. I recognised some faces, but not enough to go over to say hello, besides, I was here with my team, so I was content to stay in our corner of the bar. I was going to try and make small talk with John and see if I could change his opinion of me. I didn't want his personal disdain for me to be contagious, as I had a good thing going with Julia and Demetri, so I was keen on making sure he didn't cloud their judgment.

James appeared out of nowhere and the mood suddenly heightened, as though the main guest had finally arrived. He gestured at the bartender to bring over a couple of bottles of champagne to our table, and it had to the best kind of champagne of course. I liked the way he carried himself, he commanded everyone's attention without even having to try. When he spoke, it almost seemed as though everyone was spellbound by him. In addition to his idiosyncrasies, he had an unusual influence over the women in the office, they would become over-enthusiastic when he was around, and I noticed this, more so, especially with Julia.

On a typical day, Julia was rather ordinary, she would keep to herself, and only engage with others, during coffee or lunch breaks, but when she spoke to James, it seemed to me as though she would put on a mask of a character that was completely different to that which she wore on a day to day basis. She would seem more self-assured, sexual, more deviant with a dash of haughtiness about her that made her stand a few inches taller and sashay as she walked, swinging her hips from side to side, in what could only be described in the style of a peacock. I couldn't quite put my finger on, but it was obvious that she was attracted to him.

As the night went on, everyone seemed to get more and more inebriated as more champagne flowed. I found myself way over my usual limit, so by 11pm, I was completely blurry-eyed and unsteady on my feet. James on the other hand, managed to maintain his composure, he clearly had a stronger stomach and could handle more alcohol, for he still seemed quite sober.

A few people decided to head on to a club, which in

such an intoxicated state, should never have been suggested, but Julia, Demetri and James persuaded me to join them, and off we went in a twenty minute cab ride to a night club on the other side of town. I hadn't had much experience on the club scene, so I was quite excited at being included in the group. We arrived at the club at about 11.45pm, and James insisted on paying our entry fee, but this time, it almost felt a little disingenuous, as though it was his way of stamping his authority on things, and signalling to us and everyone within listening distance, that he was the man in charge. Nonetheless, out of courtesy, I let him pay. We handed in our coats and jackets to the lady in the cloak-room, who looked unperturbed by the fact that everyone in our group looked out of sorts and overdressed for the usual clientele that frequented the club. We then headed straight to the dance floor, eager to get the party started.

The club was spread across two floors, with scantily clad eclectic dancers on platforms, gyrating away, and everyone else dancing as though they were all in a drug induced trance. It all seemed so surreal. There I was, middle class Ms. Fiona, who had never been in a night club, and was always miss sensible with the drinks, suddenly immersed in a different world. I never really ever stayed out past midnight and always had good judgment when it came to things such as this, but this new and improved version of me, was mixing with the cool folk, in this hip world of high class investment bankers, who worked hard and most certainly played hard.

James of course appeared, as usual out of nowhere, with a bartender, who was holding a bottle of Grey goose, some Russian Vodka, and a tray of Jager Bomb shots. I shrieked with excitement. James looked over at me, he smiled and as if he wasn't already charming enough, he pointed his finger at me, in a very Tom cruise style and winked.

After about an hour had passed, Julia was starting to take a turn for the worse, so Demetri decided that he would put her in a cab and re-join us after a few minutes. James however insisted that he should be the one to take her. That really should have been my signal to leave as well, as the others had also somehow disappeared or had got lost in the crowd, but by that point, all sense of reasoning had escaped me, and I was just pumped and not ready for it to end yet. Demetri grabbed Julia and headed for the exit, and with that, James took my hand and started to dance.

He wasn't really the best dancer, but with this kind of music, it really didn't matter. I humoured him and started to shake my hips and wave my hands in the air.

"Are you ok Fiona, having a good time?" he asked.

"Hell yeah, this is amazing James," I slurred.

He moved in closer and grabbed me by the waist as we continued to dance. This was certainly the closest I had ever stood next to him, and perhaps it was a little inappropriate, given that he was my boss. I looked at him encouragingly, commenting on his dance moves. This excited him. He suddenly pulled me closer, to avoid bumping into a highly intoxicated dancer, and our lips almost touched. I blushed, which perhaps might have been construed as a signal that I liked it.

"Fiona, are you alright? That was close. This place is great isn't it, except for the occasional bump here and there. Right?"

He laughed, continuing to dance.

"Yeah, it's pretty cool, I take it you come here a lot then, you seem to know the bartenders, or least, they know you."

He laughed again, hysterically. "Well I guess you can say I'm a regular, I spend a lot of cash in here, so I would be offended if they didn't show me a little respect. Anyway, you too will soon become a regular, just you wait and see. To be honest, it's the music that brings me back here every time, I love to dance, not very well I know, but, you on the other hand, you're an amazing dancer, I really like how you move with me, and it helps that you're pretty hot too- you have it all ."

He smirked. I felt extremely flattered; no one had complimented me in this way, not anyone who mattered anyway.

"I just love working with you, I love having a pretty face to look at in the office, certainly makes the day much easier," he continued.

I didn't know whether to speak, as I wasn't sure what words would come out if I did. He was my boss, and undoubtedly, this conversation was improper, but like with most things, had I misinterpreted his intentions? It was too difficult to decipher, too presumptuous and audacious to make assumptions. I would be ill-advised to think that he thought of me in any other way, than just his colleague, someone way low down the pay-roll; and so, the pragmatist within me chose to dispel any inappropriate thoughts that were floating around my head in my state of insobriety; it was unprofessional and downright misguided.

Suddenly, a sparsely dressed tequila shot lady appeared, in front to us offering us some shots, to which James accepted enthusiastically, and grabbed a couple of shots from her. He pulled out a fifty-dollar bill from his pocket, handed it over to her and signalled that she could keep the change. He then grabbed my hand to try to offer me one of the shots, but I winced, gesturing that there was no way he was going to get me to drink a tequila shot, and before I had time to speak, he drank both shots back swiftly, almost animatedly.

What followed this was then completely unexpected, as I am sure I heard him say the words, "Ahhh, screw it," immediately after drinking the tequila shots. He then, with both hands, grabbed my waist with such fervour, and pushed himself against me, and kissed me.

I couldn't believe what was happening. It hadn't been a figment of my imagination, after all. It was all happening too fast. I didn't know how to respond, so I just kissed him back. The kiss was passionate, alcohol fuelled, and lasted only a few seconds. I blushed, as our lips parted, confused that as to what to do next. I didn't understand why he had kissed me, especially given that Julia literally threw herself at him daily. He could have had her at the blink of an eye, if he wanted to, so, why me?

He suddenly pulled away, and seemed quite embarrassed, rubbing his forehead nervously.

"I am so frigging sorry Fiona. That was totally out of line, I didn't mean to offend you."

I didn't say anything, but instead, the girl inside me, couldn't help but smile. It had been a while since I had been kissed. In fact, the last person to kiss me had been my geeky next-door neighbour, back in London, after I had been dealt an unlucky hand at truth or dare.

It had been a wet, humdrum dribble, of a kiss, that left much to be desired.

This kiss, however, was incredible. A fully formed French kiss, by formula; our tongues had brushed lightly against each other's, savouring, and sampling our taste buds, with just the right amount of moistness to lubricate, interlink and synchronise our lips.

I was glad that I didn't have to ruminate for too long, as at that exact moment, Demetri appeared.

"Hey guys, Julia is in a cab, poor thing. Do you guys want a top up?"

James looked over at me, hinting that it was up to me whether we continued the night. The kiss had certainly been unexpected, but nonetheless, I knew liked it, and perhaps, on some level, I had willed it.

He was a good kisser, and I think the kiss made me realise that perhaps I was a little attracted to him after all.

"Yeah sure," I replied, smiling at James. "I'll have a top up."

Chapter Five

Saturday was a bit of a blur, as I woke up with a pounding headache, feeling slightly nauseated; the after-effects of the Jager Bombs.

I sat up in bed, cradling my pillow, willing it to comfort me. I slowly started to recall the events of the night before, the night club, the flirting, the dancing, the kiss. How could I have been so stupid as to let that happen? How could I have kissed my boss? I went over to the kitchen, made myself an espresso and set myself on the sofa, agonizing over the events and trying to ponder over parts of what I could remember.

I didn't know whether this 'good thing' was going to be a problem. Would he fire me, or should I be a little excited at the prospect of him showing interest in me?

I hadn't been particularly attracted to him, at least not up until the kiss, but there was just something about him that made me gravitate towards him. He had a magnetism about him, which made him just so unashamedly alluring to the opposite sex.

After the kiss and the sudden reappearance of

Demetri, we hardly spoke to each other for the rest of the night. I spent what was left of the night, either looking for the rest of the group, dancing around Demetri, or making conversation with random revel goers. I didn't dare make eye contact with James again until I left the club. Even after hours of sleep, and three cups of espresso later, in full flashback mode, I could not believe my own recollection, and on some level, I felt that I had imagined the whole thing.

I spent most of the morning indoors, in full recovery mode.

I wasn't really used to the heavy drinking, so the whole post-night hangover phenomenon was all too new to me. At about 2 p.m., I was suddenly jolted out of my late afternoon slumber, by a knock on the door. I hadn't been expecting anyone, given that I knew so few people. I opened the door, and there stood a delivery guy with a huge bunch of white Lilies.

"I have a delivery for a Fiona McCullum?"

I stood there in silence, unable to piece together the picture in front of me.

"Ma'am, are you Ms Fiona?" He seemed a little irritated.

I looked at the flowers and then back at him.

"Yes, that's me."

He huffed and then pulled out an electronic device from his messenger bag.

"Please sign here Ma'am."

I did as I was told, and he handed over the flowers and walked off hurriedly. I rolled my eyes and slammed the door. I wasn't familiar with curtness of this kind, so I didn't really appreciate it. I placed the flowers on the coffee table and stared at them.

Back home in London, the idea of someone sending

me flowers would have excited me to no end. Still, here I was, hesitant, suspicious, and slightly apprehensive at such a strange occurrence, strange in the sense that such gestures were never usually directed at me. I didn't dare look at the card. I had a slight suspicion as to who they were from. After minutes of pacing up and down the apartment, I finally took up the courage to read the card.

> Hey Fiona, hope your head is ok this morning. Just a little something to brighten up your day. Hope I wasn't out of line last night…? See you on Monday--- James.

The message wasn't easy to decrypt, and I didn't want to make any assumptions.

I pondered whether to call him and thank him for the flowers or call Christian and tell him what had happened. My head hurt terribly, and in no state to make a decision, I decided to ignore it and go back to bed.

I could wait until Monday, put on a brave face, and face him then.

L ater that afternoon, I decided to go out for a walk, to ease away the remnants of my handover.

The Saturday farmers market seemed like the right choice for a distraction, this had been my new obsession. I particularly enjoyed walking around each stall, taking in the delights and the free samples of cheese and cold meats, which were on offer. Julia had recommended this to me, something I could do on my own without feeling out of place or all alone. I arrived at the market at about 3.45pm, and luckily it was still buzzing with people.

I walked through the market, stopping between each

stall, sometimes making a purchase or two, or just making conversation with the traders. Market traders always had a knack for making people feel at ease, and of course, making people part with their hard cash. I walked past one of the flower stalls, and immediately remembered the flowers James had sent me. At that exact moment, my phone started to ring, and as I looked at the screen, lo' and behold, it was James calling me.

I didn't know what to do.

I stared at my phone, almost too afraid of what was waiting for me on the other end. It rang a couple more times and then stopped.

"Shit," I yelled. I'm not sure if I was annoyed at myself for not answering, or that he would now be expecting me to return his missed call.

"Shit… shit … shit…" The phone suddenly started to ring again, but this time, I didn't hesitate.

"Hi James," I responded too enthusiastically.

"Hey, I got ya, I tried you already, but I didn't leave a voicemail, so I figured I'd call you back and leave one."

His voice was deep and croaky, almost as though he had just woken up.

"No, sorry, I missed it. I'm just out and about, so I didn't hear it ring," I lied. "Thank you for the flowers, it was really nice of you, I wasn't expecting anything like that." I rambled on.

I was nervous, and so to hide this, I continued to fill the space with words. He must have sensed it because he cut me off mid-sentence.

"Fiona, Fiona, don't even mention it, I just figured that I made you drink too much and maybe things got a little out of hand, and well, I just didn't want you to feel uncomfortable or anything. I really did have a good time and hope you did too?"

As I listened to him speak, I could almost sense that he was by no means apologizing, but instead revelling in the events of last night.

"I had a nice time too. My head's still quite sore, but, yes, it was fun. Thanks for taking us out."

I made a point to say 'us,' highlighting the fact that this was a work thing and nothing else.

"So, Fiona, what are you doing this evening? I feel I should continue with the apology, and maybe take you for a bite to eat... just dinner, nothing major. It kills me that I was less of a gentleman, and well, I must make things right, you know, this sort of thing, well... I just need to fix this. Let me buy you dinner, just dinner, that's all."

I didn't respond immediately, hesitating for a second. Would accepting his offer constitute as a date? Would there be another kiss? Would it be wise to start something of this sort with him?

He sensed my apprehension, but he all but shut it down. He was persuasive, almost on the border of demanding and would not take no for an answer, promising to pick me up in a couple of hours. I didn't really appreciate his forcefulness. It was no secret that he was confident, but I figured from his tone, that he was also probably not used to being rejected, so I had no choice but to indulge his ego.

Deep down, I was excited about the whole thing, and it probably wouldn't have taken much persuasion. I also wanted to see what else he had to offer, and perhaps dig deeper in uncovering whether there were feelings involved that had led to him kissing me, or whether it was just the effects of alcohol.

I rushed back to my apartment, not wanting to waste any time. My hair was a mess, and I still looked ashen from my hangover. The whole time I was getting ready for my get-together with James, trying on several outfits and shoes, I kept on deliberating on the specifics of our soon to be encounter. It wasn't a date, he had even said so himself, and yet, I doubted the veracity of this. I couldn't trust that it was a simple, platonic meeting of minds, a friendly meal as a gesture of kindness, an apology for a misguided kiss.

With only a few minutes to spare, I finally picked out a cute little red mid-length dress, and layered it with a black cashmere cardigan, as a token of my blameless modesty.

The doorbell rang at about 7 p.m., just as I had finished layering on a copious amount of mascara.

I looked at myself in the mirror, loathing my outfit choices, and the spider web appearance, which my eyelashes had now taken the form of. It was too late to obsess over it, so, I grabbed my bag and bolted towards the door.

"Wow, you look amazing Fiona." James smiled as I opened the front door.

He stood there, both hands in his pockets, confident as ever. I had been used to seeing him in a suit jacket, so when he arrived in nothing but a light blue shirt and blue denim jeans with brown loafers, I couldn't help but notice how different he looked. He seemed more relaxed, and the informality of his outfit gave him a younger, more attractive appearance. He stepped forward and kissed me on the cheek, a chivalrous formality. I suddenly felt butterflies in my stomach, much like a teenager, being kissed by her teenage crush.

It was inexplicable, I felt as if I had regressed back into my childhood, the giddiness almost overpowering, albeit that my face held an expressionless form, hiding my internal plight.

———

The restaurant was only a fifteen-minute cab drive away, and yet, it was the most painstaking fifteen minutes of awkward conversation about work and other nondescript topics.

I was unashamedly relieved when we finally arrived, jumping out the cab and rushing toward the restaurant, almost tripping over a piece of rock that was carelessly sticking out of the sidewalk. James hadn't noticed my inner turmoil and seemed to be preoccupied with paying the cab driver and deciding on an appropriate tip.

We were greeted by the doorman and shown to our table by a highly spirited Italian maître-d. James had called ahead and requested a corner table, somewhere where we could sit privately, away from any disruption.

As we sat, James whispered something into the maître-d's ear, who then walked off hurriedly, with his hands flapping in excitement.

'What was that all about?" I said and looked at James quizzically.

He smiled, and then winked at me, as though to hint that it was a secret. A few seconds later, the maître-d reappeared with a huge chocolate cupcake, lit with a single candle, coupled with a bottle of champagne.

"What in god's good earth is this for?"

He had apparently organized a surprise for me, as a gesture for having survived my first month at Du Greys.

"I know you've had to hit the ground rolling, and we have literally been in the middle of this big contract, so for you to start at such a time must have been difficult, but

Fiona, you have made such a big impression on the partners - they love that you bring some freshness to the team,
and I'm sure your team members would say the same
thing, right?"

I was in shock and a little confused. I couldn't imagine
that he took all his new employees out for celebratory
dinner and cupcakes. Naturally, I had assumed the dinner
was in aid of the kiss, so all this talk of Du Grey's was
taking the emphasis entirely off what I really wanted to
focus on.

"Wow James, this is too much. Are you serious? This is
for me? I don't get it, I thought…" I paused, not wanting
to sound unappreciative.

I quickly blew out the candle, and we both took a swig
from our champagne glasses. The cupcake looked delicious, so I dipped my finger in it, and scooped up some of
the chocolate icing, only then realizing that I might have
come across as uncouth.

I quickly licked my fingers coyly. James's eyes were
locked on me the whole time, making me self-conscious. I
wasn't a naturally sexual person, and my intentions had
not been to seduce or sexualize this, but I could tell that he
liked the way I licked the icing off my fingers.

"Oh, I'm sorry, would you like some?" I teased him,
trying to lighten the mood. Taking this as a queue to
mirror my playfulness and perhaps endorse my crudeness,
he dipped his finger in the cupcake and scooped up some
of the icing and tasted it.

He kept his eyes locked me, and then playfully, he
wiped the remaining frosting from his fingers unto the tip
of my nose. I giggled, thrilled to witness this side of him
that no one else at Du Greys got to see, a playful, more
spirited James.

"So, about last night, Fiona."

I froze, the giggles turning into a strained and awkward smirk. He continued to speak.

"I know I was out of line, but if truth be told, ever since the minute you walked into my office, I haven't been able to get you off my mind, so when the opportunity arose, and of course the alcohol was flowing, I sort of let myself go with the flow. I guess, what I'm trying to say is, well, sort of an apology, except deep down, I'm not actually sure that I am sorry. It won't happen again though, I can assure you that, strictly professional here on in, Deal?"

I bit my lip, hard, as if making sure that I was still conscious. I felt timid, not knowing how to respond to what seemed like a rhetorical question. He had clearly thought through what to say, throwing me off guard, with the distraction of baked good and his excellent showmanship, and I, like a fool, had been led into a false sense of security. I didn't have a dignified response for him.

Was I supposed to say that I wasn't expecting him to kiss me, but didn't recoil at the fact that he had kissed me? That I secretly enjoyed it, and the longer I had to think about it, the more it roused something within me, that the thought of not having the chance to at least explore it, would be somewhat disappointing? Instead of saying anything that would allude to the thoughts that were spiralling in my head, I just nodded in agreement, and continued to drink the champagne, refusing to let the glass part my lips for fear that he would read the disappointment on my face.

Eventually, the maître-d approached to serve more drinks and to take our order. When we were served the main course, we continued to talk about other conventional topics, anything to avoid talking about the kiss.

We drank copious amounts of champagne, and once

our inhibitions were thinned by the dopamine effect of alcohol, and its ability to act as a social lubricant, I was in full swing, making the rest of the evening, more of a delight than anything else.

A s the night ended, we called a taxi and James insisted that we share. When the driver pulled up to my apartment, I didn't really want the night to end. For lack of a better reason, other than that I was still affected by the champagne and perhaps utter madness had finally prevailed, I invited him up for a nightcap.

I had never really had company in my apartment, so when we were both stood in the lounge area, I suddenly became very conscious of how small the apartment was, or perhaps I was just aware of his presence.

"How do you take your coffee"? I asked him sheepishly.

He sat on the sofa and seemed to make himself comfortable. "Do you have anything a little stronger?"

Shit!

When I invited him up for coffee, I should have realized that coffee never really meant actual coffee! I didn't have any hard liquor, other than half a bottle of red that I had left over from the week before.

"Will a glass of red suffice?" I asked.

"Sure, that'll be fine."

I walked over to the kitchen area to grab a couple of wine glasses, and as I turned around, James was standing right behind me.

He moved in closer, just like he had done the night of the kiss, and grabbed the wine glasses from my hands, placing them carefully on the kitchen worktop. He then took hold of my waist, gently pressing me against the kitchen isle, his eyes locked on my lips, as he slowly brushed the hair from my face, with his fingertips.

I took a deep breath and closed my eyes for a second, in anticipation.

"I know I said I wouldn't do this, but my god, look at you. I am going to kiss you now, and I don't even care if it's wrong. I just… I can't… I must… stop me if you don't want it."

He brushed his fingers lightly against my lips, and then he kissed me softly. He stepped back for a second, as if to gauge my reaction, and in my state of submissiveness, with no hesitation, he kissed me again. This time, he let his tongue slide in, caressing my whole mouth, in an all-encompassing passionate and tantalizing kiss.

His hunger was undeniable, he wanted me, and I, him.

I could feel my body get warmer, as I kissed him. The heat of the moment made my skin tingle with pleasure, creating a glistening layer of perspiration over my rosy cheeks. He kissed my neck, letting his tongue tease me.

I moaned encouragingly, breathing rapidly as I ached for more. He then started to kiss me all over my body, my lips, my chest, every bit, more arousing than the previous. A thirst had taken over him, he was no longer gentle. I could feel the coarseness of his day-old stubble, against my skin, and I liked it; the combination of pain and pleasure.

He ripped open my black cardigan and lifted me on to the kitchen counter. His hands reached under my dress and stroked my thighs. I gasped; it had been a long time since anyone had been this close. He reached under and pulled down my underwear. I could feel his pulse racing, the desire, the excitement.

His hands moved back up between my thighs, feeling my arousal. I had lost myself entirely by this point, and I grabbed hold of his shirt, pulling at it as a blaze of desire emerged from deep within me, aching to erupt.

We toyed with each other in our nakedness, until the foreplay was too much to bear and, as he finally thrust himself into me, I knew things were never going to be the same again.

Chapter Six

So much for his promise that the kiss was just a one-off.

After we had exhausted ourselves, we drifted off to sleep, and in the morning, as he kissed me goodbye, I was relieved that he had not chosen the awkward one-night stand, middle-of-the-night runaway approach.

I laid in bed, now alone, still covered in the perspiration of the two of us, and I couldn't help but muse over the fact that we had just crossed a line that could now never be uncrossed. When you have been intimate with a person, it creates a bond, it connects you to that person on a physical and an emotional level; or perhaps, these are just the illusions of a hopeless romantic.

I knew that it was just sex, but at some point, during the night, I realized that I was very much attracted to him, more so that I wanted to allow myself to admit. It wasn't one-sided; we were both attracted to each, and although this was the act of two consenting adults, on a subconscious and untapped area of my mind, I felt a slight uneasiness lurking, as though I had just done a disservice to myself.

In the light of the morning, however, as the sun shone through the gaps of my Venetian blinds; a prized possession of mine, that I had purchased in an attempt to make my modest bedroom look somewhat elegant; the excitement of now being the centre of something this exhilarating and audacious was overwhelming. I was determined to ride this high for as long as I could.

"Oh shit, Fiona, you don't want to get involved with James, he's… somewhat impulsive. I'm telling you, just be careful. Why did you go and do that, for Christ sake? Relationships with co-workers are also a no-go area, and I know James, he says one thing, but he means another. Just keep your wits about you, that's all I'm saying."

I couldn't help myself, I had to tell someone the titillating details.

I couldn't talk to Julia - she would absolutely hate it, and I couldn't keep it to myself. I was too excited, too confused as to what it meant, and how I was supposed to go on with life as if nothing had happened.

So, after James had left my bedside and I had gathered my thoughts, I called Christian and asked him to meet up for a coffee, so that I could dissect the details of my encounter with James.

On hearing about my escapade, his response was all too cynical and wasn't quite what I had expected. He seemed concerned and didn't share in my excitement. His approach was that of the antagonist, trying hard to dissuade me from pursuing anything further; to nip the whole fiasco in the bud, and put it down to a reckless one-night stand that should never have happened.

"I don't get it? Aren't you two buddies? Why are you trying to put me off? Besides, it was just one night, it's not a big deal- Chillout Christian."

He didn't buy into any of it. He persisted in trying to talk me out of considering James in any capacity other than my boss, to the point that it started to annoy me.

Perhaps he was jealous?

I decided to change the subject, feigning a lack of interest for James; it was just easier to take the easy route out of the conversation and blame it all on the alcohol.

"Fiona, it's not that I am saying he is a bad guy, I'm just saying, keep your wits about you. These kinds of dynamics can be quite tricky. He is your boss remember. What happens if you want a raise or you want to go for a promotion, you will never really know if it's by merit or by some other means- and if people get wind of it, they too will start to talk. Besides, James is a bit of a lady's man, so I don't want you getting mixed up in something you can't handle. As long as you're not going to get too deep in it…"

He laughed, trying to defuse the situation, and sensing my hostility.

We finished off the coffees, and he gave me a ride home - that was to be the end of the topic.

It was not to be mentioned again.

Monday morning started off on a wrong foot. I had overslept and was late to work for the first time. I walked past James's office to get to my desk, and his eye met mine. His face was inexpressive, almost stoical, which stumped me.

Perhaps he was annoyed that I was half an hour late, or maybe he was trying to keep it relaxed and casual.

Whatever the reason was, the fact remained that I was

late, and I had heaps of work to do. I hurried to my desk to meet a sea of angry faces.

"Fiona where the heck…" Julia started off.

"Yes, I know I am late, I overslept. I think the battery on my alarm clock has gone. I'll get you guys the start of day reports ASAP. I'm good, don't worry, I've got this."

I didn't want anyone thinking I was slacking on work as I was still trying desperately to make a good impression.

Later at lunch, I found out the reason for the hostility that I had been greeted with. In the morning, the team had lost one of our major clients to a competitor, so James was in a frenzy. It seemed that whenever this sort of thing happened at work, someone usually got fired, or James would see to it that everyone worked extra hard, which put everyone on edge.

I hadn't spoken to James all day, and I thought it peculiar that the subject of the other night had not been addressed. I couldn't focus on anything other than replaying the details of that night repeatedly.

I decided I would approach him after lunch and submit my daily report to him personally, by hand. This was usually done by the team assistant, but in my exasperated state, I decided that I would purposely wait until she had gone on her lunch break, and causally drop by his office. I would use this as an opportunity to get some closure.

James, of course, beat me to it, and after lunch, I was summoned to his office.

Julia looked concerned when she saw me marching off. She had thought that perhaps I was the one who would be in the firing line.

"Hey Fiona, how are you doing," he spoke softly as I walked into his office.

I stood by the door, waiting to be asked to approach.

He stood up from behind his desk, and walked over to me, smiled, and shut the door behind me, making sure that he looked as nonchalant as possible, so as not to arouse suspicion. As the door shut, he turned to me, and moved closer, so that I was nothing but a few centimetres away from him.

He then suddenly pressed me against the door and kissed me. I was stunned by his boldness, not expecting to carry on with this until we'd had a conversation to define the boundaries or definition of what 'this was.'

"I've been waiting all day to do that. I thought you would have popped in this morning, but then I got the news about the Cheval file, and well, it's been manic all day.'

He moved in closer again and kissed me again, lifting my chin and looking at me straight in the eyes. He seemed so intense, and his every movement was laboured, as though he was trying hard to restrain himself.

"I hope you had a good time the other night?" he asked.

I smiled, still a little stunned and more confused than ever. I didn't really know what to say. Nothing about the way he kissed me, suggested that it was just a one-night stand and yet, I had no cues, no experience in dealing with anything of this sort.

His brashness was presumptuous, almost forceful, but it was this forcefulness, his brazenness and the brevity of his movements that aroused me.

"Oh, like that then?" he asked, sensing my coyness.

He reached under my skirt, gently tugging at my underwear.

I gasped. "We are at work, James, STOP!"

He pulled back abruptly, a look of horror in his eyes, as though he was not really used to being rejected. It seemed as though I had somehow offended him, but then he quickly regained his composure and walked back over to his desk and sat down, gesturing for me to take a seat.

I straightened up my skirt and walked over quickly and sat down.

"I'm sorry Fiona, I don't know what came over me, seeing you like that and then, all of Saturday just coming back to me. Can you blame me?"

I didn't mind that he wanted to ravish me and that I had somehow become the object of someone's desire. I was completely and utterly flattered, but nonetheless, I needed to set some boundaries. The fact that it had happened once did not automatically mean that I was his to be had, even though every fibre in me wanted it.

"James, it's fine, I just meant, what if someone walked in? Christ, can you imagine what they would think, can you imagine the scandal?'

I laughed nervously. "Yes, but that's one of the perks of being the boss, I don't really give a damn what they think. If they don't like it, I can always just fire them."

We both laughed.

He saw that I was a little more relaxed now, so he stood up and walked over to my side of the desk, bent down and grabbed me by the waist and lifted me up onto the desk. He pulled back my hair and kissed me on the neck.

"Fiona, you know you enjoyed the weekend with me, so why stop there. I want to feel every part of you, kiss every bit of your body, and I think you want it too, don't you?"

I felt too coy about responding. I knew he wanted affirmation that I wanted him, just as he wanted me. I didn't know how to be this person, the sort of person who could speak and act so freely, so confidently, so, instead, I smiled and nodded sheepishly.

He sensed that I wasn't going to engage in conversation of the sort, and not wanting to lose momentum, lifted me off the desk again, and carried me over to the sofa in the corner of the room, placing me down gently.

"We shouldn't, someone might walk in, this isn't me James... I can't..."

He bent down and put his hands over my mouth, "Shhhh... Don't say a word, just go with it."

His eyes were deep and dilated, and I could tell that there was nothing I could do but succumb to this. He wanted to let me feel his dominating presence, to let me know he alone was in charge.

"Don't say a word Fiona, just got with it."

I blinked and took a deep breath in, and when I opened my eyes, his pants had already hit the floor. For all my virtues, values and seeming incorruptibility, it was now clear that Monday's had taken on a wholly different meaning.

━━━

T he rest of the month took on the same pattern. We would work hard and then towards the end of the day, I would go to James to submit my reports, and he would ravish me. It almost became a routine, one which was so exciting.

I relished the thought of being wanted by a man of his standing. I enjoyed the danger of our illicit affair, the notion that someone could possibly walk in on us and catch us made it even more alluring, more forbidden, all which made me keep going back for more.

Before I knew it, I was hooked on him, whether it was just the physicality of the whole affair, or whether I was falling for him, I just couldn't tell at that time; all I knew was that I wanted him, all the time. I craved his touch and his kisses. I craved his body in its fullest, devouring me, making me feel womanly in so many ways.

Up until then, I was just a small-time middle-class girl, in a new city, with a great job, and a great boss. Now, here I was, James's new flame. This was the icing on the cake.

It just couldn't get better than this.

A fter about a month of our office delights, we took it a step further, not only were we now making love in the office, we were finding any excuse to meet up during the weekend.

I had never felt anything like this, and James was such an expert. I didn't really have much to compare with to be fair, but at that moment, it was more the excitement than the act that I was hooked on.

One Saturday afternoon, in the middle of summer, James phoned me and asked to take me out on a proper date, something we had not really done since before we had slept together.

The gesture pleased me, as it signalled that perhaps our illicit encounters might somehow now prove to be more than just a casual fling. It indicated that we were moving into that space between casual sex and exclusivity, albeit that from my limited dating experience, this was where murky waters chose to reside and doubt seemed to thrive.

He picked me up at 7 p.m., and we grabbed a cab to the restaurant. We pulled up to a lavish-looking hotel restaurant, in an upscale area of Chicago, somewhere where the more affluent spent their time and money; decadence and flare combined in a bubble, a place for the more opulent and privileged of our society. We were seated swiftly by an overly dressed and polished Maître-de, who, it seemed had been assigned to make sure that we were shown the five-star experience.

James, all too pleased with himself, told me I could order whatever I wanted; that he wanted to spoil me. No expense was too great for the lady who had finally given him a reason to get up in the morning. He said he had never met anyone like me, and that the girls he met in Chicago just didn't fit the bill.

The flattery was insurmountable and somewhat over-whelming, and most importantly, I felt that there was a sincerity in the way he conveyed his intentions. I was trans-fixed by his confidence and valour, laying down his feel-ings; his vulnerability triggering a more profound emotion within me.

I decided at that moment that I would lay my cards down and just go with the flow. I would be whatever he wanted me to be and allow myself to go into this with an open heart and an open mind.

The evening flew by, emotions intertwined with an intoxicating cocktail of aperitifs, flowing uninterruptedly. By 11pm, not wanting the evening to end, James suggested we go back to his place. I had never seen where he lived, nor had I ever been invited back, so naturally I was excited. I would finally be able to piece together a few things; see where he slept every day, how he lived, and what made this man so exciting. I imagined it would be grand and luxurious, but when we pulled up, it just didn't meet my expectations.

It was a tiny unexceptional apartment downtown. One could mistake it for a studio. He made good money and had a high-flying job, so what was he doing living in an apartment no bigger than a studio.

I tried to hide my disappointment, but I just couldn't piece together why someone who was always so generous and lavish when it came to be spending in front of others, chose to live such a modest life.

I decided it didn't matter, maybe he was putting away his money for early retirement or something, after all, just because you have it, doesn't mean you should spend it. I sat down awkwardly on the corner sofa, in what was supposed to be the living room, and tried to make myself feel at ease. The room had a false partition wall to separate the living area from the sleeping area, but it felt too cluttered and small for its purpose.

Sensing my apprehension, James explained that this was his weekend 'pad.' His real place was being redecorated or something along those lines. Alas, it all made sense, and now I could enjoy the rest of the night without any suspicion or derision. It was entirely reasonable for him to have several houses, these sorts of people usually invested heavily in real estate. Hence, it was not strange that he had a weekend getaway place.

The rest of the night took on a similar pattern. We talked, we kissed, we made love, and then we repeated it all over again. I stayed over, and just before we drifted off to sleep, James asked if we could make our relationship official. He didn't want me to date anyone else, and he was sick of sneaking around the office. He would announce it tastefully at work, and hopefully, no one would cause any issues.

It made sense, as if we were going to carry on dating, someone was bound to find out sooner or later, so it would serve better to come from the horse's mouth. Of course, this would mean no more lunchtime escapades in his office, as it would be too crude if everyone knew what we were up to, while we were up to it.

"No more sneaking around sweetheart. I could kiss you in the corridors, and it wouldn't be taboo, I could take you away for the long weekends, and no one would care if we both didn't show up on a Monday. Fiona, don't you worry, I'll take care of you. I mean it. You won't have to worry about a thing here on now. Anything you want, it's yours."

Things were on the up for me. Everything I had dreamed of was finally coming true, and I was so happy to finally be in a place where I could say that I was indeed content.

———

"Oh shit, Sarah! He said he was falling for me," I said to my sister, the next day when I phoned home.

My mother was out at the supermarket picking up some ingredients for a roast dinner, and my father was out golfing with some ex-work colleagues, so I only managed to catch my sister, who was by a stroke of luck, just visiting for Sunday tea. Sarah was ecstatic.

"Well, do you think he will say the L-word?"

I bit my lip. "It never crossed my mind, it's only been a couple of months, slow down."

Sarah was laughing hysterically. She always got ahead of herself. I think she thought that because our parents got married so soon after dating, this sort of good fortune existed for everyone.

"Well, he says he's falling for you right? That's pretty much the same as saying he is falling in love with ya. First comes falling, then comes the real LOVE, then comes marriage." She shrieked.

I pulled the phone away from my ears to shield it from her screeching. This was ridiculous, it was just too soon to be having this sort of conversation.

"Sarah, seriously, like I said, it's too soon, but yeah, I guess so, you never know. I mean, I'm very fond of him too, but love is a long way off. We're just exploring each other at the moment. Who knows where this will go, he may turn out to be a jerk? I don't even know where he actually lives, so, yeah, I think love, that's way off."

She didn't sound convinced, but we agreed to disagree, and I promised to call back later that day so I would get a chance to speak to our parents.

Chapter Seven

When James finally broke the news to the team at work, there were mixed emotions, some people seemed surprised, while others were irritated, although they didn't dare show it.

One of the senior executives gave James a high-five, and there was some heckling going on in the corner amongst some of the younger interns.

Demetri gave James a blank stare and then turned to me and nodded his head mockingly, making sure to check that James hadn't seen this.

He didn't say or do much else on the topic but just carried on as per usual. Julia, on the other hand, looked concerned. It had already been established that she was infatuated with James, so naturally, this was never going to be good news for her.

She came up to me several weeks after the news broke to ask if I was happy dating 'the boss.'

My response was casual, hinting to her that it really wasn't anyone's business and that I didn't really think it was an issue.

Her retort was somewhat strained and hostile.

"You know these office romances never work. You break up, and then you'll have to quit, or worse, he'll fire you."

Her response was undeniably bothersome, and I must have responded impolitely, giving her impetus to launch a counteroffensive.

"I've seen James with lots of chicks, so what makes you think you are so special? I love ya, hun, but men will be men, so don't get your hopes high. He is no different from the rest of them, in fact, I can't count on both hands how many women I've seen him get involved with from this building alone, only for it to go downhill."

Her animosity was unpalatable and abrasive, and what followed was a diatribe of patronizing advice, which was masked by her skilled passive-aggressive tone.

"I bet you'll get a promotion now. The things us women do to get ahead, eh!"

By the time the conversation had ended, so had our friendship, and there onwards, our exchanges at work became limited to small- talk, pleasantries, and discussions about the weather.

A jealous friend is just as dangerous as your worst adversary. I had unwittingly propagated the seeds that would later spawn a bed of thorns in my perfectly trimmed rose garden.

Six months went by so quickly, and we seemed to be in a whirlwind romance.

I had finally been granted the pleasure of staying over at James's house, as opposed to his studio apartment. His house was very grand and ostentatious, an ample amount of space, and too much for someone who lived alone. I had come from a middle-class background and was used to having nice things, but this was just on another level.

The house also came with a housekeeper, in the form of a curvy, twenty-something-year-old female Spaniard, in the name of Maria. She wasn't like a typical housekeeper in any sense of the word, as she seemed to have the authority to choose what type of housework she would do. This meant that she would occasionally cook; but would not clean, and so, there was a weekly cleaner to do the menial tasks.

Maria spoke English to James, but then would pretend she couldn't speak English whenever I was around her.

I immediately took a dislike to her.

She reminded me of the receptionist who I met at my interview with James. That receptionist had long been fired, and I later found out on the grapevine that it was down to some 'misunderstanding' with James.

On my many sleepovers at the house, I would probe James about Maria. Why was she here? Why was she so lazy? Why was she getting paid to do hardly anything?

My incessant inquisitions would always seem to be received poorly; with James indicating that I was displaying a badgering tone, like that of a petulant child, or a typical female who perhaps felt some jealousy towards the other woman due to her God-given assets.

"Why not? She can cook, she's cheap. No brainer really," he would retort, so I could never come straight out with my uneasiness about her for fear of coming across as insecure.

This issue had to be put to bed if I wanted to continue to maintain my dignity and security.

We took our first trip away together, to Paris in late November.

I thought it was quite extravagant, and a bit excessive, but James, of course, took pleasure in splurging. He called it our six-month anniversary trip, and he made sure that all expenses were paid for.

We stayed at the Four Season's hotel V Paris, a grand and luxurious hotel in the centre of Paris. Built-in 1928, it was now a luxurious landmark hotel off the Champs-Elysées, located about 1 km from the Arc de Triomphe and 2 km from the Eiffel Tower, a perfect location for a touristic adventure.

All the time we were dating, he would never let me pay for anything and always looked insulted when I offered, so after a while, I just stopped offering. I was a feminist on some level and believed in my financial independence, but James thought it was very un-ladylike, or at least that was what he told me when I questioned him on the subject.

The trip had been a success, a perfect mini weekend trip, with all the clichéd activities one could expect. We visited The Louvre, Notre Dame, Sacre- Coeur and even had croissants overlooking the Seine.

It was magical, and in between all the lovemaking and sightseeing, James took to perfecting his French, soon picking up whole phrases and making some conversation with the locals.

━━

"So…?" said Sarah, as she quizzed me excitedly when I visited home for the first time in almost a year.

"So what?" I responded.

I knew what she was implying but chose to feign ignorance.

"Did he propose in Paris?" she asked impatiently.

Oh, here we go, I thought to myself, irritated to be getting a grilling on my first day back at home.

I had been slightly homesick after the Paris trip, so a week after we got back, James decided to surprise me with one return flight to London for the weekend. He had wanted to cheer me up and thought that I should go home and see my parents. I was so happy. No one had ever been so thoughtful except for my immediate family. I jumped into his arms when he showed me the flight tickets.

"This is a business class return flight to Gatwick, my darling. Anything to turn that frown upside down."

He waved the tickets in the air excitedly.

"Flights home? Wow, but Christmas is just around the corner, you realize that don't you? They'll be expecting me home then too."

He nodded, indicating he had thought it through already.

"I know, but don't forget that we have that business deal on the 27th, so you'll have to be back in the office straight away. I figured you could see them now, just in case, you know?"

James always thought ahead. The thought hadn't even crossed my mind that I may not be able to go home for Christmas, or that if I did, I would have to rush back, as the firm had a huge deal which was due to close just after Christmas.

Some of the team would have to stay on board to see it through, maybe even work right through Christmas Day. It was ok for the rest of the team as their families lived in Chicago. For me, this was a major inconvenience.

Mom was undoubtedly excited when I informed her

over the phone later that evening, I would be making a fleeting visit, courtesy of my boss and my new beau.

She wanted to know everything about James. How we had met, how we got together and why I thought he was so incredible.

She'd known I had been dating someone new but had been skeptical about it, given that Sarah had refused to give her all the juicy details.

I also certainly hadn't divulged too much on the relationship. Being an enthusiast of keeping the peace, and a believer of not doing anything to jinx a good thing, Mom had been kept in the dark about James. Secondary to this was also the fact that my mother was the type of parent who would be setting up a wedding dress fitting the moment I told her I was seeing someone special.

She had done the exact thing to Sarah when she brought Ian back home for the first time. Ironically enough, that worked out for her, as she did, in fact, end up marrying him.

By the end of the conversation, Mom was utterly sold and convinced that I had literally scored a knight in shining amour; at least this is what she referred to him as when she regaled my father on the details of this new love affair.

So, there I was, flying back home for the weekend, all expenses paid by the one and only, most generous, loving, sexy man in my world.

———

"No, Sarah! Calm yourself down, right down. It's been like six months. We're hardly walking down the aisle yet. Jesus woman, what's the matter with you?"

Sarah threw herself into Mom and Dad's armchair in disappointment.

Why was she so set on getting me down the aisle? I wasn't in any rush. I was 25 still, so I had lots of time, and if it was about babies, I had lots of time for that as well.

Mom walked in and caught the tail end of my sentence, and she just couldn't help but add her two cents in.

"Well Fiona, at 26, I was already married and having kids. Things have changed now, you know, you young 'un's think you have all the time in the world. If you find the one, why wait. I just don't get the kids of nowadays. In my days, you had to marry a man before you even got to see what was under his belt? Marrying your dad was the best decision I ever made, and I didn't have to wait a whole year, I didn't, and look at me and your pops, happy as Larry."

Mom had an old-fashioned view of dating, and she just couldn't get her head around why you had to date so many people before finding the one. She surely wasn't comfortable with the whole concept of sex before marriage, so when she started on her rant about this, that was my queue to leave the room.

All this talk of marriage had got me thinking. What if he did propose? Was I ready for such a commitment? I adored him at that point, but I just didn't know enough yet to commit myself to him forever. I decided to take any thoughts of marriage out of my head. It was ridiculous to have such ideas so soon into a relationship. No one ever got married within a year of meeting, not nowadays - it just wasn't enough time to really get to know someone well enough to commit.

The weekend had been fantastic, the weather, although quite cold, was crisp and fresh.

I had gotten to spend time with the whole family, something I really cherished. We had a lovely dinner with Mom, Dad, Sarah and her husband, Ian, and I hadn't realized how much I had missed everyone. There was just something about being with close family that was so warming.

Although I loved being in Chicago, working at a great firm and being with James, it was always just the two of us at the dinner table; nothing like I was experiencing now. The laughter, the jokes, my mother toying with us, and father pulling his silly faces whenever mother said anything cringe-worthy, Sarah and Ian blowing kisses at each other and acting like newlyweds. I missed it all; the chatter over the dinner table, uncles and aunts visiting at the holidays, the postman whistling as he walked by, delivering the mail to everyone on my street; friends popping over for cups of tea on a cold winters afternoon, while mom fussed over which china to serve lunch from.

My life was now in Chicago, a place where friends were scarce and life was pretty much centred on James, work, and parties, in that exact order.

Ian had some news which he was excited to share with the whole family.

He had just landed a new job in investment banking, a very well-paid job. I think he was trying to shadow my father in some way. Ian was successful in his own right and was a real provider. He was also a little old fashioned, and I think he probably had encouraged Sarah to do the whole stay-at-home-mom thing, something I wasn't too keen on.

Nevertheless, it was comforting to listen to his plans. He had his head screwed on right, and I could tell that Sarah was happy.

She had found a keeper.

I managed to squeeze in some time with friends and had a scandalous night out on the town on my last night in London. Everyone was envious of my new life, my new job, and the new man. They all promised to visit, to see me in my limelight, the newly improved version of Fiona in Chicago. My best friend, Harry, or 'Hot Harry' as he was referred to by my sister, gave me some stern advice about keeping my wits about me and not rushing into anything until I was ready. He warned me not to come home un-married and pregnant.

I loved him dearly, and he was always somewhat protective of me. Harry was always the sort of person to put me straight whenever I was doing something stupid. He had a bright personality and an infectious laugh that would fill the room and make everyone warm to him, but he was also sensible. He always said that things that appeared too good to be true often were just that- too-good-to-be-true. He was elated for me and teased that I was going to get too wrapped up in my love affair and I would soon forget him, something I just thought could never happen.

London would always be my home, and Harry, my number one confidant.

———

The journey to the airport was quite emotional. Mom and Dad gave me a lift and Mom cried the whole way. She said she hadn't realized how much she had missed me, and how much she was going to miss me. I think she knew I wouldn't be home for quite some time.

"Mom, stop already. I should be back in a few weeks

for Christmas, or you can always come and visit and celebrate Christmas and my birthday with me."

Mom wasn't the best at flying and would only fly if there was no other option available.

———

The flight back to Chicago was dreadful. There was so much turbulence we eventually had to be diverted to New York before we were allowed back on to finish the journey.

I left James a message on his voicemail to say I was going to be delayed and would just grab a cab from the airport whenever I landed.

I didn't get a reply, and when I finally landed in Chicago, I still hadn't received any messages from him. James was always with his phone, he never let it out of his sight, continually responding to one email or another, or making calls. He was a busy man and always needed to be contactable, so when he hadn't got back to me, I couldn't help but wonder if he hadn't seen my message or if something was wrong.

I was too tired to hang around the airport, so I rang his phone once more, just to be sure, but when he failed to pick up, I just grabbed a cab from the airport to take me straight to his apartment.

———

As the cab pulled into his driveway, I saw Christian and a woman walking towards the cab.

Christian's eyes caught mine, and he immediately started to wave theatrically.

"She's back," he shouted towards the house, at which

point James bolted out the front door. I was flattered by such a dramatic homecoming.

James walked over to me and gave me a huge hug, followed by a long, drawn-out kiss. I indulged in the kiss, as I had missed him, but finally pulled away, aware we had company.

"Ahem, sorry guys, I haven't seen my babe all weekend, and she is looking smoking hot"

Am I?

I looked a mess after the scary journey I just had.

"Hey Fiona." Christian broke the awkward silence which followed the kiss dramatics. "So good to see you."

He moved in closer and kissed me on the cheeks. "I don't think you've met my wife, Amanda." He smiled awkwardly and gestured toward her.

I looked in her direction and saw that she had an odd expression on her face, as though she may have been crying or maybe it was just panda eyes.

"Hi Fiona, I've heard so much about you. Please excuse my appearance. I haven't had much sleep, and THIS one insisted we come out and visit James."

I stepped closer to give her a kiss on the cheek, and she seemed rigid.

"Hi Amanda, lovely to meet you. You guys look like you're on your way out. Such a shame... maybe we can get together for a drink sometime?"

She nodded but looked uneasy. "Sure, I'll get your number from Christian."

And with that, they were off and driving down the road hurriedly. The whole conversation was odd and quite contrived, as though they had been in the thick of some event which was interrupted by my sudden appearance.

James grabbed my bags, and we walked into the house to be met by Maria, who was hurrying around the place, tidying up. It smelt as though she had been cooking, so at least I would be having a nice home-cooked dinner tonight.

I didn't mind, I didn't mind at all. Even if it meant that Maria would be hanging around like an unwanted pet.

———

Maria served up a dinner of roasted chicken and vegetables, and I ate until I was completely stuffed.

James also cleared his plate and looked so content. Maria then served up some desert, but by this time, I could hardly eat another bite. James, on the other hand, finished his and then stood up and gestured to Maria that he would help her clear up the plates.

I retired to the sofa to put my feet up. I was so tired, and it had been such a long day. I started to drift in and out of sleep when I heard laughter. It sounded like Maria's voice. What was so funny? I didn't like it that the two of them seemed to have a friendship. As far as I was concerned, she was an employee and there needed to be boundaries.

Nonetheless, I didn't get up from the sofa and instead decided to ignore it. Then I heard more noises coming from the kitchen, more laughter, and then a sudden gasp. I shouted out, "Everything ok in there?"

Suddenly, I heard a scraping sound, like the sound of furniture being moved before Maria rushed out and darted up the stairs. She looked rather dishevelled and wide-eyed, and her hair, which she usually kept in a bun, was undone, her hair falling beautifully down to her waist. I never realized how long her hair was—long locks of beautifully conditioned hair that made me envy her even more.

A few seconds later, James re-appeared from the kitchen, his shirt untucked. I noticed that a few buttons on his shirt were unfastened and his sleeves were rolled up. He seemed to have a massive grin on his face as he walked towards me.

"What happened, why all the noise?" I asked, but he rolled his eyes, mockingly.

"Oh nothing, just a little spillage in the kitchen, nothing for you to worry about."

I can't say that I was particularly satisfied with his response, but with all the commotion from the flight, meeting Christian and Amanda, followed by a huge dinner, I was just too tired to think anything of it.

Before I knew it, I was fast asleep on the sofa.

Chapter Eight

The next couple of weeks rolled by, and the demands of my busy work schedule set in.

James had been in and out on business trips, so I hadn't had the chance to spend much time with him. Our schedules had become quite hectic, which meant that we saw less and less of each other, and what little time we had together, was always spent indoors with a bottle of wine, relaxing, and recharging our bodies for the busy week ahead.

James had been away on many trips and would sometimes spend a whole week away, leaving me feeling alone and anxious. However, it also allowed me the time to try to build relationships with other people, perhaps even try to make friends. At times though, I would often wonder why he was the only one of the executives that were required to be away on business trips. On some level, I felt uneasy about it.

I would often watch movies where the husband would start affairs whilst on business trips, his clueless wife, stuck at home. I once jokingly put this across to James, but he laughed it off and reiterated his feelings for me. His eyes were sincere, and I felt that I could somehow tell if he was untrue.

On some level, this gave me all the reassurance that I was the only one he had eyes for.

———

16th December came about swiftly.

I would be spending the first of many birthdays here in Chicago. James had, of course, surprised me with a grand gesture and bought me a brand-new car; a Mercedes SLK, in pearl white with unique custom-made rims. It was the most elaborate and clichéd gift I had ever received, down to the red ribbon wrapped beautifully across the body of the car.

At first, I refused to accept it and urged him to return it; this was a step too far for me. I adored his generosity, but I wanted the opportunity to provide for myself, to be able to buy my own car and whatever else I needed. The idea that I would be perceived as a kept woman repulsed me. The atypical girlfriend, freeloading off her rich boyfriend to bleed him dry. People might assume I was with James as a means of accommodating a lifestyle that had all the superfluities and indulgences of the more affluent.

James, on the other hand, could not see my side of things and couldn't understand why anyone would refuse a gift. After some stern but loving words, he persuaded me to accept it.

I had no choice. I didn't want to offend his generosity, especially after he had been so kind to me.

So, we took the car for a quick drive, and I immediately fell in love with it.

After lunch, James announced that he had also planned a party at an Italian restaurant with some of his friends and work colleagues, Christian and Amanda and, to my surprise, the housekeeper, Maria.

At the party, everyone took to talking about the lavish gift I had received, and how lucky I was to have James. And just as I had predicted, there were whispers and insinuations about my relationship with him. This, of course, made James gleam with smugness. He loved the attention this brought on him as the provider, the ever so generous, powerful James Foyler.

I chose to ignore the negative remarks and focused on the positive. After all, it was nothing but mindless gossip, which bore no truth.

I did, however, notice that Julia looked uneasy, perhaps bothered that she wasn't in my shoes. Her attempts at flirting with James were too obvious and, even though she tried to pretend that she wasn't at all attracted to him, as a woman, I could see all the signs.

To keep the peace, I made sure I stayed well clear of her; jealousy and alcohol do not mix well, and I didn't want to bear the brunt of her resentment.

On the other side of the room, I could hear some commotion; Maria had taken to be the highlight of the night, wearing a tight, short, low cut red dress, with a lacy hemline that didn't leave much to the imagination. It was evident that she wasn't wearing any underwear, as the full shape of her voluptuous breasts were visible through the dress. The length of her dress made for quite some conversation, and it seemed she had drunk one too many glasses of wine and drowned any level of refinement and decorum.

She was now on the dance floor, letting her dance partner swing her from arm to arm and dip her low in sweeping movements, causing her legs to be flung in the air and the hem of her dress to edge closer and closer to her crotch.

I noticed how the men in the party gathered around, staring at her ever-emerging orifices, much to the annoyance of their wives or girlfriends.

As I looked on from the corner of the room, where I stood with one of James's friends, I could not help but stare in amazement, not understanding how a woman could allow herself to be seen this way; to be objectified by complete strangers.

She seemed to revel in it somehow, enjoying the expressions on their faces as they jeered encouragingly, asking her dance partner to dip her even lower and lift her up in the air so that there was full exposure to that which lay between her legs.

She had now become the main attraction of the night. I looked over at James and Christian, and they too were transfixed by what had now almost become an X-rated striptease. Neither did anything to stop her, but just stared on as more and more of her person was exposed. Finally, her dance partner pulled down the top of her dress, fully revealing her breasts. This is when James gallantly ran over, grabbed her by the arm and carried her off the dance floor in a fire-man's lift, through a crowd of boos and whistles.

Christian and Amanda, sensing my uneasiness about this, hurriedly walked over to me to wish me a happy birthday. Amanda immediately hugged me and handed me a gift, wrapped in a Tiffany box with a white bow.

"This is from both of us, I picked it, and I hope you like it. I wasn't sure what kind of jewellery you liked, and of course Christian is of no help in that department."

She waved her ring finger, gesturing at the small

diamond ring. I thought it was rather crude to make fun of Christian in this way, but he didn't seem to mind.

"Oh my God! You shouldn't have."

I immediately opened the gift to reveal a silver tiffany charm bracelet. It was rather elegant and shiny, with two gold charms, dangling stylishly from the bracelet. I kissed Amanda on the cheek and waved at Christian, who was now distracted by something that was happening on the other side of the room.

"Glad you like it, it cost a bloody fortune," he laughed. "But you're are worth it."

I suddenly heard the clink of champagne glasses. "Everyone, everyone, please gather around, I have a few words to say to my special girl on this special night."

Everyone started to shuffle together, and I walked over to where James was standing. He handed me a glass of champagne and kissed me on the cheek and continued to speak.

"So, I have been with this lovely lady for about eight months now, give or take, and can I just say, this one is a keeper. This is the kind of lady you want to take home to your mother. So, I wanted to take this opportunity to wish her a happy twenty-sixth. Still young and youthful and probably has no greys yet. I am the luckiest son of a bitch ever, and I want to thank you for coming into my life and making it so much more. Fiona…"

My heart stopped for a brief second, as I anguished over the idea of him, perhaps proposing to me, right in front of all these people. I panicked, knowing full well that I wasn't ready for such a grand gesture, the grandest of them all.

He continued to speak. "… I am completely smitten by you, and I am totally in love with you. I just wanted all our friends to hear the first time I told you I love you… to make it special. I love you to bits. And with that said, let's raise our glasses and toast this wonderful woman who has come into my life and made each day that much more bearable."

Everyone raised their glasses and looked over at me, waiting for a reaction, or at least a response.

I was shocked, but on some level relieved that he hadn't proposed. Combined with this was happiness; he had finally professed his love to me for the first time. Although I was elated, a slight twinge of regret set in. I had wished that he would have kept such a private matter just between the two of us.

The thing about James was that he loved to put on a show; he loved the camaraderie and the limelight, so whenever there was a social gathering, he would always be the one popping the champagne and buying everyone drinks.

I, of course, didn't really think this was necessarily a bad thing. So, what if he liked to be the star of the show, he was the boss after all. He was also successful in his own right.

All eyes were now on me, but I didn't know what to say. Nerves kicked in, and a fear of speaking publicly suddenly overcame me, a fear that, up until then, was something I had never really experienced.

With blood rushing through my head, and an anxiety attack imminent, I crumbled, and instead of responding to the now raucous crowd, I just raised my glass to my lips and drank the entire contents in one full dramatic sweep.

There was a roar of laugher, as the crowd interpreted this as perhaps a rebuff. James stood next to me, awkwardly and joined in with the laughter, possibly to ease his discomfort.

The crowd dispersed quickly, and he went straight to the bar with some of his friends to order shots.

———

The party went on until about 3 a.m. as James had bribed the owner of the restaurant to let us have a lock-in.

Everything that happened past midnight was a bit of a blur, as the night took on a more sordid tone, with a few people making out, sexual games and too much excess and alcohol.

I didn't see James at all after his botched speech, but he seemed to reappear again at about 2 a.m. He had left the party and had given Maria and one other guest a ride home.

He maintained that Maria had drank too much and needed to be put to bed. He was always such a gentleman, and it was the sort of thing he would do for someone in need. My only complaint was why he had invited the housekeeper to my party in the first place, and why it had taken two and a half hours to drop her off at home.

He seemed irritated at being questioned, before handing me a glass of wine and walking off to a group of friends gesturing him to come over.

He still hadn't mentioned anything about the speech, so I knew something was brewing up inside him.

Christian and Amanda walked over to me, ready to go home and say their good-byes. James shouted something inaudible across the room, then walked back to where we were standing. He pulled Christian away towards the bar for one last drink, leaving Amanda and me standing awkwardly in the middle of the room.

I felt a little apprehensive but figured that this was as

good a time as any to get acquainted adequately with Amanda. We had never really had any alone time to have girl talk, so I could use this opportunity to make a new friend.

I was utterly lost in thought when Amanda immediately grabbed me by the hand and pulled me to a corner. She was a little drunk, so I let it slide.

"So, you and James, eh! How's that going? You in love with him yet? You didn't say anything when he declared his love for you. I have to say, he must have been embarrassed by that. You know you're going to pay for that later? He doesn't like to be humiliated. Usually, it's the girls who are left waiting, not him. All the girls fall in love with him, then he's gone in a flash."

I didn't understand what was happening. Was this another sabotage, much like how Julia had tried previously. And why on earth did Amanda care about James's previous love life?

"I don't want to spoil your fairy tale, but you'd better watch out with him. He is a lunatic, he's dangerous. You need to understand Fiona, all that glitters is not gold and that one there, well, he's pure brass."

She swayed and let out a couple of hiccups. A few partygoers brushed passed and gestured for us to liven up and get more drinks. Their aim was to get as wasted as possible. They cheered and danced and bumped into us a second time, irritating Amanda.

Once they had moved on, I looked back over at Amanda, but her demeanour had changed as though she had suddenly sobered up.

"Amanda, you were saying?"

She turned to me and lowered her gaze before placing her hands over her mouth in a panic. She started to walk off, and I immediately grabbed her by the elbow.

"Amanda, what do you mean, he's dangerous?"

She tried to free herself from my grip, at which point Christian and James suddenly appeared out of nowhere. "Hey darlings, are you ready to go?" James bellowed and grabbed my hand too eagerly, freeing Amanda from my grip.

"Yes, of course, let's go," Amanda replied, too enthusiastically.

I noticed that James gave Amanda a look, but I couldn't quite put my finger on it. I did see that she suddenly looked nervous and excused herself, saying that she needed to powder her nose.

Christian, who was, of course, oblivious to anything going on, laughed. "Women eh? Go on honey, go powder that beautiful nose."

As Amanda walked off hurriedly, James high-fived Christian and announced we were leaving, indicating we wouldn't be waiting for Amanda to return.

We walked out of the restaurant hurriedly, and James hailed down a cab as quickly as possible.

"What's the rush? Slow down James, SLOOOW DOWN... my feet hurt?"

He looked irritated as we jumped into the cab and slammed the door.

"Hey matey, lakeshore east, now! Quick as possible. Bloody step on it for Christ sake, you deaf or something?" he barked at the cab driver, who looked slightly confused.

I knew I was in for some trouble, and it wasn't going to be easy to get out of this, yet when we arrived back at his place, his anger had all but dissipated. He was back to his old self; flirty and loving, so I had somehow dodged a bullet.

Or least I hoped so.

Chapter Nine

The holiday season had finally arrived in full swing.

For every street you walked past, you could barely avoid all the carol singers and well wishes. Chicago was lit and alive, people rushing and busying about doing their last-minute Christmas shopping, entirely on autopilot, stockpiling turkeys, enough to feed small armies. The Du Grey office, on the other hand, was open until Christmas Eve, and everyone in my team had to work late all week, including Christmas Eve, to secure the deal James had been working on.

He referred to it as our 'Christmas bonuses. Everyone became slaves to their desks, robots spellbound by their oversized computer screens, typing away endlessly, all for the love of money; money which they were making for the institution, albeit a tiny percentage would be passed on to them in the form of a discretionary handout.

This was work, and it pretty much dictated our lives. One had to work hard to stay ahead of players who moved in sync to a melody of shuffled papers, paper-cuts, mega-bytes, and giga-bytes of incomprehensible streams of data, pirouetting across their screens. Psychedelic graphs and charts, being sent instantly from point A to point B, in a cycle of a never-ending charade of egos.

As much as I loathed the narcissism of the archetypal financier and the atypical self-importance that was usually a trait that came hand in hand, the very quintessence of the financial establishment was just too alluring. Frankly speaking, away from all the pretence, bluffing, and head-nodding that needed to be sometimes endured to fake your way through overly complicated meetings and discussions, I found the world of finance, riveting and addictive. It was also highly lucrative.

The unspoken and un-festive motto at the firm was that Christmas was for schmucks, so because of this, we seemed to miss out on all the pre-Christmas festivities and excitement. I didn't mind at all, as although I was burning the midnight oil, I was doing this with James, right by my side. Occasionally, to cut through the lengthiness of the workday, in between the tea breaks, I would sit with him in his office, and sometimes we would make love on his desk or his sofa, or he would pin me against the door and ravish me. At the same time, I tried my hardest not to scream out loud in pleasure. He did so, knowing full well that the team was just a few meters away, on the other side of the door, and could probably hear us. Sometimes there would be some role-playing during sex; other times, he just wanted to dominate me. It was fun and exciting, it made up for working too many hours of the day and the lack of festivity in the office.

Who needed Christmas fireworks anyway, I told myself. We made our fireworks happen all over his office, and it was an explosive experience.

I woke up on Christmas day, in my bed, in a bit of a haze.

We had decided to stay at my apartment the night before, as it was closer to the office, having worked till 3 a.m. I was exhausted and sleep-deprived, so when James woke me up at 9 a.m., excited like a kid in a candy store, I lacked the enthusiasm that he sought. He lay in bed, next to me, singing Christmas carols and clicking his fingers to the rhythm of the melody.

"Fiona Merry Christmas. This is our first Christmas together. I am so happy to have you here."

He paused to see if I would respond. I didn't say anything, as I was still half asleep. He sensed I wasn't amused, and then his mood slightly changed. He looked like he had something more to say but was struggling for the right words. He turned on to his side, facing me.

"I know I told you in front of everyone that I love you, I also noticed you didn't say it back and..."

My heart skipped a beat. I hadn't yet managed to brace for this topic and was altogether avoiding it for the last couple of weeks since the party.

"But Fiona, it's ok, I…"

I couldn't bear it anymore; he had a wounded look on his face. I had to stop him before he made the situation more awkward.

"James, I'm so sorry, I was just so shocked. I had wanted to tell you for ages, even before you said it, I just didn't, I couldn't find a good time, I just…"

I took a deep breath and sat up and held his hands in mine. "Of course, I bloody love you, I love you, James, I freaking love you."

He smiled a look of relief on his face. I think he

already knew that I was falling for him, he just wanted me to say it.

He pulled me in closer and kissed me on the lips, then rolled me over so that he was on top of me. He kissed my neck and then unbuttoned my night-shirt with his teeth.

He then, slowly with his tongue, brushed against my nipple. "I freaking love you too, Fiona, and I am gonna bloody show you how much right now," and with that, he thrust himself into me.

A fter the morning's exertions, we got out of bed, showered, and grabbed a taxi.

James had booked a table at an upscale restaurant called Les Chambres, which was located atop the Chicago Stock exchange. This place was indeed at the height of elegance, with fantastic views across the city. The menu was divine, with perfectly executed dishes, each with an Alsatian flair. We were attending the Christmas brunch, which was booked for noon. When we arrived, we were welcomed to an array of cocktails and delicious looking appetisers. We sat at a corner table, as James wanted some privacy.

We then exchanged gifts before our meals were brought to the table.

I bought James a Swiss watch, and he topped this by giving me a diamond bracelet. I was overwhelmed again, but after the gift of a car, I was starting to get used to the lavishness. To make the day special, James had personally seen to it that we did all the Christmas related effects one could imagine. He didn't have much of a family to speak of, being an only child, and both his parents had already passed away in a tragic accident when he was still in college.

For his last Christmas, he had flown first-class to the Bahamas and spent it on a hired yacht with a nineteen-year-old he had met the night before. It was his escape from reality and the pain from losing his parents. By 4 p.m., after too much food and alcohol, we finally headed home, and James, unsteady on his feet, retired upstairs to bed.

I headed to the kitchen to make a call home to wish everyone a Merry Christmas. I had only broken the news to my parents a few days earlier that I was not going to be able to fly home. Naturally, they just couldn't understand why I wasn't allowed the time off from work. Everyone was allowed time off during the holidays and to them, by defin-ition, the holidays were meant to be spent, holidaying.

I dialled the numbers slowly on the keypad, and the phone had hardly even begun to ring before I heard my mother's voice on the other side.

"Hello, stranger, my daughter from another Country. Merry Christmas, love." She sounded annoyed, as though I had personally put a somber mood on the McCullum Christmas, and her voice quavered as she spoke.

I overheard my father in the background, who also sounded disappointed, and when I asked to talk to Sarah, my mother seemed to get even more upset.

Sarah refused to speak to me. She'd had an announce-ment which she had been waiting to break to the whole family on Christmas Day. It turns out she was expecting and was six weeks pregnant. For as long as I could remem-ber, it had been a family tradition of ours to always be present for important events, birthdays, Christmases, weddings… and that year, I had missed all the above.

As I put the receiver down, I felt a sudden wave of

emotion. I missed being with my family, and I missed having lots of people around me, especially during the holidays, and before I had a chance to compose myself, the tears rushed from my eyes. It flowed down my face in waves, so heavy and so full of sadness.

I couldn't hold back and sat there, sobbing, until sunset. That Christmas wasn't the best, it was as though the words 'Merry' had been lost on me.

Feeling sorry for myself, little did I know that the events of the next coming months would mean this Christmas would be by far the merriest of all the Christmases I would have for a very long time.

A week later, after all the festivities, I arranged to meet Amanda for lunch at a local café, not too far from James's apartment.

I wanted to get to the bottom of the conversation we had started the night of my birthday party, and I hadn't spoken to James about it either.

"Hey Amanda, thank you for meeting me at such short notice," I said sheepishly as I kissed her on the cheek before sitting down for lunch.

The place was a bit of a dump, and I hadn't expected it to be so crowded, which wasn't ideal for the type of conversation I was planning on having. Most of the restaurants and cafes in James's neighbourhood were quite upscale, so I was quite surprised at how un-swanky this place turned out to be. It had been Amanda's idea to come here, so perhaps she just wanted something casual, away from any prying eyes.

There were only a few items on the menu, none which tickled my taste, so I only ordered a coffee. Amanda, on the other hand, just opted for sparkling water and a slice of lemon. I guessed this wasn't going to be a long lunch by the looks of things.

"So, what is it you wanted to talk about, Fiona?" She looked concerned, as she spoke.

She must remember the bombshell she dropped on me, just a few weeks ago.

The words 'he's so dangerous' kept running through my head, as if it was trying to find an escape route, but was being pulled back in.

I cleared my throat before I spoke, taking a sip of my coffee. "Do you recollect the night of my party, just before we left the restaurant? You know, when James and Christian went off for a few shots of tequila? Do you remember what you said to me? You said something about James."

I didn't want to give her any clues. I wanted it to come from her. If it was indeed true, then she would remember.

She rolled her eyes and waved the waitress over. "Can I have a glass of Chardonnay." There was an awkward silence, as the waitress took her order and then walked off, without checking if I also wanted anything.

I admit I was nervous at what she might say next, but at the same time, I was annoyed that she could be making up the whole thing.

"Ok, Fiona, fine. I just wanted to warn you that was all. I've seen this pattern with James before, and it never ends well."

The waitress approached with the glass of wine and finally asked if I wanted anything. I quickly hurried her away, irritated at being interrupted again.

"Look, I probably said too much, it's just that, well, James and I had a fling, years ago, before I got with Christian and I have to tell you that guy he is deeply troubled. I can't go into too much detail as it's personal and I have put it behind me, but there are some dark issues within him, something troubling. I guess I just think there are sides to him which he doesn't always reveal, but if he does, then you'd better steer clear. It's not my place to interfere like this, but please, just be careful. Maybe it's different with you, maybe he has learned to deal with his demons. But if not, you'll soon find out. Just know one thing, don't bloody have kids with him."

Was that all I was going to get? I wanted details. What did she mean? Was I in any danger, or was it something else?

I was disappointed by the lack of any discernible information. It was as though she had handed me a puzzle, but with parts missing.

I tried fruitlessly to get more information out of her, but she was like a closed book. Maybe she was too afraid to tell me, or perhaps she just wanted to put it all behind her. Whatever it was, it scared me.

I'd now lost my appetite, so I thanked her and left a thirty-dollar bill on the table and walked out of the restaurant. I couldn't do anything with what she had said.

I couldn't ask James about it, and I didn't want to burden Christian.

I had been warned, and yet, was none the wiser.

Chapter Ten

The next six months went by, effortlessly.

It was the middle of summer, everything seemed to feel better, the glow of the sun, beaming down on us, basking in the rays each day, as though we had no real problems.

That's the issue with the sun, it brightens up the day and masks away any darkness, so much so that, you soon begin to forget any troubles you may have.

By now, I seemed to have a handle on things at work, and I fit in nicely with the team. The firm had now also secured a few more deals, and so the bonuses kept flowing in, which meant that everyone was happy and in good spirits. I had already left my rented accommodation and officially moved in with James, after he had surprised me one night after dinner, and asked me if I would move in with him.

I was thrilled at this, as in some way, to me, this signalled that he was ready to move forward with me and that whatever issues he might have faced with other women, were now entirely in the past. I was his, and he was mine. Our love story, much to the envy of everyone, was blossoming into something great. The passion we felt for each other was insatiable, it kept on growing stronger, day by day, fuelled by my desire to make him my prince charming, and his unquenchable thirst to satisfy me sexually and emotionally.

We were unable to keep our hands off each other, and that so-called honeymoon period glow never seemed to dim. I settled into life with him, and even though Maria hovered around from time to time, I chose to ignore her antics. She would walk around the apartment in tight fitted clothes, revealing an ample amount of cleavage, much to my disdain. I had already tried to convince James that I thought her services were no longer required now that I had moved in, but he seemed to feel responsible for her and didn't think it would be fair for her to lose her job.

He promised that he would revisit the subject in a few months, but we never did.

O n the weekend of James's birthday, I arranged a small get together at our apartment with a few of his friends.

It was supposed to be a small event, which turned into a huge party that lasted into the small hours of the morning. James got completely drunk, and I seemed to lose him for a few hours. He had a habit of disappearing at parties, just like the same stunt he pulled at my birthday party. This time, I went looking for him. I couldn't find Maria either, so I decided to call him on my phone. As the phone connected, I could hear the distant sound of ringing in the room upstairs, in Maria's room.

What in hell was James's phone doing in there?

I ran upstairs as quickly as I could, daring not to jump to conclusions, albeit that there was lump now forming in my throat making it difficult for me to swallow. I knocked on Maria's bedroom door, my phone in hand, listening to the ringing coming from the other side of the door.

Maria appeared quickly, hand on hip. "Yes madam, you need something?" She spoke nonchalantly. The ringing had stopped by this time.

"Have you seen James, I can hear his phone. Is he here?"

She smiled at me, pushed open the door to let me have a peek inside and then walked over to her bed and sat down gingerly. "Oh, ya, I see him earlier, he asks me to charge his phone, he go outside with some people. I think they smoke cigars," she responded.

I suddenly felt relieved. It was plausible that he had asked her to charge his phone, even though there were several charging ports around the house. But why would she need to take it into her bedroom?

It didn't add up, but for the sake of not sounding like the nagging shrew, I decided to let it go. Besides, I had guests downstairs, waiting with empty glasses that needed to be filled.

I walked back downstairs and, waiting for me at the bottom, was James.

"Hey you," I said, relieved at seeing him. "I was looking for you," I added and kissed him on the lips softy.

He looked a mess; he had clearly been drinking too much. I often wondered how his liver coped with all this drinking, it wasn't all that excessive, but when he was in that kind of mood, it was more like, go big or go home.

"Maria says you were outside smoking some cigars. She's got your phone, right? Why has she got your phone?"

I sounded a little accusatory, albeit trying to sound as

nonchalant as possible. He looked puzzled, as though he had no idea what I was talking about.

"Eh? My phone, what about it?" He dipped his hands in his trouser pocket as though he was searching for something, but as my luck would have it, Christian walked over with some drinks and interrupted us.

"Fiona, James has something to ask you." Christian stepped behind James and rubbed his shoulders excitedly. "Go on, Romeo, ask her."

What was the secret, and why was Christian so excited?

I looked around and saw that people were starting to gather around. James was blushing now, whatever it was he was about to ask me was obviously a big deal, big enough to make another speech in front of everyone.

I daren't think what it was as I didn't really want to get ahead of myself, but just like with my birthday party, here he was, making another big display in front of everyone.

"Fiona, the love of my life. As you managed to arrange this lovely party for me to celebrate my birthday, I figured now would be as good as any time to do what I have wanted to do for a long time.

For Christ's sake, what was it he had wanted to do for all this time?

I was getting nervous and excited, but all I could do to calm myself was to take a deep breath and wait for him to say whatever it is he was dying to tell.

"Fiona, I want to spend the rest of my life with you. From the moment you walked into Du Grey's, it's like a switch went on in me. No one can light up a room the way you do... no one can put the spring back into my steps like you do. No one. Fiona McCullum. I want you to be mine. I want to grow old with you."

He smoothed back his hair, reached into his inner jacket pocket and slowly brought out a small red box.

Everyone gasped as it was now quite apparent precisely what was about to happen.

This was the moment of every girl's dreams, the moment when she is transformed from a girl into a woman; chosen by a man who would make her whole.

James moved in closer and held my hands and kissed me on the cheek, and down he went on bended knees.

"Fi, Will you marry me?"

Part Two

Chapter 11

They say the most dangerous lie is the one you tell yourself and I suppose this part of my life was mainly based on the delusionary tale I kept telling myself.

A part of me wanted so deeply to hold on to the first part of my life in Chicago, my blissfully unaware life with James, the man who fulfilled me, emotional, physically and mentally. I couldn't understand how I could go from being so unapologetically happy to something of a shadow of my distant self. How could I tell the tale of the next chapter of my life, how could I lay down my soul for all to bear witness? I had reached a precipice and I was at the fight or flee stage, and yet I just wanted to pretend it was nothing but a dream, nothing but a fictional story.

Life has a funny way of letting you know who is in charge, and when you feel that everything has almost reached a perfect state, it has a way of pulling the rug from under you and showing you that no one can be eternally happy, for happiness is nothing but a myth.

I was about to be wed to the man of my dreams, that should have been the finale, however, my life was about to be turned around full three-sixty, and I had no control over it. I could see my world slowly tumbling around me, I could see all the signs and all the while I felt helpless to control the situation. Maybe it was weakness, maybe it was fear, fear of being deserted or perhaps fear of failing, whatever it was, I knew deep down that I was but a mere spectator in the events that were about to unfold in my life.

I had front row seats to my descent, and all I could do was to watch, bear, and endure. The old African proverbs says, do not look where you fall, but where you slipped, and I guess to reconcile fully the events that took place over the next year or so, it is of crucial importance to fully understand exactly where it all started to crumble, where the first signs of a failing youth manifested, where a darkened destiny emerged and where a tale of misadventure began to unfurl.

The vow that binds too strictly, does eventually snap itself.

"*I, Fiona McCullum, do take thee, James Andrew Foyler, to be my husband. With elation, I come into my new life as your wife. As you have promised to me your life and love, so I too thankfully give you my life, and in confidence surrender myself to your leadership as the head of the home. I will love you, obey you, care for you and always seek to satisfy you. God has prepared me for you and so I will support, help, comfort, and inspire you. Throughout life, no matter what may come, I promise wholeheartedly to you, my life as a dutiful and faithful wife.*"

Chapter 12

I was, finally, Mrs Foyler.

I liked the sound of it and how people would respond when I introduced myself. It had been a week since the wedding, and we were now getting ready to go on our honeymoon. The wedding itself had been quite a lavish affair.

In all, there were about two hundred and fifty guests, which consisted of forty-five family and friends from my side and two hundred and five guests from James's side. When we had sat down to organise the seating plan and the guest list, I was taken aback as to how many people James had wanted to invite. It was like a free for all, from his neighbours to every single person at work, to what seemed like the janitor at his old school.

This was turning into a circus, but his justification was that being an orphan meant that it was important to share this precious moment with everyone.

I, on the other hand, had settled for just close family as well as friends and their plus ones. As James enjoyed being the centre of attention, there was no better time to show

off to every single person he knew, that he had a perfect
life. He had it all; a fantastic career, more money in the
bank than he knew what to do with, a lavish lifestyle and a
young trophy to call his wife.

He was the archetype of perfection, and so, when it
came to planning the wedding, he would do everything in
his power to make sure that if possible, the whole world
could relish in his delight. James had chosen Christian as
his best man, with a total of six groomsmen in tow.

I had chosen Sarah as my maid of honour, and Harry
was my honorary bridesmaid, much to everyone's humour.
I opted out of having a bachelorettes party, instead
choosing to spend the time with my sister and family who
had arrived in town early. I didn't have too many female
friends in Chicago, and the friends I had were only flying
out to Chicago a day or two before the wedding. James's
bachelor party was something out of this world. He had
flown all his groomsmen, all expenses paid, to Las Vegas
for a bachelor weekender, and unsurprisingly, several
sordid stories were floating around after the wedding,
which made my stomach turn.

My family adored James when they finally met him a
couple of weeks before the wedding. He had paid for business class tickets for my parents, Sarah, and Ian, to fly to
Chicago for the wedding and had insisted that they stayed
with us for the whole duration of their trip. His house had
four vacant bedrooms, as such, it fell to him to insist that
they stayed with us, a gesture that pleased me.

Sarah had since given birth, and I finally got to meet
my new niece Ella, who was only a few months old at the
time of the wedding. Having her around made me
maternal, all to James's discomfort. Up until then, we
had never really discussed having children, I was still
relatively young, and some would argue, a little imma-

ture, so as a result of this, the thought hadn't really crossed my mind.

James had never brought it up either, so coming to terms with the fact that he might be averse to the idea of having any children of our own, was something I didn't dare accept.

The wedding took place in an old courtyard, in an area surrounded by lush green meadows. It was unequivocally beautiful. James had organized and paid for a wedding planner, who had planned a few C-listed celebrity wedding in the past. It was quite the event. My family was surprised as to how much had gone into planning it, given that it had only been four months since James proposed. James had refused any help from my father and had insisted that he wanted to pay for it himself.

No penny had been spared. There was expensive champagne, beautiful gift bags for all the guests which were filled with designer perfumes, designer sunglasses and luxury chocolate, specially flown in from Belgium.

There were also unique hand-picked presents for my extended family, Swiss watches for the men, and Tiffany and co. Jewellery for the women, all paid for by James. James had presented my father with a gold Rolex watch, to my father's delight and surprise, and for my mother, he had bought flowers and a diamond-encrusted necklace. When it came to his side of the family, it was quite sad in some respect as I did not have the same pleasure of presenting his parents with gifts as they had already passed.

Instead, I had presented James with a pair of engraved diamond cufflinks which read – *'forever yours, love always. F.'* This was the only thing I had paid for in the entire wedding. It was quite expensive, but nowhere near all the expense James had incurred.

The day time entertainment was a string quartet that

played romantic tunes in the background to keep the ambiance, and then for the after-party, James had hired a famous local band to keep the party going until the early hours of the morning. My wedding dress was quite exceptional, it was every girls' dream wedding dress, an ivory-coloured dress with a pearly white fitted lace bodice, with a trumpet illusion and a sweetheart neckline. It was lined with Swarovski crystals, with a long flowing trail. I wore a Tiara to top it off, which was a gift from my mother.

Earlier in the process, I had told James that I was happy to go for something more modest and was even willing to wear Sarah's old wedding dress, no point in it going to waste, but he insisted on me having the best. He hinted on coming along for the wedding dress shopping to give me ideas on what he wanted me to look like on our big day. He said that there would be over two hundred eyes on me, so I had a better look the part. I assumed this was a joke, what kind of man would want to go wedding dress shopping with his bride to be and wasn't there some sort of rule against seeing the dress before the wedding.

To my surprise, he turned up to the first dress shop I visited and brought Christian along for moral support. On this basis, I knew I was in for a hell of a ride. He didn't get to see the final dress that I picked, but he certainly influenced my choice as well as the choice of a wedding shop.

The day was magical, and I was over the moon. I was so happy to be marrying the man of my dreams and to have my father walk me down the aisle. There were no hiccups, and everything went smoothly, nothing but perfection. James, ever the showman gave a few speeches and so did Christian, but the most heartfelt speech of the day was that of my father. It had a twinge of sadness, hinting that he was forever losing his youngest daughter and that life would no longer be the same. He talked about working hard to keep a marriage going and not to give away my sense of identity.

It was as though he had a feeling of what was to come. Just after dinner was served, he read out loud a famous Charlotte Bronte quote.

"I can live alone if self-respect and circumstances require me so to do. I need not sell my soul to buy bliss. I have an inward treasure born with me, which can keep me alive if all extraneous delights should be withheld or offered only at a price I cannot afford to give."

I wish amongst all the champagne clinks, the laughter, and the chatter, I had heeded his words. We danced the night away, blissfully happy, and full of excitement for what lay ahead on our journey of unity.

This was to be the start of the rest of our lives.

W e boarded the flight at 8 a.m. on route to Hawaii. James didn't want to venture too far, and as I had not been before, it was a perfect choice. We had first-class seats to luxury, and I felt spoilt rotten. The total journey time was about nine hours, and James had slept through the entire flight. Poor thing, I thought to myself. He must have been exhausted from the events of the week, juggling the wedding, work commitments, and the holiday preparations. I, on the other hand, was too excited to sleep.

Not wanting to miss out on the indulgence, I made sure that I made use of all that first-class had to offer. I had flown first-class before thanks to James and his lavish gifts, but still, it was something to be relished.

We arrived in Hawaii at about mid-day on the same day, which was a little disorienting as Chicago is five hours ahead of Hawaii. I made a joke that we had stepped back in time, to which James didn't seem amused. He was still exhausted and mentioned that he needed a few more hours of sleep before we could begin 'honeymooning.' A driver came to pick us up from the airport and took us to the resort, where we would be spending the next five days.

As we arrived, I was utterly overwhelmed by the opulence. Our suite was very grand and had a Jacuzzi and private swimming pool, with a private terrace that over-looked the ocean. I had never seen the sea so blue, the waves soft and smooth, so mesmerizing to the eyes, that it beckoned me towards it, a perfect, postcard setting.

James dragged himself across the room and dumped his laptop on the bed. He looked drained, so I insisted he take a power nap now so that he could wake up fresh for an early dinner. I decided to go out and explore the resort while he napped. At the bar, I met a couple of honey-mooners who had been at the resort for a few days and decided to sit with them. The bartender served up some cocktails, and as it was an all-inclusive resort, I decided I would indulge. He looked at me with intrigue, wondering why I was all by myself and if I was holidaying alone.

I must admit, I felt a twinge of embarrassment, having to admit that I was at the bar alone on the first night of my honeymoon because my new husband had fallen asleep.

After about an hour of friendly conversation with the bartender and probably far too many cocktails, I decided I would head back to the suite. I called out for James, but he was nowhere to be found, so I curled up in the overly sized bed intending to wait for his return but fell asleep almost instantly. I woke up abruptly after about four hours, confused as to where I was.

It was dark outside, and in the darkness, I could barely make out my hands in front of me. Once I had my bear-ings back, I got out of bed and switched on the bedside lamp; it was 11 p.m. I searched for James but he was still nowhere to be seen.

Eight missed calls later, I decided I would call the reception desk. They advised that they had not seen him and that he was not at the bar, and perhaps he had gone for a stroll. I didn't want to sound concerned, so I lied and said I had forgotten that he told me he would be going into town. As I put down the receiver, I realized I had no idea where he could be.

This wasn't exactly the perfect honeymoon night I had envisioned.

Chapter 13

The restaurant at the resort was already closed, and as I was now quite ravenous, I decided to order some room service while I waited up for James to return.

I felt a wave of sadness at the prospect of eating alone in the room, but I hadn't eaten anything since the flight, and I was starting to feel a little light-headed. I tried James's phone several more times, and there was still no response.

The room service was swift, and before I knew it, I heard a knock at the door. For a moment, I hoped it was James, but when the food arrived, I can't deny I wasn't relieved as my energy levels were so depleted. I sat on the edge of the bed and put down the tray. I had ordered a vegetable pasta dish and a hamburger, quite the mix.

As I took a bite of the burger, I heard the front door creak, and suddenly, James walked in. It looked as though he was trying to be discreet, tiptoeing into the room like a thief in the night, but his efforts were short-lived, as he knocked down a flower vase that was placed on a corner table by the door as he walked across the room. I just stared at him apprehensively, dismayed by his frazzled appearance. His hair was wiry, and his shirt looked all crumpled up. I could smell the pungent aroma of bourbon, wafting across the room, as he tried to walk, unsteadily, over to the bed, where I was sat.

I put down the burger half-heartedly, annoyed that it would probably be cold by the time I got to eat it. I was happy to see him, of course, but at the same time, I felt a slight annoyance at seeing him unhurt and indifferent. It meant that he had intentionally chosen to leave me alone on the first night of our honeymoon. It might have stung a little less if something dramatic had happened to him, which had meant he wasn't able to get back to the hotel to be with me; nonetheless, I flung my arms around him in a tight embrace and then kissed him.

"Heeeey baby girl, you're still up."

He released himself from my embrace and kissed me on the forehead. "I thought you would be asleep. You're only just eating your dinner? It's late?"

No shit Sherlock. It is bloody late.

Why would he think I would just go to sleep without knowing where he was? He didn't even seem concerned that he was stumbling into our hotel suite on the first night of our honeymoon, with a putrid stench of booze, and looking like he had been rolling around in the hay.

"Honey, I waited, I was hungry. Where were you?" I asked nonchalantly, trying not to seem like the nagging wife this soon into the marriage.

He walked over to the bed and grabbed the burger on the plate and took a big bite, which annoyed me slightly, but I daren't say anything. He then stumbled over to the minibar to pour himself a drink, and without even stopping to offer one to me, he filled a wine glass and drank the entire contents in one gulp.

"Baby, I met a few wayward people outside, then went for a walk into town. I tried to wake you, but you looked so peaceful. I had drinks with some more people in town, and then we went to another bar, then another bar, you know how it goes, I think we ended up back at their suite for an impromptu gathering, house party, whatever you want to call it."

He walked over to me and grabbed me by the waist and kissed me.

"You should have come, it was fun and baby, I'm sorry I left you all alone. Let me make it up to you. Ok?"

I was still a little hurt, but more so about his indifference on the matter, but his kisses were so intoxicating, and I let myself be carried away by them. He kissed me on my neck and then made his finger work downwards between my thighs. I wanted to resist as we had unfinished business to discuss, but he had a way with his hands. I could feel myself getting aroused by his magnetism, but then I was jolted back to reality.

"Babygirl, I need a shower first, I must stink, so hold that thought. Don't move a muscle, I will be right back."

I sat down on the bed sulkily and took a bite of the half-eaten burger, waiting for him to wash off the dirt and delights from his night out so that he could come and ravish me, the way honeymooners are supposed to be enchanted, and as I waited, my mind would not settle. It wasn't a big deal. He got carried away with a few random strangers, then went to paint the town red and left his new wife in a hotel suite all alone on their honeymoon.

It wasn't a big deal, right? He turned up at almost midnight, smelling of booze and a whiff of some strange perfume, with a crumpled shirt which looked like it was covered in brown dirt or was it make up?

Too difficult to tell without further inspection, but I

daren't pick up the shirt to look. I told myself I needed to be cool about it. I needed to show James that he was married to a chilled and relaxed going person who didn't just always jump to conclusions, albeit that the findings may or may have not been a clear as day.

The only issue here was that I was neither chilled nor easy-going; this was getting to me, but I wasn't about to accuse him of anything, especially on our honeymoon. I couldn't imagine how he would react. I didn't want to spoil our holiday, I didn't want an argument, and so, I let it go— no point crying over spilled milk. No point sticking pins in the cracks and best to let sleeping dogs lie for these tiny cracks in the foundation would soon smooth themselves out. Surely?

James seemed to take an infinity in the shower. I could hear him singing, surely pleased with himself and therefore not a hint of guilt on his conscience. This slightly irritated me as I wanted him to understand why it wasn't ok to leave me the way he had. He didn't, and the matter was never brought up again.

That night he didn't make love to me. He kissed me on the lips, perhaps intending to start something, but then rolled over and just went to sleep. This was out of character for a guy who liked to have sex for breakfast, lunch, and dinner. This time, he seemed disconnected, as though he had already had his fill, even the passion in his kisses were lacklustre and uninspiring.

I had to put it down to the fact that he was drunk, but even drunk James was always on top form- and this was our honeymoon, had I missed a trick or was I reading way too much into it.

|⊐   ⊏|

The next day, James seemed to be almost back to his usual self, sex for breakfast and then some more for brunch.

I was so relieved on some level that at least perhaps it must have just been the alcohol rendering him without an appetite for our usual sexual delights, but there was a distinct difference in the way he made love to me that morning. It was as though he didn't see me, as though although we were having sex, something was not quite right. He seemed to rush his way through the whole thing, and all the time, he did not even look at me once. He appeared as though, on some level, he was looking through me. He would screw me on autopilot and then go at it all over again, faster, and harder, as though he wanted to pound his way through to the other side of me.

I felt on some level violated, but this was my husband, if he wanted to make love like a porn star, then so be it, we all have our vices, but there was rough sex, and there was sex that was hard and rough enough to leave you with bruises.

I was bruised, I was sore, and although I tried to convince myself that this was just sex, it has to be said that there is a fine line between sex for pleasure and sex for pain, and on all accounts, I must admit that was I very much on the verge of the latter.

When he finally wore himself out and realized that I was no longer enjoying the act, he retreated and decided that we should go out for breakfast. I was exhausted and sore but decided to trooper on. We arrived at the tail end of the breakfast service, and as such, the remaining options on the breakfast buffet were limited, which annoyed James. He was on edge, as though he was ready to pounce on anyone who dared to anger him.

He shouted at the waiter and ordered that they made special items that weren't on the menu. He seemed out of control, a side I had never seen, except for the time he was irate with the cab driver who drove us home after my surprise birthday party. He finally finished our late breakfast and went down to lounge by the pool.

A welcome break.

The pool was lovely and fresh, and having a dip must have reset James's mood, as he seemed to relax again. He no longer looked angered or on edge. He kissed me passionately in the pool, to the delight of the older couple next to us. They didn't seem bothered by the overzealous performance he was putting on, and instead, they cheered us on. James was back in full swing. We spent the rest of the day like couples do, walks by the beach, lots of food and drink and relaxation. I tried to put the events of the previous night behind me, but something kept me on edge, something pulled on my subconscious, telling me that this was the start of something dark and uninviting.

———

On the last day of our honeymoon, we decided to venture out of the resort and take in some of the sights and try to be somewhat like typical tourists for the day, soaking up all Hawaii had to offer.

Our resort was based in Waikiki, so we decided to stay around the area and visit the sights nearby. We visited the USS Arizona Memorial, did some last-minute shopping at the Royal Hawaiian Centre, and finally checked out the International Market Place.

The day was full of surprises, and adventure and James was the perfect husband, attentive and not once did he complain as we paraded around the shops aimlessly, looking for something that would catch my eye. He seemed to enjoy the time spent together, just the two of us, away from the distractions of real life; away from the office, away from the constant need to ingratiate himself with others or impress some nonentity. It appears any worries or stresses he may have been harbouring for the last few weeks had dissipated, and he had been given a new lease of life. As night-time fell, we opted for dinner at a casual dining spot by the beach.

It was nice to just be ourselves, to remove the pretentiousness and just for once, have a burger with cheese at a place which didn't even require one to sit down or use any silverware, a simple, quaint beach shack, no-frills, no superfluities, just plain old good cooking.

As we sat down to eat on the bar stools at the front of the shop, James took my hand and smiled. He shifted nervously, and I could tell he was struggling with whatever it was he was about to say. I stroked his cheek, to reassure him that he should feel comfortable to talk to me about anything.

"Fiona, I love you so much. I need you to know that. Ok?" He paused for a few seconds and moved his stool closer to me and then continued "I sometimes get ahead of myself, and I may say things and do things that are out of character for me, but I love you. I need you to know that. I need you to know that, no matter what, no matter who may to try and pull us apart, no matter the journey, I need you to know I love you."

I didn't understand why he was saying this. Was there something wrong, or was he just speaking generally?

"James, what's the matter, did something happen, are you ok?"

I wanted to know what brought on the sudden declara-

tion. Did it have something to do with his strange
behaviour as of late, or was I just reading too much into it?

"Nothing baby, I just know what I am like. I don't want
to ever hurt you. I just want you to be happy, I don't want
to do anything that will ever make you doubt me. There
isn't anything bothering you or that bothers you about me,
right? Are you happy? You would tell me, wouldn't you?"

I still didn't know what was going on. I was happy, at
least I thought I was. I had no significant reason to be
unhappy at that point. I had just gotten married to the love
of my life, and I had my whole life ahead of me. I had so
much to look forward to. Love, friendship, family, and a
sense of accomplishment. I didn't have much to be
unhappy about, not really, so nothing about what James
was saying made any sense to me or made me concerned.

I was oblivious to the clues that lay in front of me, from
his suspicious behaviour with the housekeeper, his assertion
that he didn't want kids, to his violent outburst and super-
ciliousness. Oblivious, or simply choosing to ignore them?

With all the conversations that I decided not to have for
fear of rocking the boat, perhaps this sudden declaration
should have been a signal and a lightning bolt to jolt me
out of my subservient behaviour and allow me to voice or
unburden myself of any uncertainty. He was, after all
asking me if I was happy and if there was anything that I
was concerned about that may make me doubt his love.
And yet, at that moment, when I was offered the low
hanging fruit and the chance to speak up and ask the
uncomfortable questions I had swept under the rug, I
chose to brush them aside for fear of starting down a path
that I didn't wish to go.

My mantra was, if you think it, you will find it.

"James, I've got this. There is nothing I want more

than you, and as far as I am concerned, I couldn't be happier."

And with that, I had inadvertently set the wheels in motion. I had declared that I was happy, and as it would later turn out, from that day forward, I had no right to rescind on that declaration. I was to be held to testimony no matter what; I had avowed the oath of my irrevocable and absolute happiness.

From henceforth, no matter what the situation, it was yielded into his brain that he was all I wanted, and I could never be unhappy with him, no matter what.

This was to be the start of my undoing.

Chapter 14

We returned to normal life, with a post-honeymoon glow that was still ever so palpable.

I went back to work the very next week, and James, busy as usual, kept the office on their toes. Marrying James didn't mean that I would automatically receive any special treatment at work. I think he went out of his way to see this wasn't the case.

He didn't want our relationship to affect my work or the morale in the office, so we kept it professional, well, except for the odd sexual rendezvous on his office couch. He hadn't lost his fervour for me, and I loved it. It had been drilled into my head from an early age that married people seemed to lose their passion for each other. It had been six months since the wedding, and I had now settled into my routine with James.

We worked hard, we partied hard, and we made love almost every night. He was insatiable, his sexual appetite grew so much that I started to feel that I could no longer keep up with him. I would often catch him pleasing himself, even after we had had three to four rounds of lovemaking. I couldn't quite understand the compulsion but didn't think it was an issue. Maria stayed on as our house-keeper, much to my dismay and as ever, she would parade the house in next to nothing, and when confronted, she would blame the heat.

I didn't buy it, but the feebleness in me meant that I chose to let her get away with it. It didn't bother James whatsoever, and although he never admitted it, I think her fleshly display added to his new compulsion and erratic sexual behaviour.

I was always afraid to leave both of them alone, not so much because of lack of trust for James, but more so that he may realise that she had more to offer from a physical aspect.

She was voluptuous, hot-blooded, and from the looks of things, her craving for sexual affection was all too obvious.

———

By late February, I had decided I would go home for my mother's birthday, it would just be a quick long weekend trip to surprise her as I had not seen her since the wedding.

I mentioned this to James, but he seemed irritated and said we would talk about it later. I thought nothing of it and hadn't even considered for a second that it might be an issue. As the weekend approached, we decided it would be a good idea to go out for dinner as we hadn't been out together as a couple for quite some time. We seemed to have hectic social lives, but it always seemed to be based around some overly pretentious dinner with his friends. I still hadn't made many more friends, but I put that down to my busy work schedule and my motivation to spend time with my husband at home.

I hadn't tried to address the conversation about starting a family again. Still, I had hoped spending some quality time at home together might inadvertently lead to a natural progression of the next phase in our lives.

We arrived at the restaurant at about 6 pm and sat at the corner table, our usual spot. James ordered a few drinks and then decided to order for me, which was very odd. He seemed in a rush, as though taking me out for dinner had become suddenly become a chore, an obligation, an act of duty, rather than an act of love.

"Hey, what's the matter darling? You seem awfully tense" I asked him affectionately.

I wanted to have a pleasant dinner with him and didn't want the stresses of work, or whatever was on his mind to get in the way.

"Nothing, I am just a little tired. Do you think we can just eat and go, I'm rather tired and to be honest, not much in the mood for all this?"

In hindsight, perhaps I should have chosen a better time to bring up my upcoming trip to London, but I had no idea that this would antagonise him. I started to speak about the journey and my intended date of travel, but I wasn't given a chance to finish before he cut me off abruptly.

"What the hell. Didn't you just see them a few months ago when I paid for the whole bloody family to come and stay with us?"

I couldn't understand what the issue was and why it was such a big deal.

"Do what you like, but you're bloody paying for it and forget first-class, that ship has sailed now. You'd better book coach and not waste any more of my money."

I had never once heard James complain about money, and, I had never asked him for a dime. He had always just splurged out on me and always seemed to be offended whenever I offered to pay my way, but here he was now, a few months after our wedded bliss, at the top of his voice, shouting at me for wanting to get plane tickets to visit my family. I hadn't even mentioned flying first-class, and even if that were to be the case, I earned a living and had my own money and was very happy to pay for it.

"And don't think you are getting any time off work, we are too busy now, so it better just be a weekend trip."

Shock and dismay filled me, as I took in his total change of behaviour. He seemed annoyed about something, perhaps the cost of the flight, or that fact that I was going away and possibly asking for a few days off work.

I sat still, as the shock of his tone weighed me down, and I just stared at him in horror. His brazenness was startling, and he had a grave look in his eyes, something I had never seen before, and I could only describe it as resentment. It was as if all the love had been drained out in a moment. This was pure contempt.

"And, as for the bloody honeymoon we, we were both there weren't we, so it's only fair you fork out half the cost. If you ask me, it was a bloody waste of money. We could have spent it here in Chicago with friends, out on the town, showing everyone how it's done. Anyway, I may just deduct that from your next salary. I am not a bloody bank, you know."

I suddenly snapped out of my momentary paralysis when a teardrop fell from my eye and rolled to the corner of my lip, the saltiness, waking me up from my stupor. I was humiliated at being spoken to in such a manner, and as I stood up and grabbed my bag, ready to head for the door, he grabbed me by the wrist and gave me a bloodcurdling look.

"DON'T you dare Fiona, sit down, I'm warning you. Sit your ass back down and don't make a show of me."

I freed myself from him and responded. "Then watch your tone with me. Why are you overreacting, you are the one making a show here, not me? I didn't ask you for money, and I shouldn't need to ask for your permission to go and see my family, what's all this about."

He snatched my hand again. "I said, sit down for god sake. You just saw your bloody family a few months ago, and just because you don't ask for my money doesn't mean it's not being spent by you some way or another, who is paying for this bloody meal, huh?"

I grabbed his hand with my free hand and pulled away, then grabbed a fifty out of my bag, placed it on the table and ran out the door in tears. Not only was I humiliated, but I was also so hurt that he would start a fight over money. I caught a taxi and went straight home to contemplate what had just happened. I never asked him for money, I never ever had. He had always insisted fervently on paying for everything, much to my discomfort and objection, and there he was insinuating that I was eating away at his money, money which I never cared for, or didn't need. I lay in bed in floods of tears, wondering why my prince charming had suddenly turned sour.

It didn't make sense, the rage, the hurtful words; this wasn't the charming man I knew, there had to be more to this. I contemplated for hours on the many reasons for his possible outburst, much of which I seemed to blame myself for, but nothing made sense.

James turned up in a drunken state at about 3 am, and I was awake, waiting for him.

I was no longer angry about the argument, more so hurt than anything and very much expecting an apology. I got out of bed and walked to the lounge where he stood pouring himself a whiskey. I was relieved to see him, and all I said was, "Baby, are you ok? I was worried."

I was about to walk over to him, but he turned around suddenly, bloodshot red-eyed, bolted towards me and threw the glass towards my head. It missed me by about a couple of millimetres.

Shock, horror and fear, as I trembled, trying to compose myself from what had just come to pass. As I bent over to pick up fragments of the shattered glass which had been scattered across the floor, he pulled violently on my hair and grabbed me by the neck with his other hand, lifting me up against the wall.

"Baby? Don't call me baby, you bitch. You think you can embarrass me like that and get away with it? No one walks away from me. You whore, you walked out on dinner and left me there looking like a loser. You know how people talk."

His grip tightened, and all the while he was speaking, I was grabbing at his hands frantically, desperately trying to free myself from his murderous grasp. I could feel my lungs constricting, tightening as his grip grew more forceful. I started to gasp for air but could feel the life draining quickly out of me. I could no longer struggle.

I had no fight left in me.

My body had started to give up for lack of strength, and as I felt a teardrop fall from my eyes unto my cheek, hitting the side of his hand which was full of veins from his lethal grip, the teardrop almost marking the curtain drop at the end of a performance, he suddenly let go.

The air rushing back into my lungs, filled me with life as I fell to the floor in a thump, with streams of tears falling down my face, shaken and fearful of what he could possibly do to next.

"Oh, hell, what have I done, I'm so sorry... shit, Fiona, are you ok" I heard him say, his voice trembling as I looked up at him, still dizzy from the lack of oxygen.

His expression had changed from that of anger to disbelief, disbelief at what he had just done, something which could now never be undone.

I had now become one of those women, beaten, bruised, or abused; you name it.

He had done the most unforgivable and had lashed out at the one he was supposed to hold true—his most beloved. After the event, we went to bed in separate rooms. We didn't speak that night. I think it was the shame on both parts.

The shame that he had been so cruel as to physically hurt me and the guilt that I had let it happen, I was now a victim.

We awoke to the break of dawn and a new day.

It was a cloudy February's day, and the rain was threatening to make an appearance. I so desperately wanted to leave the apartment to gather my thoughts, as I could not bear to make eye contact him with. I was ashamed. I didn't understand where this shame had come from, but it took hold of me completely. Was it my fault that he had done this? Had I provoked this kind of emotion from him? Had I evoked an evil within him and was this what Amanda warned me about?

The words, "He is a lunatic, he is dangerous" kept ringing true in my ears.

I could see Amanda's face, as she said those words to me in that small café less than a year ago. Was this what she was alluding to? I had so many questions, but no answers. James was still sound asleep upstairs in one of the bedrooms, he had not yet made an appearance, and I was glad that I had some time to think before having to deal with him. I walked over to the on-suite bathroom and looked at myself in the mirror.

I looked pitiful. My eyes were red and angry from crying all night long, but what stunned me the most were the bruises on my neck. Purple and angry, a picture-perfect reminder of my battle scars. They reminded me of the anguish I felt from his tightening grip, sucking some of the life out of me. I was reliving the events all over again. I touched my neck and felt the tenderness where his hands had been. It hadn't been a dream; this really had happened. Suddenly I heard the door open, and James popped his head in the door.

"Morning baby girl, are you ok?"

He walked in and put his hands around my waist and kissed me on the cheek.

He looked rested and guilt-free. I said nothing, a little bit in disbelief. I just stood there, slightly frozen. His eyes met mine, and he noticed the redness in them, and I think this jolted him back to the events of the night before. He spun me around gently and delicately put his fingers on my neck, examining the sight of the bruises.

"Oouf, that looks painful. Baby, I'm sorry. I guess I was drunk last night. No harm done, right? Just a bit of teasing never hurt anyone. It's just dramatics."

No harm done.

I wasn't sure I had heard him right. I was still stood, frozen, perhaps a little afraid, but his nonchalance made me get a little riled up inside, but I didn't dare speak up.

"Just put some of that make-up thing you got, what's it called again?... congealer… no, concealer. There, put some concealer on that. No one will notice, and anyway, they will think you are covering up a couple of hickeys."

He laughed. "Yeah? Will you do that, baby girl?"

He lifted my chin with the tip of his finger so that he could see my eyes.

"Will you do that for me?"

What else was I supposed to say? If I had said no, would that invoke round two? I agreed to comply with his request. It was all fun and games, no one got hurt, and he was drunk, so I basically would have to get over it and put it down as a one-off, a sexual game that went awry. Except, I don't recall it being sexual, or a joke.

Had I imagined the whole thing? Had I misconstrued what had happened? James had a way of making you believe him even when you knew he was wrong. He kissed me again and lifted me on to the bathroom vanity. He wasn't going to address anything from last night, as far as he was concerned, I had imagined the whole thing, or at least, I had exaggerated it. I needed to get over it.

This was the message in his eyes. Get over it! I closed my eyes and took a deep breath. I didn't know what to do.

This was the man I loved so much. He would never do anything to hurt me, not on purpose and perhaps it was all a misunderstanding, a joke gone too far, an alcohol-fuelled event which had gotten out of control. It would never happen again; I was sure of that. He loved me too much to hurt me. After all, I was his baby girl.

He lifted me off the vanity and carried me over to the

bedroom and lay me down on the bed.

"Are we good? He stood there, waiting for my response. I had no choice. Would I just let it slide? Could I?

"Yes, James, baby, we're good." He smiled and then bent over and pulled off my underwear.

"Good, let me make it up to you the only way I know how."

He laughed, pleased with himself. It was now all right as rain. He bent down on his knees and pulled me toward the edge of the bed so that my legs close were to his face. He then rolled up my dressing gown and spread my legs apart.

"Come here you, I missed you like the desert missed the rain." He then licked his lips and then lowered his head and then started to tease me with his tongue. He was more passionate, more intimate. He took his time on me, making sure that he hit all the right spots.

I was weak, and I succumbed to his seductive nature.

I know I should say I resisted, protested, or perhaps pushed him off and made it clear that what he had done was unforgivable, but instead, the more he touched me and kissed me, the more I softened under his command.

I just laid there, melting under his touch.

He would not stop pleasuring me until all my senses had erupted with pleasure. When he was done with the foreplay, he stood up and pulled down his boxer shorts, proud to show me that he was ready to take me.

"Now for the finale. You won't even remember last night by the time I'm done with you, that's all in the past now."

He lay on top of me, and although I was distracted by his movements, I couldn't help but come to the realisation that perhaps there was just something not quite right with him.

Chapter 15

B y the next month, the weather was starting to get more spring-like, so I began to spend more time outdoors.

I frequently visited the farmer's markets, much like I did before I got with James. James hadn't had any more episodes other than the odd raising of voices. Everything was getting back to normal, and I had all but forgotten about the event of the last month. I had even been allowed to go home to see my folks.

Of course, I didn't mention anything about the events that had transpired that night, and when asked, I pretty much painted a rosy picture. The fact is that, other than for that moment of insanity, James was just like I had imagined any other husband would be.

He was attentive, he was caring, devoted and still had an insatiable appetite for pleasing me. My sister had grilled me on my plans for starting a family, but I had said that I wanted to wait at least another year.

This was the truth, I wanted to enjoy married life

before having a screaming baby take away all the passion me and James had built between us. Mother was also none the wiser about James's moment of madness. To my family, he was a saint, he could do no wrong. I spent a week at my parents and a couple of days at Sarah's and Ian's. I babysat little Ella, my niece, which gave my sister a few days well-deserved break, and it perhaps made me realise that I should wait to start a family.

It was bloody hard work looking after a toddler, but I did enjoy it, and I decided that I would wait no more than a year. I left London feeling revived and rejuvenated, while also looking forward to getting back to Chicago. I didn't want to miss any more work. I didn't want anyone at the firm having to use that as an excuse for me missing out on my deadlines.

At the airport, on the way back to Chicago, I had rung James to tell him what time I would arrive and where to pick me up. He seemed distant when he finally picked up, and I could hear strange voices in the background. He reassured me that it was the Television and that there was no one at home, just him and Maria. He said he would pick me up at the spot we had agreed, and with that's said, he hung up. I didn't think much of it. James was a busy man, no time for chit chat. I arrived in Chicago on time and picked up my bags and headed straight to the parking area to meet James. He was nowhere to be seen, so I rang him, but unfortunately, after four missed calls, he still had not picked up.

I decided to wait just in case he was stuck in traffic.

After about an hour, I tried him again, but no response. At this point, I was getting tired and decided to grab a cab. I sent him a text message to say I had got bored of waiting and would make my way home myself.

▭

S ometimes things happen because they were meant to be, and perhaps there is such a thing as destiny.

There is a saying, there is no smoke without fire, and if you suspect it, then there's a chance it may be true. I was always a big believer in the law of attraction, a concept that the universe hears and listens to your thoughts and that, if you think it, you will find it.

For this reason, I always chose to see the positive in everything, sometimes much to my detriment, even when a higher force such as instinct would pull me in a different direction, I would not falter on my approach on positivity. Instinct or intuition plays a huge part in our lives, and we are always told to trust our instincts, that deeper voice in the pit of our stomach, which tells us when we are being led astray.

With James, there were some signs which, despite that feeling in the pit of my stomach, I chose to overlook. So, on that day, it was as though destiny or faith had decided to step in, open my eyes to the deep, profound culpability of my naivety.

I had got an Uber straight from the airport to make my way back to our apartment, exhausted from the long flight which was worsened by the long wait for James in the car park. I couldn't wait to get home, drop my bags and head for a long hot bath.

I tipped the Uber driver generously as he had sympathized with me and hadn't bothered with nonsensical chit chat on the 45-minute drive home from the airport. He had been silent the whole way and let me sit back and relax. I walked into the apartment, excited and relieved to be finally home, to be back to the solace and stillness of our suburbia apartment. As soon as I stepped in, I could hear noises coming from Maria's bedroom upstairs. I didn't know who it was, but I didn't want to jump to conclusions.

I shouted out for James to say I was home, but no one responded. Instead, the noises from Maria's room got even louder. I wondered who she might have in her bedroom. She knew better than to have guests upstairs with her.

I walked quickly up the stairs, not knowing whether to interrupt her and then I heard it—his voice coming from the other side of the room, Maria's room. I ran up to the door and pushed it open, and there they were, naked, on Maria's bed. They hadn't heard me and were still going at me.

James had his head in between Maria's legs, just like he would do to me. There it was, intuition, instinct, rearing its ugly head.

But screw the laws of attraction, because I hadn't willed this, I had been positive even when I thought something was going on between the two of them, I had wanted positivity, and yet the laws of attraction had royally and unapologetically screwed me over.

I screamed out so loud that I hurt my throat. "Screw you James, you bastard, you low life, how could you?"

I was so angry, not only that I had caught them in the act, but that I had to bear witness to the two of them, right in the act. James immediately jumped up, his face wet with perspiration and Maria's arousal.

Maria didn't seem bothered, she just laid there, smirking, as though it wasn't a big deal.

"Shit, baby, it's not what it looks like" these were the words he uttered which were quite laughable given the fact that he still had bits of Maria's orgasm on his lips and his face. He must have thought me a fool. I immediately ran out the door and down the stairs, hysterical and in tears. I grabbed my hang bag and burst out the front door. I couldn't believe how quickly my world was crumbling. I half expected James to run after me, but he didn't. I guess there was no excuse he could have given me that could rectify this. I had seen the unthinkable.

There was no lie he could tell that would make me unsee what I had just seen. There would be no redeeming himself this time.

He had gone too far.

I ran into the street, floods of tears streaming down my eyes. I held up my hands on my head, in desperation, spinning around, hysterical.

I didn't know how to stop the tears. I had just seen the man I loved with another woman, someone who we had invited into our home to keep it whole.

I fell to the ground, dizzy and feeling like I wanted to die, for it all to end. I had never felt pain like this. It was not the physical kind of pain, more so a deeper pain that would cause a wound so great that I thought I could no longer live.

A young lady on a bicycle came riding around the corner and saw me laying on the ground. She quickly dismounted her bike and ran over to me. She bent down to see if I was breathing

"Hey, you are alright? Lady, are you ok" She tapped on my shoulder, but I did not respond.

She tapped me once more and still, I just laid there unresponsive. I think at that point, I was too despondent to understand what was going on around me. I could just about make her silhouette, but my eyes were blurry with tears, and I was holding on to my chest as though I was having a heart attack.

One might say that the pain of seeing a loved one do

such a thing to you can be as painful as having a heart attack. The lady started to shout out for help. She got up and ran up the street shouting and then ran back over to watch over me. She was dialling for the ambulance and screaming for someone to come and help to lift me so she could see if I was still breathing.

With all the commotion going on, James must have heard, as he came running out the house. He ran over to where I was laying on the ground and bent down. He took my pulse and then stood back up again. He exchanged some words with the lady for a few seconds.

She sounded irritated, but he must have convinced her that everything was ok because she then shook his hand and walked off and rode off away on her bicycle. James bent down and shock me. I could hear him shouting out for Maria to come outside.

He then lifted me up and took me into the house. He laid me on the sofa and started to call out my name. I was so dejected that I looked blue in the face. I could make out his voice, but something in me just wanted to stay under. To remain in that vegetative state and pretend none of it was happening.

I think my body was still in shock. They say a person can die from a broken heart, I wanted so much to be taken by death, for the pain to stop and for my heart to heal. I willed for death to carry me away and bring me back when things could be right again. It now seemed that this place was not real for I had stepped off the plane and walked into a parallel dimension where everything was upside down, a world where I had no place, where the left was right and where James was no longer mine.

James ordered Maria to get a glass of water for me to drink and a whiskey for him.

She complied dutifully. "Baby, snap out of it, you are scaring everyone."

I thought to myself, who is everyone? It was only the three of us in the house, and two out of the three were culprits in this fiasco. Maria walked over with a glass of water. She was sipping on the whiskey she had poured for James. She handed the water to me, and something jostled me out of my mini coma, perhaps it was the sight of her hands, but as soon as she put the glass to my lips, I jumped up and grabbed her by the hair, sending the glass flying across the room.

I wanted to hurt this woman so badly; this woman who had been so full of malice as she tried to steal James away from me. She had seen how much I had doted on him, and yet, without any remorse had seduced him. I felt like a woman scorned, and at that moment, I swear I could have killed her.

I grabbed her face and started to scratch. I kicked, and I pulled at every crevice. James was shouting out something inaudible, but I refused to stop, he then grabbed me by the waist and threw me over his shoulders, he had seen enough.

He marched up the stairs, with me kicking and screaming for him to put me down. He wanted to get me as far as possible away from Maria as he could. I was a woman who had been deceived, and I was out for blood.

"Put me down you son of a bitch, why are you protecting your whore? Are you trying to get rid of me so you can just go and screw her? Screw you sonofabitch."

James did all he could to ignore me. He carried me to the bedroom and threw me on to the bed. I was still screaming and crying at this point, all manner of cursing flying out of my mouth.

I was angry at Maria. I should have been mad at James, he was the one who had screwed up, and yet I was focusing all my hate towards the maid and forgetting to see the bigger picture.

"Fiona, I told you to get yourself together, what the heck was that performance downstairs, are you out of your bloody mind, she could bloody press charges. You went for her, are you crazy?"

I could see why he thought so, I was not the sort of person to pick a fight with anyone. I was miss sensible, and here I was, acting like a raving lunatic, kicking, and screaming and trying to gorge out Maria's eyes.

Nonetheless, I still couldn't believe I was the one being scolded, scolded for his infidelity, scolded for what he had done to us. I began to compose myself, as I realized fighting wouldn't fix anything. James said he would go and check to see if Maria was ok and would be right back. He shut the door behind him, and I heard him run down the stairs.

Why was he checking on her? I was his wife. Why did it matter if she was ok. She was a home-wrecker.

At the point, I heard sirens in the distance, Maria had called the police.

———

It turns out that fighting in Chicago is taken quite seriously, as Maria filed for assault charges.

I had hurt her more than I had intended. Her face bore a few bruises, and she had a bludgeoned eye. I had not known the might of my strength.

I immediately felt remorseful, for no matter how much someone had hurt me emotionally, it didn't give me the right cause them any grievous bodily harm. If anyone needed to take the brunt of this, it was James. When the police saw the state I had left Maria in, they didn't take to it very well.

They questioned Maria briefly in the kitchen and then asked me some questions, to which I admitted that I had lost my temper in a blind rage. I tried to explain to the police how I had walked in on James and Maria, but they seemed so dismissive, hinting that they didn't deal with domestic issues.

I said I would apologize for the bruises, but I could hear Maria in the kitchen shouting out expletives.

"She was trying to kill me. She is lucky I'm only asking for assault; she is crazy. Si, no? I swear if my boss was not in la casa, she would have killed me. Murder! asesinato Papi, la quiero fuera ahora, PUTA!"

I guess sorry was not going to be enough to heal her wounds, but everyone had seemed to forget why we ended up in such a state in the first place, and with the whole commotion, no one had stopped to say sorry to the one left with the broken heart.

The police had heard enough.

They read me my Miranda rights and then dragged me into their police car. As they put the handcuffs on me, I looked over at James, expecting him to come to my rescue or at least protest, but instead, he was over by Maria, consoling her.

Not only had I been betrayed by the one I loved, but I was also being abandoned. Humiliated at being dragged out by the police, as the neighbours gathered to see what the commotion was, I lowered my head in shame.

Everything seemed so surreal - one minute I was in London telling my family how amazing things were in Chicago and talking to my sister about plans, only then having to fall right into this upheaval that I could have never foreseen.

Life was never going to be the same again, I had been dealt an unlucky hand, and if I didn't get a handle on things, my life would inevitably spiral out of control, and fast.

Chapter 16

I arrived at the police station, still in floods of tears, not knowing what was in store for me.

I had never in my life been arrested. I was always on the right side of the law and pitied people who by whatever means found themselves in a jail cell. Yet here I was, mug shots taken, a criminal statement signed and about to have the prison bars locked, with me on the wrong side of it. I screamed as they led me into the cell. It felt like my world was crumbling right before me, as though once those bars were locked, that would be the end of me.

I wanted to protest, I wanted to punch my way through, but there were heavy-set guards on either side of me, I had no fight left in me. The cell was a little crowded, nothing like I had imagined. It was more of a holding cell, for those waiting for their sentencing or bail. There were a few angry-looking faces and one or two who, like me, just rolled up like a rock in the corner of the cell, cradling themselves, waiting to be bailed out or perhaps to be taken to a proper prison, off-site.

I looked around and noticed that I looked nothing like

these people. I didn't have any tattoos or piercings, or the common stereotypes which one would usually associate with someone who was on the wrong side of the law, a huge misconception. I didn't look the part. I was no criminal.

Luckily, I didn't have to spend more than a couple of hours in the holding cell, as James paid the bail quickly, a small glimmer of hope that he cared for me at all. I grabbed my belongings and headed for the exit, where he was waiting for me with open arms. I deliberated whether to return the gesture, but I was still too hurt from his infidelity.

I walked past him, leaving him standing there. He quickly turned around and grabbed me by the hand. I stopped, not knowing what he might do. He pulled me closer and hugged me.

"Oh, baby girl, I am so sorry. I was so worried. I can't believe all of this. I am so sorry."

He released me from his embrace and lifted my chin and pecked me on the lips. I could see his eyes were red, as though he may have been crying. He looked so sincere.

"I can't believe I let this happen. I have no words. I am so ashamed. I am dying inside baby, seeing you like this, I am all cut up inside. I just need you to know that I am a fool for ever letting a hair on your body suffer like this."

I didn't know what to say. I wasn't sure if he was apologizing for his infidelity or for the fact that his mistress had landed me in jail, whatever it was, I sure as hell was not going to discuss it at the police station.

"James, can you please just take me home. I need to rest. I need a shower, I need some food, and I just need to get away from this place. Please!"

I walked off, headed for the car park. I wanted out of there as soon as possible.

"Sure thing, anything you want," I heard him say as I was walking away.

We didn't say a word to each other on the drive home.

―――

One could cut the tension with a knife, and I was apprehensive as to what I would find at home.

Would Maria still be there? Where was I going to go once I got myself together? Would I move out, should he? Would he?

I couldn't think straight; thoughts kept flowing around and around in my head.

James still looked distressed. Perhaps he too was thinking the same, would I divorce him and most importantly, what next? We pulled into the driveway and there in the distance stood Maria, hand on hips, clearly still outraged by the events of the day. I dreaded what she might say, although, in all reality, she was the one who perhaps should have been apologizing. It was as though everyone had forgotten why we ended up in this mess.

Everyone's thoughts were on my out of control behavior. Once we were parked, James jumped out of the car quickly and opened the passenger door for me. He was threading carefully. He helped me out the car, a gesture that did nothing to soften my heart.

Maria started to walk towards us, and James stuck his hand out, making her stop dead in her tracks.

"I got this. You've done enough already, Maria. I got this."

Maria looked irritated but complied. She figured she'd better do as she was told, after all, astonishingly, James was still allowing her to stay in the house. We walked past her, and I gave her a wry look and nothing more. She knew I wasn't sorry for the attack, but now, a still calm had enveloped me, as slowly, the realization of my delusion set in. There was James, trying to play the innocent party, pretending everything was going to be okay.

Everyone was always pretending to be happy, pretending that we had a perfect life, pretending not to acknowledge the inevitability of the affair, even now when everything was crumbling. Life as we knew it could never return to normalcy, we all still trod carefully around each other, with a sense of deception, acting as though the events of the last few hours were something which we could all get past.

———

I awoke to the sound of the TV coming from the guest room.

I had sent James there last night as there was no way I was going to let him share a bed with me, not after what I had seen. I couldn't get the picture out of my head, his face dripping with the sheen of his betrayal, wet and saturated with all of Maria. I opened my eyes to a new morning, hoping desperately for all of it to be a dream, for all the pain to have been my imagination.

It couldn't be real. It was too unexpected. I pondered on this for a minute or two. Was this true, was his betrayal really that unforeseen? Was I just a naïve and inexperienced little girl trying to fill the shoes of a woman, who was desperately trying to be a wife to a powerful man, one who was notoriously known for his womanizing ways?

I had always sensed something was not right with him and Maria, even from the very first day I laid eyes on her. The times I had seen them together acting questionably, the strange behavior from James whenever he was around her, which I had chosen to ignore.

Perhaps I wasn't a victim of this, after all. Maybe I was complicit in the fact that deep down, I knew something was going on all along, and because I had chosen not to act, this meant that I was amenable to it. I had planted a weed which was so inconceivable, as now, I had indeed witnessed his betrayal, and as faith would have it, I had been a willing accomplice to my eventual demise. I stirred in bed, unwilling to leave the bedroom.

About half an hour later, I heard a knock on the door. It was Maria. She brought in a breakfast tray, filled with muffins, an omelet, fruit, and some coffee. For all the time I had lived in that apartment, she had never once brought me or James breakfast in bed, so this was an obvious ploy, one which I could see right through.

"Good morning, Miss Fiona. You sleep so long I bring you something to eat."

I looked at her in amazement. She looked composed, perhaps hoping that everything could be fixed with a little bowl of fruit and muffins. She wouldn't make eye contact, and although her words sounded sincere, I knew deep down the callousness in her heart. She didn't care for me, not really, she had ulterior motives.

If she could continue to play the part of the 'help', perhaps she would be allowed to stay on in the apartment, to satiate my husband.

"Miss Fiona, Mr James, is asking for you. I tell him that I will bring you breakfast. First, you take a shower, and then you go downstairs, he is waiting for you, I think to talk. And miss, I know nothing I can say can make up for my stupid mistake. I am so stupid, Miss Fiona, I am so sorry. First time and only time this happens. Don't blame Mr James. He drank too much, and me, I felt sad about my father, who is sick in Cartagena, and maybe I needed someone to console me. I make a mistake. I cannot erase this, but truly, I swear, on mi Papi, that this is mistake that I wish for your forgiveness."

Her voice croaked as she bent down on her knees, and then she started to cry. "Miss Fiona, please, por favour, please. Perdoname. Por favor, please, forgive, perdonanos, forgive Mr James and me. He loves you. I know that. I see every day."

She carried on with her speech, floods of tears falling down her face. I didn't know what to make of it. The whole speech seemed a bit rehearsed, but even so, the tears moved me somewhat.

Maria was always so stoic around me, and everything about her always seemed to irritate me, from her accent to her poor use of English, and her overpowering perfume. Here she was on bended knees, asking for my forgiveness, asking for me to forgive James, begging as if her life depended on it.

I didn't want to be swayed by her tears, so I got up from the bed and stood up, helped her to her knees and handed her back the tray of food.

'Maria, you and James have left a hole in my heart, one which won't be fixed by a couple of chocolate muffins and coffee. I need some time to think. Besides, I already took my frustration out on you yesterday. You don't mean anything to me, it is not you who has hurt me, and I don't care for your feelings or your tears. It is James who broke me. He broke us when he chose to bed you. It is with him that the wreckage is, not you, so, please get up and go back to work. I have no space in my heart to watch you cry. Did you have mercy on me when you called the cops last night? So why should I even listen to this? Because of you Maria, I have a record with the police, my marriage is damaged, beyond repair, because of you, I have seen the unthinkable. You beg for forgiveness, but I will not stay here and listen to any more of your words. Your actions were callous; not once did you think of me. You knew I was out of town, so you decided to seduce my James. That is truly unforgivable. But you see Maria, in all honesty, you are not the problem; you are the enabler. I should have known it was only a matter of time."

I brushed past her and walked out of the bedroom. It wasn't her words I needed to hear. She was a nonentity as far as I was concerned—a thorn in my bouquet, an unnecessary element.

I needed to find James. It was time to talk this out.

———

I went into the guest bedroom, where James was still lying in bed.

He had his bathrobe on in bed, watching the television. There was a documentary on TV about some washed-out girl band, so I knew he couldn't have been paying attention to it, as he never watched trash TV, as he often referred to it as. He was always of the opinion that only simple-minded people could tolerate such nonsensical TV. I watched him, as his eyes were affixed on the screen, in some kind of stupor.

He looked tired and tortured, as though he had been awake all night. I walked over to the bed where he lay and picked up the remote control and switched off the television, but his gaze remained on the screen.

How odd, I thought to myself. He looked like someone who had just been through a great ordeal. It was I who should have looked this traumatized.

Was this an act, or was he genuinely relenting on his

actions? I moved closer and tapped him on the ankle. He jerked, suddenly acknowledging my presence.

"Fiona shit I didn't even notice you standing there. Sorry baby. I was deep in thought there. I wanted to come and talk to you after you had some time to have breakfast. Did Maria bring it to you?"

I walked over to the patchwork rocking armchair, next to the bed and sat down, the same chair, where we had made love countless times, except now, the colors looked washed out and uninviting.

"I wasn't very hungry, James. You expect me to eat after all this?"

I looked at him, waiting for his response. He looked wounded, like a disobedient puppy who had just been told off by its master.

He didn't say anything; he then moved to the edge of the bed and sat up so that he was facing me. "Fiona, I know we need to talk. I just need you not to be so angry, so that you can hear me out. I'm not going to make excuses for my behavior or anything like that, but I do need you to hear me out."

He nodded, signalling that it was my queue to respond. I paused for a second, feeling the urge to walk out.

How dare he try to manipulate the situation, and even try to control the structure of the conversation.

He moved closer, and then I spoke immediately, that was my signal that I didn't want him anywhere near me.

"I am done being angry. That didn't do much except land me in a police cell, besides, what happened? How come I was bailed out?

He got up and walked over to the door and shut it, then walked back and sat down on the edge of the bed again.

"After you were taken away, I got into a heated argument with Maria. I guess with all the commotion, she panicked. She said she thought you were going to kill her. She panicked, Fiona, that's why she called the feds. You see, the minute they took you away, and I explained what would happen, should she persist on filing charges, she immediately backed down. We both went to the station, and she retracted her statement and downgraded it to a domestic situation."

Ha! I thought to myself. Why didn't she retract the whole charges, why downgrade?

I think he could tell from my expression precisely what I was thinking.

"I asked her to retract the statement, but she said that she couldn't trust that you wouldn't try to hurt her, so at least for her safety, she wanted the altercation on record. Something about her cousin's friend being in the same situation, which led to her cousin being stabbed in the arm."

I couldn't believe what a dumb excuse it was. As if I would ever try to kill her or anything like that, it wasn't worth it.

"Right, some bullshit James, so now I am left with a record because your mistress thinks I'm a raving lunatic who brandishes knives about, trying to kill her, as if I am capable of that, you know me!"

I could feel myself getting angry. I needed to calm down if I was going to have a proper conversation with James.

"Fine, let that be, I don't want to hear about her. We need to focus on the elephant in the bloody room, James."

I took a deep breath to stop myself from crying. I needed to refocus on why I had approached him in the first place. I wasn't here to talk about the maid, I needed answers, and I needed them fast. "

How could you, James? How could you do that to me? How could I have deserved this?"

James rubbed his forehead, frowning. He seemed lost for words, whatever he said now would pretty much shape our future together. He cleared his throat and then held my face with both hands, looking deeply into my eyes.

"Baby, if I could go back and undo all the wrong I have done to you, I would. I love you so much that I would lay down my life for you."

He let his hands drop, and then he lifted my chin with his fingers like he always did. I looked at him, trying my hardest not to cry.

"What can I say? I was stupid, a stupid drunk. It wasn't planned. I have never touched her before, and I promise, I never will again. You must forgive me. Please, give me one more shot at this. I love you, and I know you still love me, why else would you still be sat here, after that? Baby? Let me make it up to you."

He smiled, knowing his words were starting to take effect on me. As always, I was so weak, inexperienced and too fragile even to contemplate the idea of divorce.

Surely that wasn't the answer. This was the first time, he said. It was just an unfortunate mistake, fuelled by alcoholic delights and a scavenger of a woman.

I pondered on whether to retaliate, call him out that it was all bullshit, but something within me wanted our marriage to work. Something in me could not allow me to accept a failed marriage.

What would my parents think? They would be so disappointed. I didn't believe that his indiscretion had been a one-off, but his eyes sang a different tune, a melody of sorrow and regret.

I still loved him dearly, and other than the odd times, he was perfect. Marriages are not always easy, and no one is perfect, I thought to myself. With a heavy heart and churning stomach, I decided to accept his version of the truth, that this was a one-off.

He certainly wouldn't do anything like this to hurt me ever again, so I made him promise to give up drinking, and for the most part, Maria had to go.

So, as with every argument or indignity that we would and had endured, James as always, ended the conflict with the might of his salaciousness.

We made love on that patchwork rocking armchair, with each thrust in sync with the undulating rhythm beneath us.

Chapter 17

I was consumed, mind, body, and soul.

It was as though I had voluntarily chosen a path to insanity. Why else would I forgive his immorality so easily? The stars and the planets aligned themselves perfectly to let me in on his unfaithfulness, and yet I chose to look the other way. I decided to let myself be succumbed by his zeal, by his words, by his audacity. I was drunken by the ecstasy of my insanity and naivety. The putridness of his misadventure fell upon deaf ears and my inexplicable blindness. I wanted us to work, even at the mercy of his actions. I would not give up on us.

His symphonic words fuelled my foolishness, for I chose to cling on to them with all of me, every fiber drank in his words, every morsel of him just simply became my all.

Two weeks had passed since that faithful day. Maria was now gone, a distant and fading memory. She took with her, amongst all her belonging, the shadow that she cast over my marriage. Her departure brought light into the house. It brought brightness, where it had once been over-shadowed by darkness. I felt alive again.

All the insecurities I had felt every day, watching her parade her womanhood in front of us, like a low hanging fruit for James to devour, had now dissipated. She was like a serpent in the garden of Gethsemane, there to tempt James, just as the devil had tempted Adam through Eve. The darkness before the dawn had lifted, and I could finally see beyond the horizon, to a future with James, one which was nontoxic and impenetrable.

I could finally breathe again.

Life had all but returned to a reflection of the conventional. Our work-life, sex-life, and everything in between, returning to the normalcy of the time before all the chaos. We busied ourselves with the fallacy of working through it, trying hard to forget the harshness of the reality that a shameful act of adultery had forever tainted our marriage.

Although I had forgiven him for the mishap, my heart could not forget. I could still see the look on his face, buried between her thighs as he devoured her right in front of me. I could smell the scent of her orgasm as she lay there, undisturbed by the fact of being caught right in the act.

I wanted to forget it all, not just pretend, but forget, so I wrapped myself up in work, burning the midnight oil and volunteering to take on extra cases at work, anything to water down the clarity of my memory of that day. James, ever the more attentive husband had sensed that my mind was in angst with itself, and so, he had planned another romantic weekend away, this time to New York. As he had done previously, he surprised me with first-class tickets for two and had said that he would lavish me with all that money could buy.

I had hesitated, for the memory of the argument we had at the restaurant had surfaced in my mind.

Here he was again splashing the cash and reveling in it.

I hadn't asked for any luxuries, I hadn't asked for first-class tickets, I hadn't asked for any of it, so this time I did not want to be accused of squandering his cash. I did not want to fall victim for the same mistake twice, and so I insisted that I would pay for half. James protested.

He said he hadn't meant what he said at the restaurant and that I was free to do as I pleased when it came to his money. He said that his moment of madness had passed and that he apologized for his behavior.

I was no fool. Once bitten twice shy, and as much as love had made me lose all sanity, I wasn't looking for another beating. So, I rejected his offer and contributed to the flights, albeit, much to his dissatisfaction, that we then had to downgrade to coach, as I sure as hell couldn't afford first-class tickets, not on my salary.

In all my time in Chicago, I had not ventured out to any other US states, other than Hawaii, so this was as good as any time to start.

We took a day off work and made it a three-day weekend trip. James showed me all around New York's finest, the Empire State Building, the Chrysler Building, Brooklyn Bridge, Rockefeller Centre, Madison Square Garden, and Coney Island. We even took the Staten Island Ferry to see the Statue of Liberty up close and then finished up the weekend with a romantic Horse and Carriage ride in Central Park.

The weekend had been a success, I had contributed to some of the costs, but eventually could not keep up with the expense, as James consistently booked for things which were way above my pay grade. James had not been perturbed by this and said he would cover for the rest of the stuff himself. He was happy to, and I said that I shouldn't have to go out of my way to pay for things which he had booked without telling me. He hinted that he had wanted this whole trip to be his treat, somewhat of an apology to make up for the not so perfect trip to Hawaii.

I was satisfied; he had pulled out all the stops, as he always did. The thing about James was that he had such good showmanship. Wherever or whenever he had seemed to mess up, he could still remedy it by being the big shot he was and flaunting all the wealth he had amassed, whether it was by an extortionate number of gifts giving or by hypnotizing his target into submission through splendor. I had fallen hook line and sinker for the tricks of his trade and succumbed because of the delights he had shown me.

He had drowned me with gold and glitter, and through my unwariness, I had drunk in the valley of his deceit.

———

A week after the trip, we had returned home early from work only to find Maria on the porch with all her possessions.

She looked dishevelled, and she had been crying. James quickly parked the car and jumped out. He quickly approached her. I, on the other hand, didn't move. I just sat in the car, not able to believe my eyes. Why on earth was she here? I had just got rid of her, but like a bad smell, she was back again. The two of them seemed deep in conversation. Whatever it was that they were talking, it seemed important as James was pacing up and down. Suddenly they seemed to be arguing about something, but I couldn't hear what was being said.

All I could see was a lot of fingers wagging and pointing at Maria's stomach. James looked wildly angry and kept pacing, hands on his head. He looked anxious, maybe even a little scared. Maria was shouting something in Spanish, still in floods of tears. I wanted to get out of the car and see what the commotion was, but I didn't want to get in the mix of things, not after my behavior last time.

Maria starting to hit James across his chest, then on the face, she was getting out of control and beginning to cause a scene. James grabbed her by the wrist to stop her from hitting him anymore, but she was unrelenting. He couldn't calm her down, and he seemed to get angry at this. It almost seemed as though he felt that she had wronged him somehow. He then let go of her wrist; this was when things got out of hand. He unlocked the front door and pushed her inside, perhaps to avoid the neighbors seeing what he was about to do.

At this point, I got out of the car and ran towards the house. This is when I saw James stood over Maria, who was on the floor. He was kicking her in the ribs and then bending and punching her in the stomach.

She was screaming hysterically and saying something in Spanish. "Ayudarme por favor." She kept on screaming as he hit her, and in between screams she would cry out, "Basta, basta, es tu bebe. Es tu Bebe."

I ran over to try and stop him, shocked at what I was seeing. As much as I hated Maria, this was just crazy.

I tried to grab him by the hand and pull him away from her, but in the frenzy of it all, he resisted and through his need to prevent me from getting in his way, he struck me in the face that I fell to the floor and blacked out.

W hen I eventually came to, it was dark outside.
I had probably been out cold for an hour or so. James was nowhere to be seen, and neither was Maria. I sat on the same spot that I had fallen and tried to gather my thoughts and piece together fragments of what I could remember.

What had happened?

Why had James lost it and why had he been going for Maria like that?

Even though I had seen James angry, when he had grabbed me by the throat a few months earlier, I had never seen him like this, especially when he was sober. Both of his previous indiscretions had happened in a stupor of intoxication, but here he was, stone-cold sober, that devil within still burning as bright as ever.

I stood up, feeling a wave of pain on my head, as the blood came rushing back to the site where he had hit me in his moment of madness. I steadied myself and made my way upstairs, calling out for him. The house was empty, neither of them anywhere in sight.

An eerie feeling overcame me, as though something dark had come to the pass in those moments when I had laid in my unconsciousness. There was a ghostly feel in the house as I walked back downstairs. The front door was ajar, and Maria's belongings were still on the front porch where she had left them. I looked outside to see if perhaps they were there, but James's car was not in the driveway.

The welcome mat on the porch had bloodstains on it. The same bloodstains trailed on to the gravel, to where James' car would have been parked, and then the trail stopped. I gasped, wondering what the hell could have happened and as I stepped back, I noticed a smudge of blood across the door ledge. It looked like fingerprints, as though someone had tried to grab hold of the door.

Was that Maria's blood and if so, why was there was much of it? I felt a knot in my stomach. How badly had he hurt her? I wanted to ring James, but something held me back. This was a conversation that needed to be had face to face. There was no denying it though, something unholy had most certainly occurred here.

My instincts, too loud to ignore, was telling me to run, run as fast and far away as my weary feet could take me, but where would I run to? James was my husband, I loved him with all my heart, but he had gone mad. What had Maria's said to him to make him explode in a rage of madness. No matter how much I despised Maria, I needed to know she was alright.

Maybe he had taken her to the hospital.

Whatever had happened to cause yet another fiasco, I had a right to know the truth, and most importantly, I needed to know who the hell I was married to. At that very moment, in my despair and fear, I remembered the vows that I swore, the very same vows that James had insisted I read at our wedding.

"Throughout life, no matter what may come, I promise you my life as a dutiful and faithful wife."

Hopeless in my plight to find some truth and perhaps, appeasement for the malediction that seemed to take asylum with me, I shut the front door in exasperation, slowly walked upstairs, turned on the television and, as a dutiful wife, just sat there and waited for my beloved to return.

Chapter 18

"What the hell have you done, James" I screamed as he finally revealed what had transpired after I had blacked out the night before.

After the episode with Maria, I had waited at home for James' return, but he had failed to come home that night. His phone had been switched off, so I was none the wiser as to his whereabouts. Maria had also not reappeared, so all I could do was wait at home, and hope that nothing horrid had happened.

As the night drew in and I sat and waited, desperation started to fill me, as though I knew some impending doom was about to befall or had already occurred. Nothing about the night was right, and as I waited, slumber weighed heavily on my eyes, until they finally succumbed.

I must have been asleep for about two hours when James finally appeared at about 5 a.m., wretched-looking and as pale as the sheets on our bed. I got up and walked over to the door where he stood, and I held his hand.

"James, where the fuck have you been? Where is Maria? What happened? Why did you go crazy on her?

What did she say to you? For Christ's sake, James, say something."

I had so many questions, and I just let them pour right out of me, it was as though I was trying to drain a bucket full of woes. James stood firm, quiet. He had a glazed look in his eyes, as though he was there in body, but not in spirit. He let go of my hand and walked over to our bed and sat down slowly.

He was now ready to tell me what had happened that night which would invariably change the course of our lives forever.

⸻

M y suburban life, as uncomplicated as it had been, was now circling around me in a whirl, spinning as though it was about to be swept from under me.

When I first moved to Chicago, I had thought things were a little unstable, but then my luck seemed to turn and suddenly, what had felt like an uncertain and shaky time in my life, was turned around completely when I met James. He completely swept me off my feet and provided me with all I wanted and needed.

He cherished me and loved me beyond my wildest dreams, and here he was now, slowly transforming into something I could no longer recognize. That light that I first fell in love with, slowly dimming away and leaving behind it, remnants of a man that bore hardly any resemblance to my charming beloved. He was turning from an angel into something indescribable. He had hurt me, cheated on me and now this. I wanted my old life back. This was not what I was promised.

Could I love a man who had committed the vilest of all sins?

Could I still love him the way I once did and how I held him true to my heart, could I?

"It was an accident, the bitch wouldn't shut up, and before I knew it, I dunno, I just lost it. Fiona, you must believe me, it was an accident, and I didn't mean to hurt her, not like that. She's…"

He sighed heavily, and as I listened and waited for the worst, he closed his eyes and put his palm to his face as if to shield his words.

I knew exactly what he was going to say. My gut had been right all along.

"She's… sh… she's dead Fiona, I killed her."

The blood drained from my body as I stood there white in the face, unable to speak. I wanted to ask him to repeat what he had just said, perhaps hoping desperately that I had misheard him, but I knew it, there was no misinterpretation or lack of apprehension. It was as clear as day. He had killed Maria in cold blood, and here he was, my husband, ashen with dread for what he had done.

What was I supposed to say?

I had no words. I had no thoughts, other than for the face of Maria covered in blood, taken too soon, punished her for misdemeanours, that which she had now paid dearly for with her life.

I walked over to our bed where he was sat, and I sat next to him. I must have been in shock, as I could not speak, nor could I barely breathe. I just sat, next to my husband, as we waited for the dawning of day to wash away the sins of the night.

Neither of us slept a wink, how could we, when this wreckage was affixed on our minds.

The debris of the dead, the ruins of the murdered.

We hadn't said a word to each other for the rest of the night, so as the morning broke by shinning the glorious sun on our insipid faces, gently mocking us, we knew it was time to face the music. I got up from the bed and went downstairs to examine the state of the hallway in the daylight, the place where James had begun his attack on Maria.

In the cold light of day, everything seemed magnified. The bloodstains which had looked like nothing but smear on the door handle now seemed to be in vast quantities.

There were small pools of blood in the middle of the hallway and splashes everywhere. It looked like a murder scene from one of those science fiction television shows I often watched, except this was not television, this was real life, this was my life. James appeared downstairs next to me, also shocked at what befell his eyes.

He had done this in a moment of rage, and there was no denying it now. There was evidence of his crime everywhere you looked.

This was the work of a mad man.

"I will sort this out Fiona, I promise. I have messed up. But I will fix this. I know a guy."

I couldn't believe what I was hearing. What was he going to fix? There was nothing that could be fixed here.

A woman was dead, murdered in cold blood, and his first words me were that he could fix it.

"I will give him a call. You must go into work as usual Fiona. Just as if nothing happened. I will call my contact. I will clean this mess up. No one has to get hurt. No one needs to know."

This man had indeed gone mad. He was describing a cover-up, as though it was something insignificant. Was I to go to work and pretend like nothing had happened and resume daily life without any consequences?

Was he attempting to get away with murder, in the first degree?

"James, have you lost your marbles? Are you mad, you killed her? And you are talking about cleaning up a mess"? I screamed out, unable to believe this was what had become of James. Did he not feel remorse for his wickedness?

He had done the crime, so he should surely take the punishment.

"James, tell me what happened, tell me everything or I swear I will scream."

He grabbed my arms roughly and pulled me into the living room and shut the doors. He then closed all the blinds and curtains and switched on the side lamp. It must have been about 8.30 a.m., but he poured himself a whiskey. "

Want one?" he asked.

"James, I mean it, tell me now, what happened, the whole story."

And so, he began. It spilled out of him as though he was offering a confession to the clergy. Every detail was dissected and analyzed and told. He wanted to free himself of the burden of harboring this secret, but in unburdening himself, he all but displaced it all on to me.

"You know what she said to me on the driveway? She said she was pregnant. Pregnant, Fiona, Pregnant. What the heck was I supposed to do with that? She was my bloody maid. What would people say if they found out I was with the maid this whole time?"

I winced at this revelation, as it was now confirmed

that they had been having their sordid affair behind my back for quite some time. The act of catching them in action a few weeks ago was not a one-off. As I had suspected, they had been at it the whole time, right under my nose.

James wasn't even fazed by him revelation on this part. He was more concerned about tainting his reputation, should people find out that he had screwed the maid. I tried not to let the revelation of the affair distract me from what he was telling me about the murder, so I listened on, feigning nonchalance at the detail of their romance.

"She kept on going on about being a catholic and that I would have to make an honest woman of her. Her family would not accept a child out of wedlock, and she wouldn't have an abortion. She was mad. I tell ya, she was out of control. I told her that under no circumstance was I having a child with anyone, not even you, Fiona. She starting hitting me when I told her there was nothing I could do. I was already happily married, and she would have to get rid of the child. She wouldn't get under control. She was going at me, slapping me, Fiona. I didn't want the neighbors to hear, and I guess I just lost it. I saw red and lost control.

"I wasn't trying to kill her you see; I was just trying to get the life out of that thing in her stomach, but she was so strong, she was so strong, she was resisting. Why? Why the heck was the resisting."

He started to sob, and it looked like he was reliving the moment again. I could see the darkness in his eyes. I could feel him get tense.

He started to shake, trembling as the words poured out of him.

"I made a mistake being with her, I admit it, but how could I accept her pregnancy?. I would never accept it. I hate kids; I would strangle it if I ended up having a brat. If you got pregnant Fiona, I would push you down the stairs, you see, I am that screwed up, why would anyone want me to father their kid. I want to die with my name."

I was shocked at this, I knew he was opposed to having children, but I had no idea he felt this strongly. I had already started mapping out our future, and to me, it always included a family, kids, the full package.

"I started to hit her in the stomach, that's when you got in the way. I didn't mean to push you away, but, but, dunno Fiona, I think I have a problem. I just lost it. I started hitting her. I can't remember what, but there was a lot of blood, a lot Fiona, a lot. She still wouldn't stop; she wanted to fight back."

He signed, then he knelt and cradled himself, still sobbing. "I grabbed her by the throat. I just wanted her to stop, to stop fighting back. I grabbed her throat and tightened my grip, I must have even broken her neck, I was so mad, I wouldn't let go, I just wanted it all to stop, and before I knew it, she had stopped moving. She was still, Fiona, she had just stopped. Stopped breathing"

At this point, I was also torn; the man I loved was now nothing but a puddle on the floor. He wasn't the confident, charming James anymore. He was but a distant reflection of his former self.

"What happened next James? Where is the body?" I said, afraid of what he would tell me next.

"I panicked Fiona, I didn't mean to kill her, I'm not a bloody killer. I just grabbed her and stuck her in the boot you see. I drove to the navy pier on Streeterville and... I just dumped her there Fiona, in the water. I'm so sorry. I just panicked."

He stood and poured himself another whiskey. I hadn't spoken much. I needed to take it all in.

"James, you have to go to the police. You have to turn yourself in. You must."

James slammed his glass on the table and walked over to me. He was angry. He lifted my chin and looked me dead in the eyes.

"Are you mad, woman? I am not going to prison. Are you mad? Why do you think I got rid of the body, I'd sooner be dead myself than end up in prison? You better understand that now Fiona, I am not joking, you'd better understand what I am saying, no cops. End of story."

He had said no police. He was trying to get away with murder.

How my quiet life had now turned. How could he try to cover this up? How could he possibly think he could get away with it? Surely someone would notice she was missing. Surely the bloodstains over all the place would soon be discovered.?

He read my mind as he continued.

"I will get my contact to clean this place up. He's done this sort of thing before; he's a professional. Don't ask how I know him, baby, I just do. When you reach a status such as mine, it's always handy to have these clean-up guys to hand."

I felt a chill in my spine. How had he come across such contact and had he used his services in the past?

"Fiona, we need to get our story straight. Don't screw this up, please. You need to work with me on this. Do you want me to go to prison? What will people say? How humiliating. And what would happen to you? Do you think you would be able to keep your job? Think Fiona. Think!"

I was doing nothing but thinking, thinking how this would all pan out if he were refusing to go to the police, did that mean that I was an accomplice to murder?

Did I need to turn him in, even though as per the law

in the United States, as his wife, I could not be forced to testify against my husband?

Could I digest this and put it all behind us? What if someone had seen him dump the body? How could I ever have another restful night's sleep, knowing all of this and having the threat of the police knocking down our door in the middle of the night?

How could I survive this?

"James, I just can't, I just can't live with such a secret. It will destroy us. You have to turn yourself in. I cannot harbor a murderer, please. Just tell them it was self-defense but then you picnicked and hid the body. Just tell them anything, but please don't ask me to hide this secret for you. Please don't ask me to hide a murder. I just can't, James, I won't."

James had, however, made up his mind.

He was to clean up the 'mess' as he called it, and we were to put it all behind us. I was forced not to say a word to anyone.

I had to play house and make sure not to arouse any suspicion. As far as he was concerned, it was common knowledge that we had fired Maria a couple of weeks ago, so the fact that she had disappeared out of our lives should not and would not arouse any suspicions as to her where-abouts and why we hadn't seen her. She had gone back to Spain, and we were never to hear from her again.

James made me recite the story over and over that morning until he was sure that it had stuck. He told me that he was indeed sorry for all of it and that he truly did love me, and the thought of going to prison and not being with me would kill him. He said that if it was the choice between imprisonment and death, he would choose death.

I couldn't let that fall on deaf ears. Here was my husband, a murderer, pleading for me to keep his secret, and if I didn't, he would take his own life. I was at a precipice now, trying to decide on what to do. If I told the police, he would end up in prison, and he may just kill himself, and if I didn't tell the police, I would be totally consumed by the secret, but at least James would still be alive.

Despite all that had happened, my insanity and impenetrable love for him was still stirring up deep within me. I knew what he had done, I couldn't fathom it, but for some reason, it hadn't fully sunk in. It was as though I was looking at my life from the outside in.

An observer, a spectator, watching a post-mortem into the unwitting demise of the victim, who in this story was my arch enemy, Maria. All I could do was to have empathy on the guilty, just because the guilty was the protagonist in the story, and my husband.

Perhaps such empathy for James would not exist if the victim had been entirely blameless and if the victim had not been a seducer of husbands. It might have been easier if she had not tried to steal my husband.

With an altered mind, fatigued by lack of sleep and reasoning, I agreed to keep his secret, if he was sure that no one would ever know.

He was confident he could handle this, and with that, I allowed myself to put our lives in his hands.

But would he trust me to keep his secret?

Chapter 19

The days following the incident, I tried my hardest not to think of it, to try to put it behind us and move on with our lives.

James, on the other hand, didn't seem that fazed. He carried on as though nothing had happened, as though murder was insignificant. He busied himself at work, and then at the weekend, he planned a little road trip to Nashville, Kentucky to meet up with some hiking buddies of his. I was to come along and act like the ever-endearing wife.

A trophy for him to show off to his friends, as he regaled them on the perfection of life in Chicago.

It was about a six-hour drive to Kentucky, and by the time we reached our destination, I was utterly exhausted and decided not to join James and his buddies for a midnight feast.

They had planned a long hike the following day, in the David Boone National Forest, and so I needed to get a good night's rest if I was to play the part of a happy and loving wife. The irony in all this was that a few weeks ago, I would have jumped at the opportunity for a trip to meet some of James's buddies. I would have played my part exceedingly well, as it would have been coming from a place of truth, but here I was, having to feign happiness when all along, I knew I was harboring a murderer.

It would sometimes cross my mind, in those few days after the incident that if he was capable of murder and was still able to conduct himself as though nothing significant had happened, then what else was he capable of?

He hadn't killed in self-defence, which on some level would ease my discomfort, he had killed in cold blood, bludgeoning and strangling Maria to death, with his bare hands.

He had seen the life drain out of her slowly, and he had allowed for that to happen.

———

The following day, we headed off with James's buddies for the long hike at the national park.

We loaded up with supplies for the day, as we set off. I welcomed the distraction, easing my mind, as the sweltering heat of the day allowed me to think of nothing but the discomfort of trudging through the national park, blistered feet and far away from the comforts of home. James's friends were a delight, very down to earth and the opposite of James in nature. They were small-time country guys, who took more comfort in staying home with their wives and taking delights in simple pastimes such as hunting.

They didn't drive fancy cars or splashed the cash the way James would, but instead seemed humbler in their manner. I took to them very easily, feeling more aligned to them than I did with James. I always aspired to be successful, to have nice things, to drive a nice car and all the trimmings, but looking back where my journey had brought me, I wasn't too sure now if the end now justified the means.

The weekend was a hit, and we promised to revisit the following summer.

As soon as we were on our way back home, reality crept in again, and I felt a twinge of panic, knowing we were headed back home, to the scene of the crime, to the place where James had done the most unimaginable thing. James could tell I was uneasy. He pulled the car over when we reached a quiet spot.

"Baby, thank you so much for being a sport this weekend. You did well. You did well. I was worried you might not be able to relax, but those guys are fun, aren't they? Take your mind off anything, they can. You did well. I miss that part of you. It's still me here. I am the same man you fell in love with. Nothing's changed. I love you Fi, I love you, and I need you to come back to me. Will you come back to me?"

He was asking me to be the old Fiona, the one who adored him and yearned for his touch. The one who would get excited whenever he would walk into a room, the one who would make me melt when he kissed me.

"I am so sorry, James. I am trying; I am. I am. It's hard to forget what happened."

He looked frustrated at the fact I had brought up the event at this point. He jumped out of the car and slammed the door. He paced up and down the road, muttering away, so I couldn't make out what he was saying. I jumped out of the car and walked over to him. I still loved this man, even at his worst, I still loved him.

I grabbed his hand and kissed it. "James, I am trying. I love you; I do."

He seemed to relax. Despite everything, the fact that I could still tell him that I loved him, sort of made up for everything.

"Show me, show me how much you love me" He pushed me towards the car. "You say you are trying, right? Do you still love me? Show me, Fiona. Show me how much you love me."

He pushed me again, this time, against the bonnet. I yelled, asking him to stop but he wouldn't. He pressed himself against me.

"What the heck are you doing, we are in the middle of the road, stop," I yelled, but this just made him more forceful.

He grabbed my throat and kissed me on the neck, then he lifted my skirt and slid his hands beneath my underwear.

"Baby, why aren't you aroused? I want to make you remember how good it is. You remember?"

I wasn't sure what had gotten into him, but he was sure bent on making love to me, out there, despite who might see. Perhaps it was the danger that excited him, but there were hardly any cars around.

He spun me around so that I was facing the bonnet, then he lifted my skirt and thrust himself into me. He was rough, rougher than I would have liked. I didn't resist. I wasn't afraid, nor was I aroused.

I just wanted it over and done with.

When he was done, he kissed me on the neck, pulled up his pants and walked back into the car, pleased with himself.

I pulled down my skirt and regained my composure and got back into the car for the long drive home.

———

I t was quite busy at work the following day, James was trying to secure another contract for Du Greys, and so we went from one endless meeting to the next.

The office was heaving with people and external clients, more so than any other day. At about 2.30 p.m. I was summoned to James's office, where two FBI agents met me. They had been speaking with James about the where-abouts of Maria. Her family had reported her missing for over two weeks, and so naturally, they wanted to ask if we had heard from her since her departure from working for us. I was so nervous.

I tried to play cool and calm, but my nerves gave it away, or so I thought. As soon as I saw the agents, I started to shake. I walked into James's office and was asked to take a seat. The agents introduced themselves, Agents Corrigan and Stalker.

James introduced me as his wife.

"Mrs Foyler, we just wanted to see if Maria had been in contact with you since she left your place. Her family filed a missing person report, and her last known location was at the Foyler residence. Did she call you, or do you know by chance where she could be?"

I cleared my throat, careful to make sure that my answer was nonchalant yet convincing enough.

"Agents, erm… Maria left us a few days ago. I mean weeks ago. She didn't say much, other than collect her last cheque and, erm… do you think something happened to her?… er, I mean she could just have taken some time off. I'm sure it's nothing. I mean, is there any reason to think otherwise. She's a grown-up. Probably met someone, she's a gorgeous lady, probably met a fella."

I was rambling. I couldn't shut up.

I was losing it.

James suddenly stepped in and cut me off, trying to make sure I didn't give any more away. Why couldn't I give a straight answer? We had rehearsed this over and over before and yet, when it came time to perform, I was hopeless.

"Agent Stalker, we will be in touch if she contacts us, but as you can see, my wife has no idea either, but do let us know if there is anything we can do."

Both agents stood up and shook James's hand; from the tone of James's retort, it was clear that the conversation was over. I sat timidly, trying not to make eye contact with anyone.

As they walked towards the door, agent Corrigan looked back at me. He suspected something for sure. Why had I been acting guilty?

"Ma'am, if there's ANYTHING you want to tell us, here's my card. Just call me."

He was handing me the card, but James intercepted it and took it from him.

"As she already said, agent. She doesn't know. I don't know either. We will be sure to let you know if she contacts either of us."

Agent Corrigan smirked, then looked over at me again, then they both left.

James walked over and shut the door. He was muttering to himself inaudibly. He seemed annoyed. He walked over to me and grabbed me by the forearm and pulled me up from the chair.

In all the time I had been with James, I never feared him. He had done some unspeakable things, but I had never really been terrified of him. I knew he loved me deeply, so his ill doings were always forgiven, and besides, I always assumed that if you loved someone, you could never do them real harm.

Despite the couple of times he had either struck me or hurt me, I still made excuses for him, as I had believed that love would conquer all; but at that moment, in his office, I genuinely feared him. The man I had courted for months, fell in love with, now had a darkness in his eyes. The man who had once adored me and spoilt me rotten was fading into the shadows. This man before me was different; the look in his eyes spelled disappointment.

He grabbed my arm and pulled me over to the corner of his office. He then turned me around and slammed my head against the wall. I felt a crunch in my jaw, perhaps a loose tooth finally making its escape. An excruciating pain pounded right through me, as I then felt him punch me from behind, right in the ribs. I cried out, which was a grave mistake, as he grabbed me by the throat, reminiscent of the first time I had suffered his physical abuse.

He tightened his grip, making sure I couldn't make a sound. He wasn't trying to kill me. He just liked to make a point, show me who the boss was. I had been wrong, and I needed to be taught a lesson.

James had a god complex, and in some way, I didn't blame him. Everyone around him always ingratiated themselves with him. He never suffered an objection at the hands of anyone. Yes-men always surrounded him, so if something didn't go his way, he would deal with it the only way he knew best, with the might of his fist.

"Shut up. We rehearsed that line repeatedly. Are you trying to get me to put away? Are you? I thought you loved me? Don't I mean anything to you? Don't I? I gave you a job. I provide for you, give you everything you could want.

I screw you almost daily. I made you in this town, add to that, this is how you repay me? Get the story right Fiona. Get it right, cos the next time those bastards come knocking around, and believe me, after your performance, they will. The next time they come, you better get the story right, or I will end you. You hear, I mean it, don't play with my life Fiona, I will never go to prison. I told you, I'd rather die"

He loosened his grip and pushed my head against the wall again, then let go. He had made his point, I had been told, and I would never make that mistake twice, not if I valued my life.

I tried to regain my composure. I didn't want to cry. I didn't want anyone in the office to suspect. I wasn't going to be one of those battered wives who everyone took pity on. James walked over to his desk and sat down on the chair. The anger had dissipated from his face.

I walked towards the door, eager to leave the room, but he jumped out of the chair and grabbed me.

"Baby are you hurt. I am so sorry. You see what you make me do. You know how important getting the story is, its life and death. I shouldn't have hit you, baby, I am going through so much, and I don't feel like you are behind me. I don't feel the love and support. I feel so alone, baby. I feel so rejected by you. I don't even feel as though you still love me."

I was so confused, this man had just punched me in the ribs and slammed my face against the wall, and here he was, looking for my sympathy. His eyes watered as he continued to speak. He got on his knees and begged for me to accept his apology. A grown man, on his knees, in tears, well, almost. He looked like a wounded puppy, so vulnerable. I felt a pang of sympathy. He must have been dealing with so many torments, he was stressed, on edge; I needed to be understanding, I needed to play my part well.

This was life or death. I figured I would probably be going crazy too had I been in his shoes.

I looked him in the eyes, and those blue eyes shun so brightly. I was falling for his charm again. I was totally and inexplicably insane. I told him I had forgiven him, but the violence had to stop, not so much because he was hurting me, more so that if the cops came back and saw bruises on me, that wouldn't help with their suspicions. He understood. It would never happen again, he promised.

He stood up and walked over to the door and locked it, then announced on his intercom that he would not be taking any calls for the rest of the day. He then walked back over to me and kissed me passionately.

I melted. I didn't want to, but I did. He lifted me and carried me over to the desk and laid me down and then got on his knees. I knew what was next as he pulled me in closer and pushed my legs apart.

I was immediately hurled into ecstasy. The pain in my head and ribs had subsided temporarily, as my whole body shook uncontrollably, the height of pleasure making its way through every muscle in my body.

He suddenly stood up, licking his lips contentedly, and pulled me off the desk, lowering my head gently, indicating that it was my turn to please him.

I did so dutifully, afraid to resist, and besides, in the heat of the moment, I enjoyed pleasing him - it reminded me of the old days.

This was the James I knew, he was back, and for a moment, he had somehow enabled me to forget about all my troubles.

Chapter 20

It was now mid-summer, and the investigation into Maria's disappearance had died down a little as there were no real leads, albeit that the cops were still trying to put the pieces together.

It had gone from a missing person's inquiry to something more.

Both I and James were never officially identified as suspects in anything. However, there was still tension in the air. The FBI agents would periodically drop into the house now and again to see if we had heard anything. It was all very odd. It had gone quiet, but there was still something going on behind the scenes.

James had now been away on business trips quite frequently, which left me with a lot of idle time, and for want of something to do, to get my mind away from that night. Although James had said that he would trust me to play my part and keep up with our story, he just didn't believe me whenever he was away on business. He would bug the whole apartment with cameras, and he once put a wire on my phone, so that he could listen to all my telephone conversations.

At first, I wasn't aware of any of this. It was only when he would come home and questioned me about conversations that I had had with people on the phone, conversations which he would not have known about unless he was present, had I then realized what he had been doing all along. When I finally took up the courage to confront him about it, he neither denied nor confirmed it, but made it clear that he knew everything that I was up to.

I was now a prisoner in my own home, and aside from the front door security camera we had installed for safety, he must have secretly installed a dozen other cameras inside the house. My movements were monitored, calls recorded, visitors scanned.

Perhaps he thought that in a moment of weakness, I would lose my mind and go running to the cops, especially with agent Corrigan still poking around. At the time, it had never even crossed my mind to betray him in that way. I had given my word, and in all earnestly, I honestly didn't want to see the love of my life behind bars, although I felt that his crime should have come with a level of punishment, I just didn't want him to spend the rest of his life, rotting away.

During his time away on his business trips, I did have some time to think, to think about my life and where it was headed; to think about how we could plan the next ten to twenty years together. Up to that point, I think James had always trusted my fidelity, but since the summer, he became quite suspicious of me.

Alongside the bugging of phones and cameras in our home, he would get enraged whenever I so much as said hello to a stranger. I had once ordered a pizza while he was away on one of his business trips, and upon his return, he accused me of flirting with the pizza guy. He said he had seen the whole thing on the front door security camera and that I had dressed provocatively to entice the pizza delivery guy. He questioned why I had invited him into the house, and when I explained that I had told the pizza guy to come in and wait while I looked for my wallet, he just wouldn't believe me.

It was all so bizarre, and for the amount of accusation and annoyance that this had caused me, I almost wished I had done something wrong, to warrant the amount of verbal abuse I had endured over the matter.

This was control to the next level; he was possessive, controlling and sometimes intimidating, but he would always mix it up by being attentive, loving, generous and sweet-talking. It was a balance of madness and kindness, which made it difficult for me to take hold of the situation. I sometimes wondered whether I had imagined it all.

Perhaps I was overreacting, exaggerating and over-analyzing the whole thing. I was starting to lose a grip on reality. One day I would be filled with love, desire, admiration and happiness and the next, I would be mentally, physically and emotionally drained from his torment and abuse. I was in a constant state of angst. I became an object of his sexual gratification, and at times I couldn't hide my many frustrations. He sensed this all, so he couldn't and wouldn't trust me. He had to make sure I was surveyed around the clock so that I wouldn't let our secrets out, or I wouldn't leave him.

I didn't want to leave him, but this was too much. I had wanted to call home many times to tell my sister about my situation, but I guess pride got in the way. Sarah was happily married with a daughter and now another one on the way; I didn't want to be the failure of the family, one who couldn't keep her husband in tow.

I kept it all hidden, hidden from my family, friends, and colleagues. To the world, I wore a mask of happiness, eternal bliss, but inside, I was slowly dying, diminishing to a fragment of my former self.

T owards the end of summer, the FBI agents paid us a surprise visit at home. It turns out they had a witness.

Someone had come forward saying that they had seen Maria that night on the porch, and afterwards had heard screaming, a female voice. The witness had put James and me there that night, the last known sighting of Maria.

That was it. I couldn't control myself. I was convinced we would soon be found out.

James feigned any knowledge of seeing Maria. He told the cops that the witness must have been mistaken. We were asked to provide alibi's to which James had said that we were both working all day and didn't get home until about 9 p.m., a blatant lie. The agents were satisfied but would corroborate the alibis in the morning. If someone could provide the alibi, then we would be in the clear.

As soon as the agents left, James was on the phone; he was calling Julia asking her to provide an alibi for him. He had asked her to say to the FBI, when they asked, that he was with her, working late. Why on earth would he be with Julia, and why wouldn't he have just said that he was at the office.

I suppose that would be risky, as there would have been more witnesses, and everyone knew we left early that day except Julia who had taken the day off sick. She agreed to provide him with an alibi. Her compliance was too easy;

no questions asked. She was proving an alibi, and thus lying and implicating herself, all for James.

It didn't make sense.

I asked James to tell Julia to provide me with the same alibi, but he said that Julia had refused. She was only prepared to lie for James, what a bitch, I thought. It was left to me to find an alibi. Why on earth did I need to lie, I had done nothing wrong, and by lying, I was now committing a crime. James asked me to find another source for an alibi, fast. I searched my brain for who I could ask, but I just couldn't get myself to ask anyone to lie for me, it would arouse suspicion, it was almost an admission of guilt.

I wanted to ask Christian or Amanda, the two closest people I knew in Chicago, but when I suggested it, James retorted, there was no way that he could allow them to get entangled in this mess. He mentioned a lack of trust for Christian, there was some contention between the two of them apparently, and Amanda lacked the moral fiber of someone needed to carry such an undertaking, as he put it.

He claimed that she had made several advances at him, and he had turned her down every time, as such, at any rate, she would probably refuse to help.

In some way that story didn't add up, especially given James's track record with women, it did, however, explain Amanda's peculiar behavior around James. She had previously warned me to stay away from him, desperation in her voice, hinting at something dark, an account between the both, something that she dared not speak of, or recount.

I had wondered what the actual story was, I sought to dig deeper, to demand a better explanation, but James resisted, he had no time for inconsequential conversation, an elusive method to circumvent dealing with the reality of the situation. I had no choice but to pick my battles, right now, it was more pressing that I figure out what to do about the cops and their questions.

After some deliberations, I told James we would have to tell the agents it was a mistake. We would have to say to them we were home and Maria had indeed been on the porch but had left afterwards. My 'senseless' proposal angered James. He would show me how senseless it was by acting out his frustrations on me, carefully selecting parts of my body to throw his fists, parts of my body which would be less visible to the public; the sides of my stomach, a kick to the thighs, a knock to the ribs.

I endured, acting my part as the battered but amenable wife, honoring the part of the vows which said for better or worse. Soon after the beating, we sat down, both exhausted and talked about my lack of an alibi. What the hell was I to do now? There was no one else to ask.

He conjured up another story which might appease the agents, but it lacked plausibility. I would have to use it nonetheless; there could be no other solution at this stage.

The next day, agent Corrigan followed through and visited the office asking for mine and James's where-abouts on the night of Maria's disappearance.

The receptionist confirmed, as per our calendar sched-ules, we had both left the office early on the night in ques-tion, so the agent went about asking colleagues some questions to which Julia played her part just as she had been asked. She confirmed that James had dropped off some work files at her place, as she had called in sick on that day. She told agent Corrigan that they started working on the file and had lost track of time. She had given James an alibi, so he was now in the clear.

Agent Corrigan asked if she had seen me, but she said she had no idea where I was and hadn't seen me the whole day. Agent Corrigan approached my desk and asked if we could speak privately. He confirmed James's alibi back to me and asked me once again to provide an alibi, so I told him a contrived version of the truth, the version James had instructed me to give; I had gone home alone on the night in question, but I had not seen Maria. James turned up later that night, after working late with Julia.

I looked at Agent Corrigan sheepishly, could he believe this story even though it differed slightly from what James had said to him the day before, that we both had been working late; or had I inadvertently now just strewn the seed of doubt in his mind. The witness had placed both James and I there, and yet I had said that I was alone. It didn't make sense.

Agent Corrigan scribbled some notes on his notepad and said he would be in touch. I did not have a concrete Alibi, so since the case was still open, and all fingers were pointing at the Foyler residence, he would have no choice but to investigate further.

They would re-question the sole witness.

I would now be a potential suspect in the disappearance of Maria Garcia Rodriguez. It was the first time I had heard her name in full. It sent shivers down my spine. It brought reality to what up until then, seemed so surreal. She had been a living, breathing person with a family who loved her. She was Maria Garcia Rodriquez, and I had on some level, had been a part of her demise.

I was instructed not to leave town as I would be summoned for further questioning. Agent Corrigan assured me that this was just standard routine stuff, nothing to worry about. I was instructed to show up at the police precinct the following day, to give my statement in full.

There was no going back, James might now in the clear as far as the police were concerned.

I, on the hand, was still in murky waters.

———

Once at home, I informed James about what had happened.

He was frustrated that I hadn't managed to get an alibi and had to use the back story we had created. He couldn't understand why I couldn't just ask a friend to do it. It was too late to do anything about it now, I had messed up, and we would have to find a way out of the mess. I cried myself to sleep that night. I was confused as to how I had now ended up being a suspect into a murder, something that I had no part in.

The very next morning, James, realizing that I was in such a state, tried his best to soothe me. He wanted to reassure me that everything would be ok. The agents were just questioning people. There was no reason for me to be afraid. I got angry at his composure. I wanted him to know this was serious, and that it was all his fault. I lashed out, crying and hitting him. I was hysterical. He tried to calm me down but was failing. I couldn't stop crying.

My life was a mess, and I was in a living nightmare. James seemed to make things worse; he kept on trying to console me by saying he was sorry for putting me through this. He acted sincerely; however, what angered me the most was that he kept on alluding that he had done this for me.

He had killed for me, to keep our family protected, and so I should be grateful that his love for me pushed him to such measures. He had gotten rid of the problem of Maria and her secret baby, and by doing this, had ensured that we would not be put through the shame of it.

I couldn't believe his logic in all of this. He had told me it was an accident, and here he was, admitting that he had done it on purpose, to ensure that the secret didn't get out. This man had no remorse for his crime; all he had were his justifications. He had put his self-importance, his reputation, all before her life; her life had not measured up to the shame he would have had to endure, had the secret come out, and here he was pretending that it was sheer love for me that had led him here.

After this, I would go on to pretend that I was ok. I could no longer tolerate his reasoning. It irritated me that someone I loved and respected so much could try to turn this around and try to place the blame of his actions on me. I had no choice now but to face whatever the agents threw at me.

I was innocent, and so if there was justice in this world, I would be ok.

———

I left for work alone, leaving James at home to contemplate further.

I needed to get into work early enough to have some time to confront Julia to as why she had provided James with an alibi but had refused to do the same for me. In hindsight, I wish I had not bothered, as I had stirred the beast within her, as she would go on to reveal to me more than I had bargained. It turned out that they had been casually having sex for over two years, even before I had yet met James.

They would regularly meet up at James's studio apartment to have sex. Sometimes it would involve other women, some sort of sexual orgy.

The James she described to me seemed like a distant stranger to the man I loved. He was a sex-crazed sadist. I knew that he had always had a big sexual appetite, but I never knew that it was this sordid. He could never be satiated and as such, took to other forms to express his desires and needs.

Being married to me did not deter him from his exploits. I was just a trivial distraction from his intense activities. I always knew that Julia had a thing for James, but I had never really questioned her on this, albeit that I always intended to, but after I got married, it just didn't seem appropriate. But now, here she was, telling me all the details about their affair.

On some level, I think she seemed saddened by the hurt she had caused me, but it also seemed as though she couldn't resist his charm. She wanted him for herself, and so she had continued with him, even though he had now taken a wife. She was in love with him, but he was very controlling and manipulative; something that I knew all too well.

She said there were others, many more, but she was his constant go-to person. He was like a drug to her, and she was an addict. As for the alibi, she had no choice. She believed that he wasn't involved in Maria's disappearance, so she was willing to lie for the man she loved. She wasn't, however going to lie for the woman who had taken him away from her, especially when she wasn't convinced that I had nothing to do with it.

James had told her about the altercation that I had previously had with Maria, which had left Maria, battered and bruised. He had painted such a picture, which made me look as though I was set on hurting Maria, as though I had a vendetta even before I had found out about the affair between Maria and James.

Julia's revelations were more than I could stomach, for this was deceit to the next level. They had carried on their affair right under my nose, and I had not suspected a thing. How many would more women come out of the wood-work now? How much more deceit could I endure from this man. I hated him so much for this now.

At that moment, my love, or at least what little there was left of it, had now turned sour. Once was bad enough, but this meant that he was a serial cheat, a liar and an adulterer. I needed to get away from him before he destroyed me but now was the worst time.

If I walked away during the investigation; I would have no support. I wanted so badly to tell my family about this, but what would that achieve?

Everyone would just end up feeling sorry for me. I decided that I would confront James about Julia, and that once the investigation had died down, I would file for a divorce.

Deep down, I should have spoken out immediately and admitted it all to someone, anyone, but my pride held me back, and it was this pride that led to my downfall.

They say pride comes before a fall, and I would soon plummet so far in the next few months that my life would become completely unrecognizable.

Chapter 21

I received a call on Saturday morning at about 10 am.
Agent Stalker wanted me to come to the station for further questioning. He was the less friendly of the two agents, so, naturally, I was scared. The two seemed to have the good cop, bad cop act down perfectly, and I guessed that agent Stalker would be the one asking me all the difficult questions.

I was told to come in between noon and 2 pm, so this meant I still had a couple of hours before I needed to be there. This was ample time to tell James what I had found out from Julia. I contemplated waiting for a few more days, but the sight of him angered me. His smugness and the way he carried himself around the house, something which had previously attracted me, now made me red with rage.

I asked him to sit down as I needed his full attention. I figured that since I already knew about the affair with Maria, this meant that I had the edge over him, and he couldn't try to worm his way out of this. I was wrong.

"James, I need you to listen and let me say what I need

to say. This is very hard for me, so please, please, just let me get it off my chest before you say anything."

He looked puzzled but nodded his head in agreement.

"I know about you and Julia…. and…. and please don't deny it because she already told me everything, every detail James, everything. The sex, the other women, the orgies, the crazy things you both did. I just can't understand this. I had no idea you were like this. I had no idea you could do this to me, even after I found out about Maria, you were still sleeping with Julia. You must hate me, James. You know that you are the only family I have here in this damn country, you know you are all I have. How could you? … and don't you dare deny it, I swear, I will lose it. After how much of myself I have given to you. I have loved you with all my heart. I have been the dutiful wife. I have endured the pain of your fist, the liars, but this, this here, is too much.

"How many women are there, do you even love me? Why did you propose to me, even though you were messing around with others? Do you get some sort of sick satisfaction from this? Everyone thinks you are quite the amazing guy, you splash the cash, you act like the hero, the boss, the husband, everyone's best friend, but deep-down James, you are pure evil. You must be, how else can you be this way. James, how else. Did you ever love me?"

I was sobbing now. I had just had a cathartic moment. I didn't realize how much I needed to say these things to him.

Deep down, I always knew he was a sham, but my love had deluded and blinded me, or perhaps, muted me in so many ways.

This was my moment, and everything I had felt started to spill out of me, flowing through me, unwilling to stop until it was all said. I breathed in, emptied of words, taking center stage for the first time, unafraid to speak, unafraid of what might happen.

I wanted him to feel the pain, the degradation of his existence and conduct, and the illness of the man he had become. I wanted him to know it was not ok. It had never been ok; I just had no idea what a happy marriage was supposed to look like, but my vision had been cleared, cleansed from the dirt and dust that clouded me.

I could now see clearly for the first time. This man was toxic, as toxic as they come, and I wanted to be rid of him. He stood up, walked to the door and looked back at me and smiled.

"You should have known the man you were marrying. I am sick of playing house with you. Deal with it. I love women. I love sex. Deal with it. I am not going to change. You must have been blind or stupid the whole time we were dating. I took you to my studio apartment for Christ's sake, that should have been clear to you what that was for. What guy has two places and one just left for occasional visits? You must be daft Fiona. Behave! As if you didn't know. What guy needs a housekeeper who doesn't do much housekeeping, and with a body like hers? Pfff, as if I wasn't going to taste that! The money made you stay, right, the gifts, the trips. I chose you as my number 1, out of all of them. I chose you as the wife. So, don't freaking complain now, the others don't. But, if you breathe a word of this to anyone, Fiona."

He laughed. "If you breathe a word of this to anyone, hmm, just think, poor Maria, if only she had shut that damn mouth of hers, she would still be alive. And as for Julia, I will deal with her."

He walked out, and that was all.

He didn't care. The deceit, the trickery, my naivety and my lack of experience taunting me. It was like a light bulb moment. He had been right. I had gone through this relationship with closed eyes, pretending perhaps on some unconscious level, not to see the obvious, to ignore the reality in its manifestation.

I had been coy, impulsive, playing the victim, whilst all the time, all I needed to do was unclutter my senses and see the thorns on the roses, stabbing through perceptibly. My husband, illustrious in his deceptiveness, turning from man to mammoth.

There were obvious signs the whole time, but I was no good at playing this game of charades, and I had been duped into conformity. I had married the game master, acting as his companion in his rancid display of betrayal and heartbreak. Here I was now, a prisoner in my reality. He had threatened me underhandedly. I wanted to probe for more answers; had he meant what he said?

Was he threatening my life? I looked at the clock. It was 1.30 pm.

I had no time to think. I was going to be late to the station. My life was at a precipice, but I had to leave all that for now, and bravely face my fate with agent Stalker. I wiped the tears from my face and pulled my hair back into a bun. This would have to wait until later.

I grabbed a cab to the station as I was in no state to drive. Besides, I wasn't about to drive one of the pieces of evidence which could link James and me to the murder. James, ironically, had offered to take me, but I needed to do this alone. I was angry, hurt, and shocked that he was so calm in his demeanour, as though nothing had happened.

The last thing I needed was for him to offer any sort of kindness; he wasn't going to get to play the hero anymore.

I was no longer going to be that damned Damsel in distress.

━━━

I arrived at the station at about 2.15 pm, a little later than planned.

Agent Corrigan was the first person I saw. He waved me over and offered me a coffee, which I accepted thankfully. I needed something to soothe me for the grilling I was about to endure. This was the good cop part done with. Next was his partner to play the role of the bad cop, just as I had expected.

"Good afternoon Mrs Foyler. You finally graced us with your presence. Thanks for coming in."

He looked stressed, I could see the mountain of files on his desk, caseload after caseload. He gestured for me to go into the questioning room.

"Good Afternoon Agent Stalker. I'm sorry, I just lost track of time. Please call me, Fiona."

I walked in nervously. It was just like the rooms I had seen in the movies. Cold and grey with a single large brown desk. There was a two-way mirror and two chairs, so I grabbed one and sat down.

"So, Mrs Foyler," he said, ignoring my request. "I just need to go through a few questions with you regarding the night of the disappearance of Maria Garcia Rodriguez."

He sat down and slammed his files on the table dramatically, I assume for effect.

"There has been a new development, so although I was just calling you in, to question on where you thought she might have been, given that the witness had seen you with her, things have changed a little bit now."

He cleared his throat and opened the file.

I looked down, and there was a picture of a dead woman. Her face was all beaten up, so it was difficult to distinguish her features. She looked grey and bruised. At first, I didn't recognize her, and then I saw the dark wavy hair. There was no denying it; that was Maria.

Cold, grey and dead.

"Her body was pulled out of the water, just on Streetsville. Whoever did this to her surely hated her. See how she's all covered in bruises?"

He pointed at her face and then her stomach.

"There was no sign of rape or sexual assault, just a battering. Looks like she was in a fight of some sort, see how her hands are also bruised. Perhaps a struggle of some sort. Possible dead for a couple of months now," he said.

I cleared my throat. I had never seen a dead body before, let alone someone I knew. I didn't know how to react. I knew she was dead but seeing her like that was truly awful. James had used all his strength to do so much damage. She had been in the river for over a month, her body badly decomposed but you could still tell from what was left of her that she had suffered a painful death.

"So, Mrs Foyler. How well did you know the victim?"

———

The questioning went on for a couple of hours.

I had an inkling that Agent Stalker knew James and I had something to do with it. He kept on asking about my relationship with Maria, the fight we had, the affair between Maria and James, which had been recorded by the police as the reason for the altercation between Maria and me.

He teased me about wanting revenge for the affair. I tried to get rid of the mistress, he said. Then he let the bombshell out, they had run some tests on the corpse, and it confirmed that Maria was indeed with a child at the time of the murder. This would officially now be classed as a double homicide.

I wasn't sure if that was just a threat or real, but he wanted me to know that there would be real consequences for this. I stuck to my story.

I had gone home after work. I had not seen Maria, albeit that a witness had said otherwise.

It was my word against whoever this witness was, and if they had no real evidence to put me at any crime scenes, then I just needed to keep calm.

After the two long hours, I was faltering a little. He was getting to me. It was all bad cop and no sight of the lesser evil; I was tired, hungry, and I just wanted to get out of there. I needed a lawyer. They couldn't keep me in for further questioning.

I knew my rights. I had watched many crime scenes, and detective shows on television to understand how this worked. I did not have to say one more word. This was America, and there was such a thing as pleading the fifth; so, I asked for the right to a defense lawyer, except by doing this, it signaled that I had something to be defensive about, an illusion of guilt personified.

This was it. I had powered Agent Stalkers up; he wouldn't be letting this drop anytime soon. I left the station at about 6 pm.

This wasn't over. It was just the beginning as far as the police were involved.

It was time to lawyer the heck up.

The next couple of days were hell on earth.

James hired a defense lawyer who he claimed had helped him out of a previous predicament. He boasted that this guy could even get the devil out of hell; he was supposed to be that good. I didn't bother to ask about the details, internally, I was done with James, I just needed to keep up the charade to get through this mess with the police. James was confident that it would all go away, as although they had found a body, any trace of DNA would surely have been washed away by now.

There had been no charges filed yet, and so there was no need for anyone to confess. He promised that if it got to such a stage, that my life was in any danger with the police, he would immediately come forward and confess.

This was the deal, and I was willing to go along if it was safe to do so.

Monday morning started like any other day. I got up, brushed my teeth, had a shower, got dressed and went downstairs to pour myself a cup of coffee.

This had been my routine for the last year or so, except this morning, things were very different. A few months back, I had started back on that famous mantra of mine- what we focus on will eventually materialize. I had been willing for a baby, or at least to start a family soon. Each time I would fantasize about starting a family with James, there would always be something at the back of my mind, trying to discourage me. I couldn't quite figure out what it was, but I knew that there was a reason for my anxiety; perhaps it had something to do with Amanda, something she had said to me about not having kids with James.

All this fantasizing about children had been taking place before I found out about the affair with Maria. Ever since her death, I had put this aside, focusing on trying to mend my life. Still, I guess the universe had taken note of my wishes earlier and had forgotten to hit the reset button. That morning, I randomly decided to check the date on the calendar in the bathroom, a way to keep track of how far we come since the Maria incident, but something alerted me to check on something else.

In all the madness and hysteria that had become my life as of late, I hadn't noticed that I had missed a period or two.

I was eleven weeks late. This just had to be the worst timing. I did want a baby, only not with James, not now, I hated him. How could I have let this happen?

I wracked my brain, trying desperately to piece together the dates. I hadn't slept with James in weeks, so it didn't add up. I could no longer bear for him to touch me. I would recoil whenever he would kiss me, so sex had been off the list for a while.

He, on the other hand, was by no means missing out of his afflictions, he had others to satisfy his ever-growing taste for sex. I am sure he was still being pleased daily or so, as I would frequently perceive the scent of sex on him as he lay next to me in bed, after a long night at the office, as he would put it. It was very recognizable, that lingering musty odor of sweat mixed with female juices marinating on his skin.

As I tried to recollect the last time I slept with James, it finally hit me; the trip to Nashville, his dramatic rendition of a knight in armor, enchanting his princess. Except there was no enchantment, just him violating me, right on the side of the road and me bent over the bonnet of the car.

That had to be it, a careless endeavour, no protection, no pulling it, just emotionless sex.

Damn it. This was my fault; it had to be; I yearned for success, I got it. I wished for a successful husband. He came to me; I wanted a baby, and now it was happening, my new mantra would now have to be-

Be careful of success, as it has a dark side.

I quickly pulled out a pregnancy kit from the medicine cupboard, one I had purchased when I first moved in with James. I followed the instructions thoroughly, all the time, internally praying that the universe would not be so unkind as to offer me my wishes at such a debauched time. Still, in her attempt perhaps to punish me for my corruptibility, my willingness to harbor a murderer, my acceptance of a cheater and my capacity to love one who did not deserve to be loved so unquestionably, the universe cursed me with a gift of life.

I was pregnant, and even before the screen on the pregnancy kit read as 'positive,' I knew it, I could feel life radiating from deep within. We had created something good, from all the wickedness that had surrounded us in these past few months, there was a greater good coming from it, a purpose; love had been sprung from the very depths of evil and would be immortalized in the face of our child.

Just one hitch though - James hated children, he had killed Maria because she was pregnant, he had confessed that he would be a terrible father and would suffer no such curse. Still, I was pregnant. This was happening, there would be no exit options, as no matter what, this was going to be my child, and I would love him or her regardless.

I would have to tell James, and he would have to accept it, somehow. I threw the pregnancy kit in the bin, deciding that I would keep it to myself for a few days, at least until I heard some more news about the case. I needed to focus on one thing at a time, and I did not have the nerve to break the news to James yet.

I rushed out to work, James had already left earlier, so I had to grab a cab.

———

Back at the office, everything was business as usual. The office always provided me with a distraction, well except for the times I would bump into Julia, the images rushing back through my mind, as I would imagine the wicked things they probably still got up to. She would always smirk at me, in some way, boasting that she could still have my husband whenever she wanted. She had won.

I also tried my best to avoid any alone time with James in his office; it brought back too many memories of the good times we had in there, devouring each other like animals, hungry for each other, full of passion and heat. Not anymore, those days were now long gone, he was, in my eyes, the enemy.

———

At lunchtime, I could hear some commotion coming from towards the main doors to the office, people were gathering around, whispers and murmurs, reverberating around the halls.

I stood up to see what it was, and I saw two people walking in my direction, their faces looked familiar, but from a distance, I couldn't be sure. I blinked, an attempt to refocus my eyes, and as they approached, I realized it was agent Stalker and a female officer who I had seen before at the station. Their faces were unreadable, cold as the sharpness of the outside, on a winter's day.

They walked over to my desk, assertively.

"Good Afternoon Mrs Fiona Foyler," said the female agent

"Hi, what's going on? What's this about? Are you looking for James, he's in..?"

Agent Stalker cut me off mid-sentence.

"Mrs Foyler, we have a warrant for your arrest, for the murder of Maria Gonzalez Rodriguez. You have the right to remain silent. Anything you say can and will be used against you in a court of law. You have the right to speak to an attorney, and to have an attorney present during any questioning."

What the fuck!

I thought they had no real leads, no evidence, nothing, just a body.

Where was my lawyer, my defense? Where was James? I looked over towards his office; his door was shut. Surely he could hear all the commotion.

To reduce the gossip, I did not resist, I put both hands in front of me, compliant as possible. The handcuffs went on, for the second time, just in the space of a few months.

Tight, sharp and fast, restricting the blood flow to my arms, constraining me and holding me captive in my own body. I could hear gasps in the distance as people looked on impassively.

Julia walked past me, as the handcuffs went on and shook her head mockingly, making my stomach churn even harder, as I could do nothing but swallow the resentment simmering on the surface on my tongue.

I was led away, voiceless, shivering, ashamed and in shock.

As we walked towards the elevators, I looked back over my shoulder, a moment of reflection to see how far I had come, and how far I had fallen, and there in the distance was James, standing next to Julia and Demetri. He looked shocked and yet there was some level of acceptance in his eyes.

He mouthed the words, I am sorry, I will sort this, and I just looked at him, my heart wounded and dejected.

How could this be happening to me?

It was time to wake up from this endless nightmare.

Chapter 22

It turns out there was DNA evidence, coupled with the witness and the fact that I had no alibi and a previous assault on the victim.

The case was not looking promising, and all fingers were pointed at me.

After the arrest, I spent a few days in a cell, waiting for my bail hearing. These days were torturous. I had all manner of people coming to visit me from my defense team. James had hired a whole set of lawyers to work on the case, to try to have it dismissed. He came to visit me at some point during those couple of days, but I refused to see him. This was all too much.

I had called home to break the news to my family, and my mother had fainted and ended up in the hospital with shock. I knew it would hit her the hardest, but I tried to assure her that I was not being convicted, there was still a trial, and my team was working on getting the case thrown out of court.

My father, quiet as always, didn't say much, but I knew he was hurting. They would be on the next flight to

Chicago to visit, alongside my sister, who was just inconsolable and my best friend, Harry. I hadn't spoken or seen Harry in such a long time, that when I finally had some time alone with him, I broke down and told him everything.

The abuse, the affairs, and the baby, everything except for the murder. I knew that if I told him anything about the murder, he would run straight to the cops and let it all out, making everything worse. There was also the fact that the visit was being monitored, so I wasn't about to incriminate myself or James, should one the guards hear something. Harry tried to console me as best as he could.

He was always the understanding of all my friends. He would never say I told you so and was a firm believer in the saying, that what was done, was done. I just needed to get out of this mess and figure out how to tell James about the baby. Harry, being his usual sweet self, offered to support me should James turn the baby and me away. I did, however, make him promise not to allude to the fact that he knew anything. I did not want to add fuel to the fire, to push James to act out in such a way that would be detrimental to my case.

Harry would have to keep this secret to himself, at least until after the trial.

When it came to my family, on the other hand, I couldn't get myself to admit anything, as I am pretty sure my father would probably have ended up in prison for having killed James. I just told them it was a misunderstanding. The feds had got all wrong.

A case of mistaken identity or something.

It was some relief to them; I was very convincing. I couldn't allow this burden to be put on them, especially when I thought that James would confess if at any time my freedom was in jeopardy.

Sarah was distraught during visitation. She couldn't see past the prison clothes, the clinical setting of the prison and the bars that separated us. She would not make eye contact, for fear that the image of me at my lowest would be forever imprinted in her memory.

Instead, she just talked about non-relevant topics from back home and showed me pictures of Ella. She spoke of the baby on the way, they had gone for their final scan, and it was revealed that she and Ian would be having a little boy, a perfect little family.

They had already chosen the name, Elijah, so all that remained was for the little one to be born. She was excited when she spoke of her unborn child, and I yearned so much to tell her that I was also pregnant. This was something that would have bonded us, a precious moment between sisters; but this was not the time.

It would kill her to know that I was with child and stuck behind bars. We talked for a little longer until my mother stepped in and decided to ask me about how I got into this mess.

She asked if I knew anything about the affair with Maria. My lawyers had already briefed my parents on the particulars of the case. They had told my family about the previous altercation I had with Maria, which had led to the police being called out. That made my case a little weaker, as the prosecution would jump on that as a motive to kill Maria.

Mother wanted to know why I hadn't told her any of this. My mother always assumed that I told her everything that went on in my life, so it was to be expected that she would be quite hurt to discover that I had kept this from her, something so huge, something which could potentially land me in so much trouble.

She probed for more details. Why had I forgiven James

for the affair? Why had I assaulted Maria, why was I a suspect and not James? I couldn't keep up with the questions. I was spiralling. It incensed me that the focus was still on the affair with Maria, instead of on how the hell I was going to get out of prison.

I just couldn't tell my mother anything, I guess on some level I was afraid of what James would do, should he find out that I had revealed the details of our sordid marriage. He had already once threatened to hurt me should any of his extra-curricular activities get out.

I had seen him kill once, so I knew better than to cross him, and so, I lied to mother and told her that the affair had happened well before we were married and that it was all a misunderstanding. I had overreacted and that Maria and I had sorted out our differences before her death. My father suspected that I wasn't being candid about the affair but advised my mother to keep well out of the business of man and wife.

He just wanted to focus on the case and tried to convince me that it might be better to put our legal defense team together instead. I didn't see sense in that, as the costs of flying lawyers back and forth from London would spiral. James already had an excellent team on the case.

It made no sense to change teams now. I would be sticking with James's lawyers.

———

Day six, I was set for my first initial appearance in front of the federal magistrate, a daunting but necessary part of the whole legal preceding and the judicial process.

The magistrate was an elderly gentleman of about sixty years or so. He looked quite distinguished but stressed and overworked. He must have had too many caseloads to preside over, to attach any prominence to mine.

As I stood in front of him, I was informed of my constitutional rights. I was then asked to provide details of my legal team.

The magistrate read out the charges and the statutory maximum sentence. The "statutory maximum" is the most jail time that a defendant can receive for a crime. Under the argument provided by the prosecution, the evidence pointed at Voluntary Manslaughter- murder in the second-degree murder, classed under crimes of passion; an intentional killing that involved no prior intent to kill but carries a sentence in Illinois of anything from four years to a maximum of twenty years to thirty years in federal prison.

They argued that given the cruel way that the body had been disposed of wreaked of malice and could only be carried out by a person with a personality trait of a psychopathic individual. Someone with the potential to kill again; they wanted to push for more severe sentencing, which could see me behind bars for a considerable amount of time.

After the charges were read out and the possible sentence, should I be found guilty, the magistrate then turned to the matter of bail.

The prosecuting team was trying to move for me to be detained until the trial, but my legal team fought back.

They had to prove to the magistrate that I was not a flight risk, and as this was my first real offence, there was little chance of a further felony being committed.

I was asked several questions and given a detailed back-ground check. After dissecting the details, the magistrate fixed the bond at eight hundred thousand dollars, with the preliminary hearing, set in twenty days.

I was free to leave for now, under the conditions of the bail. That was, at least, some comfort in all the madness.

━━

There were so many pretrial motions after this stage. My legal team tried to argue to dismiss the charges, citing that the whole case was just based on circumstantial evidence.

There were constitutional challenges, motions for a bill of particulars, motions to strike and so on. My legal team wanted to go for a suppression motion, which moves to suppress evidence or to prevent the prosecutor from using it at trial.

They argued that the DNA found on the victim was circumstantial and that as I had contact with Maria in the past, given that she lived with me, therefore it was not unusual that some traces of my blood and hair might be found on the body.

The prosecutors, however, were adamant that given the nature of the murder and the history between me, the defendant and the victim, it would be judicially irresponsible for a dismissal of tangible evidence linking the victim and accused.

The DNA evidence needed to be presented in court, along with the witnesses' statement.

My team argued, citing the witness was unreliable as she could not be sure what date she had seen me with Maria and that even if she had indeed seen me at the house, followed by sounds of screaming and so on, that wasn't conclusive it was on the night the victim was killed.

They moved for a motion to discredit the witness on the grounds of bias and inconsistency in the witnesses' statement. The witness, when questioned again, was unsure as to whether she had seen both me and James exiting the car and going into our apartment on the night in question.

She wavered, saying she has just seen the car pull up, and then a woman screaming afterwards. The prosecution was given ten days to respond to the suppression motion and other motions that were put forward before it would then be deliberated in front of the magistrate at the evidentiary hearing.

I would have to go home and wait to see if this case would still go any further. James was very optimistic and reassuring. He wouldn't talk too much about the case. He said there was nothing to worry about.

Leave it with the expert, Fiona, he would say. *Don't fret your little self.*

I kept busy with my legal team, going through the case and ensuring that no stone was left unturned. They didn't want to be stunned by the prosecution, so they questioned me on every aspect of my relationship with Maria. I mostly lied, as I didn't think it would help the case, alluding to the fact that I hated Maria to the core.

Our legal team also questioned James, but as the case wasn't yet going to trial, his input was limited. He came for moral support nonetheless.

In those few days, James was attentive, a fabrication I thought, all in good spirits, to keep me sweet and ensure that I did not sway from the script. He barely let me out of his sight, albeit that I was under house arrest.

I felt suffocated. If I sneezed, he would be right in front of me, asking me if I needed anything. The deception was rancid, it sickened me, but I also had a part to play, to keep us both out of prison, if not for me, but our unborn child.

If I went back on the story now and told the court that it was James who killed Maria, I might also go down as an accomplice or for obstructing the course of justice. Either way, I needed to play my part, just as we had agreed.

There was no going back now.

◁▭▷

Two weeks later, at the evidentiary hearing, the witness's statement was given to the magistrate, along with arguments from the defense and prosecuting teams.

The judge, however, despite the convincing arguments from the defense, dismissed the suppression motion and allowed for the DNA and the witness's testimony to be admissible at the hearing.

Nothing was going in my favor.

At this stage, the prosecution tried hard to push me into confessing. Deals were being thrown on the table - admission of guilt for a reduced sentence - five years instead of twenty. Someone even suggested that they could lower the case to third-degree, and I would hardly see much jail time, a fallacy nonetheless, anything to get a confession, I thought.

I would be making no such deals. I had a reliable legal defense team, and James had promised that should it go awry, he would come forward before the trial and confess. Besides, I believed that justice would always prevail and that the judicial system would never send the wrong person down for a crime that they did not commit.

One might say that I was mad to cover for James, but he pleaded with me not to speak out; the chances of there being a conviction against someone without a record were minute. He, on the other hand, as he explained, had a string of petty and financial convictions, something I knew nothing about. As such, the judge would probably not take kindly to a wealthy businessman taking the law into his own hands.

He argued that, if convicted, he would face at least twenty years, but for me, even if I were sentenced, the worst case would be that I would probably get out with not much to serve. He reminded me that, if he had to go to prison, he would kill himself, but if I were prepared to play my part, he would put himself forward if there was even a small chance that I was going to get a conviction.

I was confused. His argument was very credible; I didn't want him spending twenty years in prison, especially not now that I was with child, albeit that he wasn't aware of this.

I hadn't yet told him about the baby, but I knew that deep down, I didn't want my child to have a felon for a father, or worse still, to have to visit his or her father in prison for the next twenty to thirty years.

I trusted his judgment, even now, after everything, I trusted that there was some logic to this. In some ways, I also figured that outing him wasn't the best thing to do at this stage anyway, but if it came down to the wire, I would undoubtedly confess and admit that it was James.

The cops would release me, I might face some sort of penalty for obstructing the course justice, but I wouldn't do any real-time and James would just have to face the consequences for his actions, it wasn't as though he was innocent after all.

A few weeks later, at the plea hearing, when I was asked what my plea would be, I stood up assertively, head held up high and responded, "*Not Guilty.*" The trial was set for three months, the prosecution and defense would need to come up with a compelling case to either convict or exonerate, but until then, I was told to go home and get my things in order for the case that could define the next chapter of my life.

———

They say insanity is doing the same thing, repeatedly, but expecting different results, and so, I must confess that I must have been insane.

At every avenue, every path, I somehow managed to hide myself away from any probing issues, anything that could cause discomfort in our lives, but all the while I hoped that somehow, everything would work out, it always did.

I had always said to myself, all is well that ends well, but of course, how do you define the end if not but for dying, and if one is still in the middle of one's journey, then surely there could still be a long treacherous road to travel.

Chapter 23

I had never felt more relieved to be at home.

It would be a gruesome three months of patiently agonizing and waiting. At every opportunity, I was being advised by my legal team that they had a water-tight case; the case would most likely be thrown out of court, as the DNA was circumstantial.

The altercation with Maria was anecdotal if anything and didn't amount to guilt. The witness was unreliable and could be easily discredited in court once the defense had time to interrogate her under oath.

The jury would see right through her. Her statement was the only thing keeping this case going, as other than that, this was a clear-cut dismal or an automatic win. They even talked about what I should do once I had been exonerated, sue the state, for criminal charges and libel. It was all going to work out; faith and patience was the word of the day.

I was slightly relieved on this account. I didn't have to picture myself being carted away in three months, in an orange jumpsuit, six months pregnant and no hope for a future; I could now see past that and focus on what would happen after the trial, the baby.

I decided it was time, James had to be told, and I had to do this now.

My family had to return to London; father didn't care much for Chicago, something about it being too American.

Sarah being heavily pregnant, didn't want to risk having the baby in a foreign land, just like my mother had done with me, and mother would have to go home with them as she was terrified of flying alone.

So, the very next weekend, we said our good-byes. James had been the best host as always, but this time, it was different, my family knew of the affair with Maria, so the distaste was all too obvious. I still am not too sure how James could have assumed that it could be kept hidden from my family, given that it was being used as evidence by the prosecution.

He denied it, feigning it to be all a misunderstanding and assumed I would set my family straight. I didn't, no more lies, they needed to see him for who he was, but at such a time, we still all needed to stick together to get through this unstable period our lives.

On their last day, father was re-briefed on the case, he also was of the mindset that it was going to go in our favor. There was just not enough evidence to convict.

On the morning of their departure, I decided to tell them about the pregnancy. I was surprised that my mother hadn't sensed this; she was usually good at detecting these things. The stress of the case must have been taking its toll, as her usual bright personality had all but become subdued.

She was, however, elated when I broke the news to them, another grandchild would bring about much-needed happiness to the family, and it was even more special as I would be having the baby only a few months after Sarah's. They thought it odd that I hadn't yet told James, but under the circumstances, they felt it best to let me make my own decisions. They left Chicago with some stern words for James. He was to look out for me, keep me safe and out of prison, no matter what.

They would be back in three months for the trial. Still, until then, James was instructed to provide my father with daily updates on the preparations and evidence gathering in the case, and both mother and Sarah promised to call me weekly for progress updates on the baby.

A fter their departure, the house just seemed to lose the gleam of hope that had surrounded me as my family paraded around, busying themselves in the grandiosity of a house.

I had been filled with a wholesome desire for love, which had now but diminished into a hidden sinkhole, choking my very passion for living and turning it into dark and disturbing anxiousness.

I was now alone, with only James for company. The emptiness of the place was causing a void to be forged within the depths of my consciousness, so deep and troubled that it left a gaping hole from which acrimony rose and flourished from within. The creaks in the floorboards, as I walked through the house, full of echoes of distant voices, would pierce through me, louder than I could withstand.

I was a fragment of a person, not quite whole, like a piece of furniture cut in half, reduced to nothing of any use, crippled and unstable, too afraid and in resentment of the man that now resided in the downstairs bedroom, a twisted version of a person I once loved.

It was time for action, time to reveal to James that I was pregnant. I had no choice as I would start to show in a few weeks; my slender frame, betraying me and prohibiting me from hiding the one thing that I once yearned for. A few days earlier, I had booked a scan to find out the sex of the baby. Mom and Sarah had accompanied me for moral support, given that I couldn't go with James.

I almost felt as though I was a single mother, except I wasn't. The doctor finally did the big reveal; I was going to be having a baby girl. I was so happy, and the thought did cross my mind that, perhaps revealing to James that it was a girl would soften his heart, the idea of having a little daddy's girl.

———

I t was a Tuesday as I recall; it had rained all day, and the sky was a dark grey color, standard for the start of autumn, or fall as it was referred to in the States.

Everything about the day was ominous, from the rain to the darkness and the headache that had been brewing all day. I had made a simple dinner of chicken and vegetables and sat and waited for James to return from work.

By then, I was always nauseated, side effects of the pregnancy, and James had been concerned, thinking that I may have picked up a bug, or that I was suffering from the effects of stress. I had dismissed it all, pretending that nothing was happening, but now, today, I would finally be revealing to him the secret I had kept for over three months.

I was nervous, afraid of how he would react, fearful for myself and my unborn child. He walked in, two hours later than expected, something that wasn't a rarity for him anymore.

He was probably working late, or with one of his girls, doing something sordid as usual. I stood up from the sofa and walked to the kitchen to heat the dinner and told him that I had something to say to him, he didn't seem that interested, but sat down at the table nonetheless, ready to be served his dinner.

We ate in silence, as he toyed with his phone, always replying to messages or emails. Once dinner was made, he asked what it was I wanted to talk about. We walked over to the living room and sat down. He could tell that I was struggling with whatever it was that I needed to say.

He stood up and poured me a drink, to which I declined. He frowned at this, hesitating for a second, and then pouring the contents of the glass down his throat, in one large gulp.

"James, please don't freak out. I just don't have the energy or the will for any drama right now, so please just accept what I have to say, with open arms."

I took a deep breath. "I don't know how this happened…well, of course, I know, what I mean is that I didn't plan this. We didn't plan this, but it's a good thing, James, trust me, it will bring us even closer."

He looked anxious as I dribbled on with what could only be described as a rant.

"For the love of Christ, woman, please just spit it out, it can't be worse than the bloody murder case, so just tell me."

He was right; we had bigger issues to deal with; this was just a minor issue. I cleared my throat.

"I'm pregnant. We're having a baby, James. We are pregnant."

Saying it out loud was not only cathartic was for me, but it also felt amazing, to say those words out loud, to finally accept it to be true. James did not move an inch. He just sat still, frozen in time.

His face has turned white, as though the blood was being drained from him slowly. After what felt like minutes, which was in actual, just a few seconds, he finally rose, walked over to the bar area and poured himself a whiskey.

"Is it mine?"

The few seconds of joy I had just felt, had now been soured by his audacious question.

He repeated himself. "Is it mine?"

I looked at him, disappointed, this was a low blow.

"Of course, it is yours. What are you insinuating? I don't screw around like you. I took my vows seriously, you bastard!" This angered him. "How the hell do I know if you have been messing about, I haven't touched you in weeks, it's impossible."

He was right, we hadn't slept together in a while, but I had left out the part about how far along I was.

"Look, James, don't do this, not now. I am three months pregnant, you screwed me, and now I'm pregnant, deal with it. I couldn't tell you because of all the stuff with the case, and I feared how you would react, given the whole drama with Maria, when you found out she was pregnant. I was afraid you might do something to hurt me."

I could see his jaw clenching. It was clear he didn't want this. "Get rid of it!" He walked towards me and brushed past me in disgust.

"Get rid of it, Fiona, I'm not messing. Get rid of it, and fast. I am going out to clear my head, but sort it, sort it."

He stormed out of the house and left me there. I was unsure of my next move. There was no way in hell I was going to have a termination, especially not when I was already this far in the pregnancy. I wanted to pack up and leave immediately, but under the terms of my bail, I had to stay in that house. I was distraught, thoughts whirling through my head. I felt suicidal, as my mind played tricks on me, telling me to end it all. I couldn't face the trial or James any longer. I just wanted the pain to stop. That wasn't to be the worst of it.

There was still much more to come.

⸻

The old saying is that the darkest hour is just before dawn; these next few days would prove this right.

Hell resided within James, and he was filled with fury, so I was to feel the wrath of his scorn.

Before daybreak, James came home, he had been drinking heavily, so I knew I was in for a bad time. He walked into the bedroom and climbed into bed with me. I found this odd, as we now no longer slept in the same bedroom. He started to kiss me. I resisted.

He kissed me again, so I pushed him off, but this did little to discourage him. He grabbed my legs and spread them apart, placing the full force of his weight on me. I could hardly breathe. I cried out. I didn't t want this, I didn't want him, not like this, but he was unrelenting.

He pinned me down and continued to try to enter me. Although he was my husband, I felt I still had the right to say no. He wouldn't stop; he turned me over onto my chest and pushed himself into me. It burned as he forced himself inside me. I couldn't believe what was happening.

I decided not to struggle anymore, for fear of hurting the baby, so I just lay there, numb, floods of hot tears flowing down my face, as my beloved husband raped me in the bed we once made love in.

All the time he was thrusting, he would try to justify what he was doing.

"You are my wife, stop resisting. This is my right. You want me to show you how to make a baby, eh? This is how. Do you like it? This is how you bloody make a baby. Come on, moan like you like it, you whore. You screw around and get pregnant. You whore. You like this, don't you? You think you can just stop having sex with me. I'm a man. I need this. You need this"

I was a woman undone. I had nothing left to give and no strength to resist. I had life in me to protect, as far as I was concerned, he could do whatever he wanted, so long as he did not hurt my unborn child.

Once he was done, he wiped his brow and rolled over to sleep. I lay there for the rest of the night, too afraid to move.

I was frozen in my fear, waiting for the morning to bring about something less evil, than what was lying next to me.

Chapter 24

I was done.

James could go to hell for all I cared. He could rot in prison for the rest of his life, and I would feel no remorse.

After the rape, he would go out of his way to try to set up accidents for me; an accidental fall down the stairs, caused by an item placed deliberately in a precarious manner; a spill of wine, followed by overzealous mopping with soapy water, all accompanied by a theatrical apology.

It had got to the almost laughable point, except none of it was funny. His blatant attempt at making sure that I had a miscarriage was, however, unsuccessful.

Each time I would have a knock, a fall or a slip, the doctors would still give me a clean bill of health, mother and baby, all good to go, they would say each time, as they examined me; not taking the time even to bother to ask why I had come with so many bruises.

They thought I was extremely clumsy. No one would have ever guess the real story.

I called my sister halfway towards the fourth month of my pregnancy. By this time, she had already given birth to her second child.

It was a little early, perhaps the stress of the case had brought about the early labor, but mother and baby were healthy and fine. I didn't want to burden her with my problems, but I needed someone to confide in, someone to tell my story.

Harry already knew most of it, but I had left out the part about the murder. It was time that I came clean, I needed my family now, more than ever. I told Sarah everything, from the beginning, when everything was rosy, to the affair, the murder and his request for me to cover for him.

I told her I had no choice; he had faked an alibi and in some way, implied that if I told the police the truth, he would hurt me, maybe even kill me.

I told her about the abuse, the rape and his attempt at hurting my unborn child. Naturally, Sarah could not believe this. She was distraught for me. She wanted me to leave, to call the cops, to run as far away from James as I could. She wanted to me tell my parents, to leave the country, to flee and never return.

Most of her options were just not possible. I couldn't leave, not when I was in the middle of an investigation. I didn't want to tell my parents everything, because I knew too well that my father might just kill James.

We did, however, agree that it was time to confess to the police. She told me that I had to tell them the truth, even if it meant that James would go down for life, and I might do some time for perjury.

As far as she was concerned, some jail time was better

than a lifetime of what I had been facing. It was sure to get worse. He had all the stereotypes of a psychopath; the charm, the controlling behavior, the outburst, the abuse, and manipulation.

If I didn't stop this now, she feared that she would soon be attending my funeral. So, we mapped out a plan on how to get out of the mess. It would involve telling the police, but first, I was to tell my parents everything finally, and with their guidance, I was to reveal the whole thing to agent Corrigan; he seemed like the kinder of the two agents involved in the case.

I agreed to call him the very next day, after speaking to my parents. I would ask him to come to the house while James was at work. I no longer went to work, as James thought it best to stay away from judgmental eyes, at least until I cleared my name.

———

I t was one of the hardest things I had ever done. Having to reveal to my parents, the disaster of a marriage that I once bragged about. Both parents listened intently, as I video called them over Skype.

This was something that needed to be said face to face. I needed to see their reactions. I needed them to see my anguish, to understand why I had kept this from them. I had already told them about the affairs, but to add the extent of his betrayal was too much for my mother to take. She couldn't understand how someone who claimed to love me, would allow me to be at risk with the police for something I hadn't done.

She couldn't understand why he would try to hurt our unborn child. My father was silent the whole time, and this scared me. I told them to let justice be served. It would not help my case now if my father tried to take the law into his own hands.

Once the case was over, my father could do whatever he wanted to James, but for now, I made him promise to be calm and wait for the right time to react.

With that done, I called Harry and retold the story. This time, I made sure to tell him everything too.

———

Agent Corrigan arrived at 10 a.m. the next day. I was a little disappointed to see that he brought Agent Stalker along, as I was convinced that he didn't take well to me. I offered both agents a drink.

Agent Corrigan refused, as he said he never drank while on duty, but Agent Stalker happily accepted a beer. And so, I began, the whole truth and nothing but the truth. I relayed the entire story to them, just as I had done with Sarah and my parents, the night before, making sure not to miss out on anything that may help my case.

I had been talking for about twenty minutes without interruption, and I could see the disbelief in their eyes.

Agent Stalker was the first to break their silence.

"Well then, if it was so bloody awful, Miss, why the heck did you stay, and why would you not just go to the police?"

Agent Corrigan scowled at him. "Let her finish, don't muddle the waters."

I was done. I had said everything I needed to say, and it was now up to them to decide if I could bring this to the table.

Agent Corrigan looked concerned. His expression conveyed some sort of frustration.

"Shit, you know from the very beginning, I knew something was off, I knew there had to be more. A young woman like yourself, getting mixed up in all this mess. To be honest with you, the trial really can't be stopped now. This is bad. We can't change the course of the trial. You were already charged. You will just look like the bitter wife, trying to apportion blame. This is bad. This is bad. Besides, now it's his word against yours and his alibi. Shit, you will need to brief your lawyers on this, but to be honest, there isn't much we can do for you- it's up to your lawyers now to see if they can bring this into court, but most likely on a separate case. Why the heck did you let it get this far, to be charged. You should have said something Miss, you gave a statement, you lied, so if what you're saying is true, then the fact that you lied is a criminal offense in its self. You just better hope you don't get convicted, that's the only chance you have on pinning this on your husband. Shiiit!"

I looked over at Agent Stalker, and he seemed indifferent. I could tell he didn't believe a word I had told them. This shocked me.

I never for one second thought that anyone would discredit my story, it was the truth, and that in telling the truth, I would be no closer to saving myself. I had come too far with a lie, and it could be too late to turn around, not without it looking like a last-minute desperate attempt at avoiding a conviction. I felt a pain in the pits of my stomach. I was coming clean, and yet the truth was unlikely to set me free.

Agent Corrigan took down some notes and said he would do all he could to help me, but as the case was already taken to court, I shouldn't put my hopes on this squashing the trial unless there was some evidence to the contrary.

My only hope would be if my lawyer could find some

evidence that could lead directly to James, as the killer. He asked if I wanted to file other charges for assault and rape, something that could help put James away for a few weeks or months, enough time to keep me safe and away from him until the trial and something which may help paint a picture about the kind of person James was.

I agreed, and the very next day, James was arrested for assault, I asked for the rape to be undisclosed, I couldn't bear being labeled as a rape victim.

Even after all that was happening, I was still concerned about protecting my virtue.

━━━

A man with an abundance of wealth can never be put down.

James was out on bail after just one day and very much aware that I had told the police too much. I was now afraid for my life and felt as though I was living on borrowed time. It was time for me to flee the house, so with the permission of the court and an arduous fight by my lawyer, I was granted safe-haven at a woman's shelter with a restraining order placed against James; he wasn't to come within two hundred meters of me.

The assault charges, however, could not stick, as there was no identifiable evidence. I was told that threatening words alone would not be enough of an act to constitute an assault unless James had backed this up with actions that would put me in reasonable fear of harm. In other words, unless I had real proof that he had assaulted me, such as bruises or a witness, the assault charges had to be squashed, along with any hopes of using it as ammunition to defame his character in court.

I had to settle with accepting the restraining order

against him, as some sort of proof that he wasn't as right-
eous as everyone had assumed.

The woman's shelter left much to be desired.

It was built on an old estate, from the sixties and
looked more like an asylum than a haven. Funding for the
maintenance of the shelter had run dry. As such, the
premises lacked any of the comforts of home, each room
was decorated with furniture from charity shops and yard
sales. In those few weeks, everything happened so fast. I
settled into my new life as an abused woman, a sort of
protective custody, without any of the actual benefits of
protection from the state.

My lawyers had been briefed on everything that I had
told Agent Corrigan and Agent Stalker. Still, as it was
James who was paying my legal fees, the legal team started
to dwindle in numbers and, by the second week, my legal
team had all but diminished from a group of six to just one
lawyer.

James had stopped paying.

He was of the mindset that, by going to the police with
an allegation of assault, I had betrayed his trust, and thus,
he would rescind any help he had offered me. He didn't
care that it might mean that I could lose the ability to
defend myself for a crime that he had committed.

It seemed he had all but forgotten what had got us to
that point in the first place. As far as he was concerned, I
was not to be trusted, and he wasn't going to waste any
more of his hard-earned cash helping an ungrateful
woman. He didn't care that I knew his secret.

On some level, I don't think that he recognized that he
was doing anything wrong anymore, as, in his mind, he

hadn't specifically forced me to take the blame. It was my lack of alibi that led the police to put together some evidence that had eventually pointed the finger at me.

It was my fault for failing to get an alibi, given that he had told me to do so. Yet, there was still time, the investigation was wrapping up, so I just needed to sit tight until the trail went cold enough for an acquittal.

I didn't waste any time in asking my father to help with the legal fees, but he could only just about cover the expenses unless he was to re-mortgage the house in London, something I vehemently refused.

After I told my lawyer the truth about James, he started to try to gather some evidence against James that could at least make him a culpable suspect, but James was too smart, and nothing would stick, at least nothing good enough to present in the case.

The best chance I had now was to continue to focus on the case at hand and try to get my charges dismissed.

I spent the next couple of months at the women's shelter; as I waited for my trial to begin.

During my time there, I got to meet a lot of interesting women. Some, clearly victims, feeble and timid, undoubtedly targets for abuse, while others looked tough and menacing.

On the contrary to my usual behavior, I found more in common with the tougher looking women, those covered in piercings and tattoos, with shaved heads and all the typical stereotypes associated with criminals, except, they were far from criminal, but victims of their self-indulgent corruptibility.

These women did not fit the stereotype of the abused

and beaten woman. They looked healthy and self-assured, yet, every one of them had a harrowing story to tell: an abusive alcoholic boyfriend, a possessive girlfriend, a murderous husband, brother, father.

They were usually there, not so much from physical abuse, but from the repeated death threats and acts of life-threatening violence that they had suffered at the hands of their partners.

Over the weeks, I engaged with these women, listened to their stories, their voices resonating within me. We had a commonality between us, a shared passion for avenging what had been taken away from us. I think on some level they took pity on me.

A foreigner; alone and vulnerable. The more time I spent in their company, the more enraged I felt about my situation.

There was certainly the possibility that I could be charged with murder and spend the best part of my life, rotting away in a prison cell, missing out on seeing my child grow-up, all the while having to hand my child over to a murderous husband. I knew that if I were convicted, he would most certainly get custody.

He would never confess. This man could take my life away from me, along with the life that was growing inside me.

I could end up a convict, all in the name of love, and for what, for someone who took pleasure in beating and raping me. A blind fury began to grow deep within me. I could feel that little Miss perfect Fiona; the naïve fledgling young woman who first set upon an adventure to find herself; slipping away slowly, as this newly formed, wiser and scorned Fiona took center stage.

I had to do something before it was too late. I couldn't just sit in the safe house for the next two months, awaiting my fate; fate at the hands of a man that was happy enough to see me get destroyed. I couldn't sit back and let him get away with this, with murder, threefold. It was time to act. I would make this man pay somehow.

I had gone over several scenarios with the women in the house. They offered suggestions on how to get back at James. Some wanted him to be physically hurt, perhaps a car accident, others joked that I could hire a hitman.

All their suggestions sounded enticing; however, I needed to be smart, I needed to focus on clearing my name first, and besides, I wasn't a murderer, I had no real malice in me. I just wanted to prove I was innocent, and once I had done that, I wanted to get the hell away from Chicago and back home to safe England, where everyone I knew truly loved me.

We finally came up with a few scenarios that didn't have me committing a crime.

Scenario one: Beg him to confess- there was just no chance of that happening. I hated the man, and no way was I going to submit to him, in any way.

Scenario two: Tell everyone about his sordid past, the sexual acts, the orgies, the women. Make sure that everyone in town finally knew the real James Foyler.

Scenario three: Talk to the press, tell them everything. That would surely stir things up and shed some light on his shady behavior.

Scenario four: Trick him into confessing.

This was it. I would approach him, albeit in violation of the restraining order, and trick him into revealing that he had killed Maria, all the time recording the entire conversation. This was my only saving grace. This would exonerate me and explain to the world the sort of sordid person he was.

I had two weeks before the start of the trial, two weeks to set the record straight.

Two weeks to reclaim my life.

Chapter 25

I dialled the phone with both hands shaking, nervous from the anticipation.

I needed to hear a familiar voice.

"Hey Hot Harry, it's Fiona." I paused and waited for him to respond.

"Hahahaha. Hey, convict." He joked. He always liked to make light of a grim situation; it was his way of dealing with difficult issues.

"How have you been, Fiona? I've missed you. How are you coping with all the drama? Clear your name yet?"

He was always so straight to the point and matter of fact about everything. He, however, had a way of making me feel at ease, as though everything would always be sorted, no matter what.

"I'm afraid not-but, I do have a plan though, and I think it's going to work. I think I can get that sonofabitch to confess on tape. I have it all worked out."

I told him about the plan, in detail, asking for his opinion or advice. He wasn't too thrilled. He thought it was dangerous. The man had already killed once, and if things didn't go to plan, he was afraid I might get hurt.

Harry tried his best to dissuade me, threatening to reveal the plan to my family, but I was adamant that I would go ahead with the plan nonetheless, after all, James was still my husband, he wasn't just some stranger off the road. I could handle him. I could talk to him, just like I had done when we first fell in love.

I wanted Harry's support, I needed him to tell me that I was doing the right thing, but he wouldn't budge, so I was all alone again, and this was my only chance. I couldn't face doing this alone, I needed help and most of all, I needed a friend. I am not sure why I chose to call Amanda, but something in me told me that she would be able to help.

She had once tried to warn me off James, telling me that he was dangerous. I figured that if I confided in her and told her my story, she would be able to shed some light on what James had done to her and perhaps help me figure out how to go about with my plan.

I picked up the phone and dialed her number. She picked up on the second ring. I explained that I needed to speak to her urgently about James. She was surprisingly very accommodating.

I think she had been expecting a call from me for a while since hearing about the murder.

━━

I met her a couple of hours later, at a café down the road from the women's shelter.

She looked horrified when she saw me. At this point, I was almost six months pregnant and showing. I wrapped my hands around my bump, protectively, trying to ignore the look of horror on her face.

We sat down and ordered our coffees, and after some pleasantries, I told her my story and the plan to clear my name. We sat in silence for a few minutes, sipping on our coffees, not making eye contact. There was an intense uneasiness in the air, more so on my part than hers.

I think she was processing everything I had told her. I bit my lips nervously, then my fingernails, a bad habit I had recently picked up. I was terrified that she wouldn't believe me, but contrary to this, the expression on her face revealed differently. She wasn't shocked at what I had told her, and it seemed as though there was some recognition in her eyes, as though this wasn't the first time such a thing had happened.

It turned out that James had already done this before, or at least something not too far removed from it. Amanda, as it turns out, was now ready to speak; she had her own story to tell, a secret so deep and devastating that even after everything I had been through, this left me dumbfounded.

Amanda explained that she had met Christian through James while they all worked at Abtint Investments, almost five years ago. Although they all did not work in the same department, Amanda would occasionally have lunch with James, along with other colleagues.

At the time, it was completely platonic, but everybody knew James was a lady's man, so Amanda would always try to keep it professional with him, much to his disappointment. Christian became a part of the lunch team, when James invited him along to lunch one day, along with Amanda and one other colleague. Christian had immediately taken to Amanda, and a week later had asked her on a date.

She was reluctant to date a colleague, so things didn't

develop any further, however, a few months later, Amanda received a job offer at another firm and accepted, giving Christian, the impetus to ask her out again. This time, she agreed.

Things developed very quickly from then on, and after about three months, they were inseparable, and Amanda moved in with Christian. James felt quite cheated given that he was the one who had introduced the two, and Christian had been the one who got the girl, per se. So, on some level, Christian felt a twinge of guilt and so would always invite James along to spend time with him and Amanda.

This friendship quickly grew to the point that they looked like three peas in a pod. Amanda started spending so much more time with James, at their apartment when-ever Christian was away on business trips, and one night, after a few drinks, James seduced her. He was charming and enchanting, which made him irresistible.

This was the beginning of their summer-long fling. They would have sex, whenever Christian was away, or would both call in sick and spend the whole day together, sometimes inviting other women and men to join in for the thrill of it.

Amanda had loved the buzz of it, James was so excit-ing, he was a sexual deviant in every way. He had intro-duced her to so many sexual exploits that she could no longer recognize who she was becoming. They would even sometimes have sex in the room, while Christian was fast asleep.

It was disrespect to the next level, but it kept the fuel-burning within them, and the secrecy made it even more exciting. After a few months of this, James picked up the pace; he wanted more sex, he wanted to try more things with Amanda, things she felt uncomfortable with, but when she had refused, he along with two other guys had tied her up and raped her in a violent outburst.

They called it a sexual game, but this was no game. This was the start of the violence, and it would go on for another three months; he would come over, sometimes alone, sometimes with a group of three to four people, men, and women, whenever Christian was working late, and they would force themselves on her.

Sometimes James would just watch and instruct them on what to do, and other times, he would join in. When she threatened to tell Christian or the police, he would threaten to reveal everything to Christian and her family, along with a sex tape he had recorded without her consent. Eventually, she fell pregnant and was pretty sure it wasn't Christian's as they would always use protection.

She finally told James, but he refused to accept the baby and asked her to terminate it. Amanda had strict beliefs, and abortion was just not something she could go through with. So being the coward she was, and not wanting to admit the affair to Christian; which would then mean that she would have to tell him about everything, something James had vehemently told her not to do, she felt she had no other choice but to lie to Christian and say to him that the baby was his.

She knew deep down that it wasn't, and being the gentleman he was, Christian offered to marry her. They got married four months later in a small civil ceremony with just their parents. Five months later, baby boy Ethan was born. The first few weeks were happy times for both Amanda and Christian. They loved being parents and doted on their new-born baby, but things started to go awry when James would get angry that Amanda was playing happy families with Christian, knowing full well that the child was his.

Amanda tried her hardest to avoid seeing James, but Christian and James were good friends, as thick as thieves. So even with a new baby in the house, James would still occasionally come over sometimes and even stay over. The jealousy grew within him until he finally did the unspeakable.

One night while Christian was away on business, James visited Amanda and tried to force himself on her again. When she fought back, he lost control. They wrestled, as Amanda tried to free herself from him, but in a moment of madness, he ran over to the crib where baby Ethan was sound asleep and picked him up.

He was threatening to hurt him should Amanda not surrender to him. Naturally, Amanda was hysterical, trying her hardest to calm the situation so that James would hand over the baby. But James was too far gone by now. He hit baby Ethan over the head with his fist; one single blow to the skull and baby died instantly.

James couldn't believe what he had done, he handed over the baby and ran out of the house, leaving Amanda there, grief-stricken with a lifeless baby in her arms.

The coroner established the cause of death as an accidental fall, but Amanda knew the truth. She wanted to go to the police, but James promised he would hurt Christian, something she just couldn't allow.

Amanda had now kept this secret for over four years, all the time, having to watch James pretending to be friends with Christian. It was the hardest thing she had ever had to deal with, and even now, James continued to threaten her. She was enslaved in a lie that she could not get herself to admit to anyone, until now.

She blamed herself for the death of her child. Her infidelity had destroyed her life; she wasn't going to let it destroy Christian's life. I sat in amazement as I listened to her story. It was evident that her experience was much more harrowing than mine. There could be nothing worse than losing a child in that way.

Shock and horror ran through my body. I was angry that James had been allowed to get away with something so morbid. I was also mad at Amanda. I wished that she had possessed the courage to tell me this a year ago or even before I had married James. This could have saved Maria's life. This could have saved my life, what good would this information be to me now. This only just confirmed what I already knew, the man was evil, but I guess now, it was clear the depths he would go to and the degradation of his character.

I told Amanda what I had planned on doing, to trick James into confessing. I would go over to the house, pretending that I wanted to apologize for going to the cops with the assault charges. I would pretend that I wanted to try to rekindle our marriage and, if necessary, I would even let him touch me, kiss me, make love to me… anything to get him to catch him off his guard.

As I told her the details of the plan, she looked horrified.

She agreed with Harry. The plan was too risky. If he found the tape recorder, there was no saying what he would do. The man was capable of murder, so who was to say that he wouldn't lose control and do something crazy.

Was I willing to risk my life for a confession, was I ready to go over, six months pregnant and endanger the life of my child? I pondered over this, but I was adamant that it needed to be done. Amanda refused to listen, she felt protective over me, perhaps because seeing me that heavily pregnant must have conjured up emotions of losing her baby.

She decided that it was time, to tell the truth, we

needed to stop James before he did this again to someone else and there was only one person she knew who she could rely on, even after everything she had done to him.

She took out her cell phone from her handbag and dialed Christian's number.

"Christian, it's me, we need to talk. I have Fiona here with me. We are coming over to the house. I need your help."

We settled the bill and then flagged down a cab outside the cafe.

I t was a rather long drive over to their house, or perhaps it had felt that way because I was nervous about telling Christian about James, would he believe that his so-called buddy could be so mindless.

I was also nervous for Amanda. She was willing to possibly destroy her marriage, just so that the truth would finally come out. She hoped that in telling Christian, she could free herself from this secret that she had kept for so long. Perhaps it was also a way for her to purge herself of the guilt she carried for not having gone to the cops in the first place.

The death of her baby and the shame of a sex tape had been the price she had paid for James's silence. Because of that, another person had suffered at his hands. She felt that none of this would have happened, had she been brave and selfless enough to put aside her shame and expose James for who he was.

She also hoped that Christian would perhaps be able to help us find a safer way to get James to confess, one that wouldn't put me, a heavily pregnant woman a risk.

I had never been to Amanda's and Christian's house before, they lived in the suburbs, away from the noise of downtown Chicago.

During our long and revealing conversation at the cafe, Amanda had expressed to me that they had chosen to move there specifically, when their son, Ethan was born, as they wanted to live in a place where they could raise a family. Now, it was just a constant reminder of the child they had lost. They had continued to try for another baby, but after two years of IVF, their hopes of having a family was somehow becoming a distant reality.

As we drove through the suburbs, I noticed that the houses that lined the streets were architecturally beautiful; each one looked as though it had been designed bespoke to whoever lived inside. We pulled up to the house and saw that Christian's car was already in the driveway.

He had left work early to come home, as instructed by Amanda during their telephone call, at the cafe. Amanda paid the cab driver, who was delighted that he had gotten such a hefty fare. We walked to the front of the house, and Christian immediately opened to the door. He was surprised to see that I was pregnant.

We hadn't spoken since I had been charged with the murder, so naturally, he was shocked to see me like that, and although he had still been in contact with James, it was never once mentioned that I was pregnant, or that we had been estranged.

He kissed me on the cheek and gestured for me to come inside. The interior of the house was just as beautiful as the outside. It had a big open hallway leading to a grand staircase, with ceilings, which made the place feel even bigger. I marvelled at the grandiosity, almost forgetting why I was there in the first place.

Christian kissed Amanda on the lips and gave her an odd look, which I wasn't supposed to see. I guess he was wondering what the hell was going on. We walked over to the living room, where Christian offered me a seat and a glass of juice.

Amanda handed Christian a drink and then sat next to me, nervously. She was shaking, afraid to speak, but knowing too well that she had come too far to back down now.

"Christian, I just want you to know that you are my whole life, my everything, and I love you. I would die for you. I just want you to listen and understand that this was all a very long time ago. I was stupid, young, naïve, corruptible. If I could go back and take it all away, I would. I would give up everything, just to go back and start over. I need you to know this, and I am finally trying to come clean, to amend my indiscretion, for hurting you most undeniably. You do not have to forgive me, but I beg of you, if you can, please find it in your heart, and if anything, put aside your hurt for now, and just help us, help me, help Fiona, get past this, then we can figure out the next step. "

Christian sat across from us and frowned.

He knew that whatever it was she was about to say wasn't good news, but he was calm, and he sat and listened, as she told him everything.

As I listened to Amanda tell the story, all over again, it was quite clear that the version she had told me had been condensed. The events that had transpired between her and James had been more sordid that she had divulged.

There was so much more, so much evil and deceit. Although she wasn't completely innocent in all of it, having voluntarily taken part in the affair to start with, ending it was something she had tried to do but to no avail.

So now, she figured that she would be better off telling the whole truth once and for all. All the while, as I looked at Christian, I could see he was so hurt. His eyes watered a little as he listened to the woman he loved, reveal a chain of events, which, to some, would have been unfathomable.

He didn't say a word the whole time, he kept composed and sat motionless, letting her speak until she was finished and then he turned to me and said in the calmest voice.

"Ok, so what's your part in this?"

Chapter 26

Could this get any more sinister, is all I could think?

Christian's lack of a reaction had been a result of years of intimidation by James. He had taunted him, both verbally and physically, so much so that, on hearing about his wife's infidelity and her subsequent ill fate at the hands of James, Christian didn't need much convincing that she was telling the truth.

One thing I just could not wholly comprehend was how easily he had brushed aside the affair between James and Amanda, and all that came after. He must have loved her profoundly because once they retired that night, it seemed as though the whole affair was all forgiven.

I think he must have felt Amanda's anguish at having to keep such a secret for so long, a secret that involved the real reason behind the death of their son. He didn't blame her; he knew how manipulative James was.

He knew how we must have tormented her, and so, for him, this was all in the past. It was clear that they would have some real demons to deal with for a long time to come, but for now, Amanda needed him, and he wanted to prove to her that he could be there for her, unconditionally.

So, here he was, asking me what this had to do with me.

I signed, exhausted at having to tell my story to yet another person for the umpteenth time. He looked at me, a look of empathy in his eyes, as though wanting to let me know that whatever I had to say wouldn't shock him. I didn't say a word, nor move an inch.

I was still trying to process the additional shocking elements of Amanda's story that she had left out at the café. I also wanted to make sure that Christian had taken in the news properly, as I felt his reaction was too subdued. I expected him to shout, yell, or do something, anything that would suggest that he understood the gravity of what she had told him, but he did neither.

He just stood up and walked towards Amanda and placed his hand out. She stood up and lowered her head, ashamed about what she had just told him.

He put his hand around her waist and embraced her. I could feel the strength of love between the two of them. In such adversity, ironically, this would prove to make them stronger.

He released Amanda from his embrace and walked back over to the chair and sat back down. Since I was still unable to speak, he decided that he would take the stage. It was now his turn for some more shocking revelations.

He cleared his throat, cracked his knuckles and started to speak. He explained to us how he had met James back in college.

The two had always been very close, but as time went by, he started to see a side to James that was dark and mysterious.

It all started after graduation, after the sudden disappearance of James's parents. They had apparently both drowned on a family yachting holiday somewhere in the middle of the Indian Ocean, with James as the sole survivor. The whole story just didn't add up, as both parents had been avid sailors and strong swimmers; but the investigators ruled it out as, Misadventure.

Before the accident, James would always joke about how he wished his parents were dead so that he could inherit their millions. He would tell Christian how he fantasised about their deaths, one scenario being that on vacation, he would leave them in the middle of the ocean and sail off, leaving them at sea to drown.

Christian explained that he had chosen not to listen to James's stories, thinking that it was just his angst or sadness of being neglected by his parents. As an only child, James should have been close to his parents, but he seemed to harbour resentment for them for not pandering to him.

This loneliness had brought both Christian and James closer together at college, and it meant that James would then spend most of his free time with Christian. Even when the semester was out, James could always be found at Christian's family home, hanging out and hardly ever going home.

After a while, James's character started to change. He grew restless.

He always seemed to obsess about get rich schemes and how to make millions doing the least possible. He became arrogant and aggressive. He would justify his actions by expressing that to garner a person's respect, one needed to be ruthless in the game of life. No one ever got rich, being Mr. Nice Guy.

As a way of appeasing James's temperament, Christian pondered to his every need, in fear that he might one day lose control and do something senseless. So, when the news broke about the death of James' parents, and the suspicious circumstances, Christian had a gut feeling that James had something to do with it. The idea was too ludicrous even to contemplate; how could he murder his parents, especially for money, but worst of all, Christian could not shake the feeling that he was a disloyal friend by harbouring such thoughts, what kind of a friend would have such depraved opinions about his so-called compadre?

As such, Christian decided to let it go and never bring it up again, but in dismissing his feelings, a lingering doubt would always dwell somewhere deep down, stored away like old books, down in the attic, that could tell a story of the past.

I stood up, pacing from one end of the room to the other.

I had heard enough, and this was too much, it was clear that James's past had made an impression on the man he had grown to be. The beast that had been stirring in him his whole life had awoken and caused havoc on the inhabitants in his life.

All these revelations were doing nothing to help my case. I needed to act. I quickly told my story to Christian. I said it as though I was retelling a story of someone else's life, the disturbing facts that now surfaced, spilling as the music stopped, so that my voice could be heard.

It all made sense now, the pieces of the puzzle that were once lost in flood, soon swept back by an immense wave that threatened to drown us in a sea of secrets. It was all too much. I now wanted to be alone, to compartmentalise my thoughts and process the events of the day.

Nausea from my pregnancy was coming on strong, fuelled by the horridness of knowing that I had let such a monster impregnate me.

I asked Christian if he could help me with my plan, or perhaps talk to James and beg him to confess. James might listen to Christian, given that they had so much history. I pleaded with Christian; this was my one shot; Christian could record the whole thing on tape. It wouldn't be as precarious if he got caught in the act, as at least, he could defend himself better than I ever could.

After some thought, he agreed to execute the plan the very next day. I left their house with some hope that this could all soon be over.

If the plan worked, I could clear my name and put this whole chapter of my life to bed.

I received a telephone call from my lawyer the next day with some terrible news.

The prosecution had gained access to the home I once shared with James and had gone there the night before.

My lawyer had been trying to reach me, but I had switched off my phone while I was at Amanda's, so they had not been able to contact me. The prosecution had found some spots of blood on the inside of the keyhole to the front door.

It was Amanda's blood.

Given that I was the only suspect, and I had been charged, this was even more damning evidence against me. As if it couldn't get any worse. My lawyer wanted to prepare me now for the worst-case scenario, should even more evidence come to light. I tried to tell him about my plan to get James to confess on tape but thought it best to wait until at least Christian had completed the job. I couldn't lose hope now.

I was asked to go to his office for a debriefing to try to

find a more persuading defence to be used. This wasn't good, even my lawyer was starting to fray, I was now in real trouble, and most of all, Christian was now my only hope.

I ended the call and jumped into bed. I wanted to sleep my way out of hell, but something on the television caught my eye. I picked up the remote control and turned up the volume.

"This just in, a twisted relationship gone awry, perhaps a jealous wife, who knows, but this has left one person dead and a hot murder trial."

The case had now gone public. The screen switched to a picture of me, with the heading – `Main suspect on trial.`

I screamed and dropped the remote control. It hit the floor hard and cracked. The screen then changed back to the report, where there was a red-headed lady, mid-fifties, dressed in a navy-blue pinstriped suit. She was surrounded by reporters and a few other official-looking men in black suits. She described the particulars of a murder case, involving the callous murder of a 'Maria Rodrigues,' a twenty-something-year-old woman in the prime of her life.

Everything about the news report seemed so surreal, as though they were talking about someone else. I felt so far removed from it all; how could a simple girl such as myself, end up on the news, with my face plastered across the screen in such a tasteless way.

It wasn't even a flattering picture, and it painted an evil story. Someone in the paparazzi had dug out an old social media picture of me on a drunken night out, with red wine spilled all over my silk top and my hair smeared back, with what could only be described as an excessive amount of perspiration.

The woman on the screen described how the body was dumped in the river, as well as the marks that were found -

"... a heinous crime with one prime suspect, and a long-awaited trial that is now set to start next week."

I assumed that she must have been the pro-bono lawyer that Maria's family had hired to prosecute me. I was in shock. I didn't think that this could or should be televised.

What happened to innocent until proven guilty? Surely there was now no way I would have a fair trial, not with the media painting such a horrid picture of me. I figured the prosecution must have thought that by going public, they could potentially influence the jury to convict quickly, given that there was now a substantial amount of evidence.

They had a witness placing me with the victim on the night of her reported disappearance. They had my DNA on the body, and most of all, they had the victims' blood at my house.

To the prosecution, this was a clear-cut case of jealousy and perhaps a murderous love triangle. The pro-bono lawyer on the screen looked confident. She expressed her confidence by stating that she was satisfied she could secure a conviction. Of all the things that shocked me the most, was having the screen cut to James.

He was stood by his car, a smug look on his face. A handful of reporters were questioning him. They were scrambling to get a statement from the estranged husband of a murder suspect.

"I love my wife dearly, and if she did do this, well..." He snorted. *"Look, innocent until proven guilty right? And I am sure justice will be served. Besides, she's quite hot-headed, I give you that, but murder? I can't say for sure, but I just don't think she would ever be capable. My sweet Fiona, there is no way, I have nothing else to say, please just leave me in peace to deal with this."*

He had said my name on television, and worst of all, he had sold me to the devil by making such a ridiculous statement.

I was enraged; I wasn't a murderer on any level, but at that moment, as the rage tore its way through me, firing up my nerves, bludgeoning my eyeballs in a sea of lava flamed tears-I wanted to kill him.

If I was going to go down for a murder that I didn't commit, I might as well make the most of it and kill the person who had done this to me. My phone suddenly rang; it was Christian.

"Have you seen the news? What the heck, he's screwed you, Fiona. I am on my way over to his place now. I am going to get this sonofabitch for you, I tell you, this guy is twisted." I was silent, as Christian empathised with me.

He seemed genuinely upset for me and promised that he would try to do everything in his power to help me. I told him about the blood that they had found at the house-there was no hope, there was too much evidence now, and James would not willingly confess, so unless the confession ploy worked, I was most likely going to jail, and for a very long time indeed.

As soon as I mentioned the word, 'jail,' I felt a knot in my stomach, followed by a sudden twinge deep inside. I looked down, and my feet were completely soaked. The stress of the last few days had cascaded on top of me, and my waters had suddenly broken. I was going into labor, almost ten weeks earlier than my expected due date.

I screamed down the receiver, the shock and realisation that now, nothing was in my control, not even childbirth. The twinge started to come in waves, as though a screw-driver was being pushed through my muscle fibres. I was in pure anguish, and knowing that I was alone, made the pain even more magnified. I could not endure. I touched between my legs, and it was sticky with blood.

I was losing the baby. My world was crumbling at a full one hundred miles per second, and I was powerless to stop

it, powerless to help myself to safety. I could hear Christian's voice on the phone, which had now dropped to the
ground. He was shouting something inaudible. I picked up
the phone and tried my hardest to keep composed enough
to give him the full address to the shelter.

The plan for getting the confession would have to wait
until later. I wobbled over to the bedroom door and
screamed out for one of the women at the shelter, but no
one came to my aid. Panic had now set in; would I be
having the baby alone, on the dusty flea-infested floor to a
dilapidated house, which was now covered in amniotic
fluid, blood, and mucus.

I wasn't ready to have this baby, not when the trial was
about to start. All this stress was killing my baby. I couldn't
lose my freedom and my child, all in one full sweep.

I paced up and down, trying to mimic the Lamaze
pregnancy technics I had learned from watching online
pregnancy videos. I hadn't had time to go to any Antenatal
classes, so all my birth and parenting training had been
done via you-tube and videos I had watched online.

I suddenly heard a knock on the door, I looked up, and
it was Christian and Amanda.

They had sped over so quickly to the shelter, and it was
a good time too, as that was the last thing I could remember, as I fainted just as they walked in.

Chapter 27

My vision was hazy, as I drifted in and out of a mighty slumber.

I could just about make out the shapes of people leaning over me, almost alien-like and sluggish in their demeanour. The fluorescent lights, in my distorted state, dimmed and then ignited to create an angelic halo over the tops of their heads.

Near my paralysed form, a buzzing sound, much like a high-pitched pulsing beep, pierced through my ears, at an indeterminate pace, adding to my light-headedness. The product of a cocktail of anaesthesia and morphine which by now, had steadily made its way through my body, in an eclectic fashion, dripped into my veins, pushing me further into a fog of blissful unawareness.

I blinked for what seemed like a thousand blinks, and then, the cocktail of cures, sank further into my bloodstream, the next time I woke up, twelve hours had passed.

I jumped up, confused as to where I was, and how long I had been unconscious. I lowered the palm of my hand, to touch the place where my bump had once been, but it felt different, smaller.

I cried out, the realisation that something was not right. "What happened to my baby!?"

A nurse came running in, holding an IV in one hand, and a syringe in the other. I was screaming, unaware as to what was going on.

She quickly injected me with whatever sweet nectar was inside the syringe, and within a few minutes, I was calm. After this, a young female doctor walked into the room and held my hand and asked how I was.

To save both my life and that of my baby, they had been forced to deliver the baby by emergency caesarean. The doctor explained that there had been a placental abruption, a condition in which the placenta starts to come away too early from the inside of the womb wall, combined with pre-eclampsia, a state of extremely high blood pressure.

She explained that had Christian and Amanda not turned up at the time they did, myself and the baby would have been lost.

I lay still, numb to what was being said, always slightly delicious from the morphine and whatever else they had pumped into me. I was full of joy for having not lost my child, but at the same time, a great melancholy overcame me, for I had allowed James and his actions to get me to this place.

I was asked if I wanted to call James, but I refused the offer. He did not deserve to be a part of this. Once I was able to sort my life out, I made my mind up that I would file for a divorce immediately, even if I had to do so from a prison cell.

The doctor explained that my baby was in an incubator, and as she was saying this, another nurse wheeled her in for me to see her. I wasn't allowed to touch her, except through special antibacterial glove holes in the incubator. It was torture seeing her so fragile, so tiny and thus unaware of the world and troubles she had been born into.

Christian and Amanda burst into the room, full of smiles, flowers, and candy. They hugged and kissed me and congratulated me.

"Oh, honey, we were so worried. You were in a pool of blood when we walked in, and I swear you would have hit your head, smash, against the ground if Christian hadn't run in to catch you. Oh gosh, it was horrid, so much blood. But look at this little tiny one, so perfect, so adorable. Do you have a name for her?"

Amanda was excited. She wouldn't stop talking and asking questions.

Even though I was drained and did not have the energy to respond to her enthusiastically, I was grateful that she was there, a female support network that I needed at such a time.

I didn't have a name yet. I had always dreamed that James and I would pick one together, so this was just another low blow for which he had been the chief architect.

To the outside world, this picture looked ordinary enough; a new-born baby, excited visitors, an exhausted mother and a room full of flowers and superfluities. But on the inside, we all were very much aware of the impending doom that was awaiting me, just a few days away.

Christian and Amanda had been able to get a hold of my family, as coincidentally, my mother had been ringing my cell phone non-stop, once she had seen the news report about the murder case, which Harry had found while browsing the internet.

Amanda had grabbed the phone from my bag and told

my mother I was being rushed to the hospital and that the baby was coming. My parents, in their hysteria, had booked the next available flight and were already on their way to the hospital.

Ironically, they were due to fly into Chicago in a few days for the start of the trial.

———

After all the pleasantries had been exhausted from Amanda and Christian, we reverted quietly into a trance-like state, me on the bed, still in quite some pain from the surgery, and Amanda and Christian, on chairs next to me.

We stayed fixated by my baby, who was hooked to a kaleidoscope of beautifully coloured wires, stemming from every orifice, keeping her alive and breathing.

She was almost motionless, except for the steady ascending and descending motion of her beautiful beating heart, moving in a rhythm, not quite like mine, but almost lyrical in its musicality and flutter.

I lay still, already so in love with this child, and as the darkness of the night drew upon us, and it was time for all visitors to leave, I just continued to lay still, gazing upon the child that had been conceived from malice and yet, would bring me so much purpose.

———

The next day, at about mid-afternoon, my mother and father finally made it to my bedside.

They were thrilled to see that even though premature, my little creation was still perfected formed. They had also called my lawyer to tell him about the birth.

Given that I was still in hospital and would be in there for a couple more days, they needed to get the judge's approval to move the start of the trial to the following week, thereby delaying it by seven days, to allow me to recuperate and be fit for trial. My lawyer had already made a statement to the press to dispel any false stories about the previous news report. He also shared information as to the request to move the trial.

I was in the clear, for now. I could rest and have some time with my baby until my wounds had healed, and I regained my strength.

As soon as the news story broke about my admission to hospital for the birth, James had rung me non-stop. He wanted to play the concerned husband, but I could not allow this. There was still the restraining order, so he wasn't allowed to come and visit us in the hospital.

His incessant calling enraged me. He had tried to kill the baby before, so why was he pretending to care for her now? My parents comforted me when hysteria and sadness would come in waves.

I was a ball of emotion and hormones. I would cry for hours on end, and every time I looked at my baby, so fragile, I would get angry.

The only way I knew how to relieve my anger was to cry and scream and shout.

After the third day, I could go home, but without my baby. She would be in the hospital for another two months. Christian and Amanda invited my parents and me to stay at their house.

They could not bear the thought of me going back to the women's shelter and given that they had a huge house, it made sense for us to stay with them.

My parents became my everything.

They would nurse me, bathe me, and feed me, until day six, when I could start to walk around the house without too much pain. They would drive me to the hospital in Christian's car, to visit my baby and then watch me fall apart again, when I had to say goodbye.

By day seven, I was getting better, but the rage in me only grew stronger.

To this day, I still cannot fully remember how I got to James's house, whether I drove, I hitched a ride or called a cab. Nevertheless, in a blind fury, I picked up a knife and a hammer, from Christians toolbox, and with full determination and malice, I found myself stood in front of James in his living room.

I was still dressed in my dressing gown and bedroom slippers, cradling my stomach where the doctors had made the incision. James was sat on the sofa, watching the news when he turned around and saw me. He jumped up out of his seat to face me.

"What da heck Fiona, have you lost your mind? What are you doing here dressed like that, and what the heck do you intend to do with that?"

He was referring to the knife in my hand, and the hammer in my pocket. I moved in closer to him, almost poised for battle, ready to pounce.

I don't know exactly what was going through my head. He yelled, asking me to back off.

"Seriously, you're going to hurt someone with that thing. What has gotten into you? Fiona, damn it, woman. Put the bloody knife down. Let's talk. You are not thinking straight."

He might have been right, I wasn't thinking straight, but for every fibre in me, I knew that this man had to pay.

"You sonofabitch. Confess. You have stolen my life from me. Confess James. I don't even care, don't confess. You're a dead man anyway."

I took a swing at him, which missed him by only a few millimetres. His eyes widened. He didn't think I had it in me. I took another swing; this time, it sliced him across the face. He touched his cheek as the blood spilled out onto his shirt and then to the floor.

"You bitch" He cried out. "You cut me, are you bloody serious. Put that bloody knife away, before I end up doing something to you."

I was the one with the knife, and yet he was threatening me.

"James, I have let you get away with too much. You said you would confess; you said you wouldn't let me risk jail. You said you loved me and would always protect me. Instead, you beat me, black and blue. Instead, you raped me. I was your prize, and yet you treated me like your whore. I took a vow, we took vows, and yet you broke every one of them. You lied, you cheated, and you almost killed our baby. I cannot let you get away with it anymore. This world will be better off without you. If I am to go to prison, then you cannot live. I cannot leave my baby with a man like you as a father."

I grabbed the hammer, and with my left hand, I swung. It hit him on the shoulder. Blood streamed out of him.

He screamed out, full of rage, and before I had time to think, he ran full pelt towards me and pushed me to the ground. I tried to scream, but he had his hands around my mouth. I was in excruciating pain, as his whole weight crushed me, putting pressure on my incisions.

I still had the knife in my hand, but it was slipping, as I tried to breathe. He leaned forward and grabbed it out of my hand and stood up.

"Now, you see what you have done. What am I going to do with you now? Maria tried this shit on me, and see where that got her? Huh? Down the bloody lake. That's where you are going to end up, you whore. In the lake, just like her.

He bent down and pulled me up and grabbed me by the throat. He dug the knife into my side, not quite piercing the skin, but with full intent.

"You're a dead woman, Fiona, you tried to kill me? Really? You are dead!"

Suddenly I could hear sirens in the distance. Had someone called the police? He spun me around and put his arm around my throat.

"What the heck is that? Did you call the cops? Are you kidding me? You came here to kill me, and you called the cops? His eyes were red with rage, as he spoke.

I yelled out. "No, it wasn't me. Let go of me you monster, let go."

The door immediately swung wide open, and five armed federal agents came rushing in.

"Let her go, sir." They walked cautiously towards us. "Put the knife down."

James backed away slowly. He could see that he was surrounded but was confused as to what was happening. He released me, and immediately two agents grabbed and pushed him to the ground.

They placed handcuffs on him. He didn't resist.

"I think there is some confusion here guys, she attacked me, and she came here. Arrest her!"

He was yelling at the agents.

"Mr James Foyler, you are under arrest for the murder of Miss Maria Gonzalez. You have the right to remain silent. Anything you say can and will be used against you in a court of law. You have the right to an attorney. If you cannot afford an attorney, one will be provided for you."

They read him the Miranda rights and then carted him off to the police car outside. I stood in shock, unsure as to what was happening.

One of the agents walked over to me. 'Miss, are you ok? It looks like you dodged a bullet there. Do you need medical assistance? We will need a statement at some point, ma'am…"

I nodded that I was ok, but he rambled on about something else, which in the commotion of it, I was barely able to take a word in.

I wanted to ask him who had called the police, but I think I was still in shock. Instead, I waved him away and bent down and sat on the ground and watched as the officers left the house, just as quickly as they had arrived.

Within a few seconds, it was just me, sat in the middle of the living room, clutching my stomach, trying hard to comprehend the events that had just taken place, while trying to soothe myself of all the pain that was shooting through my body.

I sat there for what must have been a few hours until my parents showed up. The police had called my lawyer to give him an update, and with that, they were able to locate where I was.

When they walked into the house and saw me, sat on the floor, cradling myself, they ran to me, and my father picked me off the ground and kissed and hugged me. My mother was beside him, tears of joy, streaming down her face.

My father carried me into the car, and as we drove home, they told me about the new developments in the case.

Chapter 28

I had come so close to committing an act of revenge, an act so irreversible, that it would tarnish me for eternity.

I had conspired to commit murder, to take another person's life. I had wandered in the wilderness of my misdirection, to a depth, so deep and concaved, that it almost drove me to become the same monster that had enslaved me and held me captive for so long.

I never in my life thought I would ever be capable as to try to hurt someone, let alone go with the intent to kill. The madness of James and his affliction has changed me irreversibly into someone I did not recognise, but the story of my life was never meant to end in despair.

Timing is everything, and a moment, a flash, a blink in time, had now reset my misdirection and saved me from total and utter damnation.

Considering all the media attention that the case had suddenly started to receive, it turned out that there was a vital witness in the case, one who had not yet stepped forward.

On the night of the murder, a teenager had been

driving past when he heard the shouting coming from our house.

Thinking it was a fight, he decided to hide in a bush and film the incident on his cell phone to later upload it on to a social media platform, for the comedy factor.

Except this was no comedy.

He had unwittingly filmed a murder on his phone. He hadn't known what to do with it, and in a panic had locked the phone in his bedroom, hoping that the whole thing would blow under; but as the media got hold of the case, and it came to light that a woman might be convicted, the teenager realised that it was the same case that he had filmed on his cell phone.

In a desperate attempt to do right, he anonymously left the phone at a police precinct, hoping someone would find the phone and match the contents of the video to the night of the murder.

It worked, and the day I went over to James's place to attack him, the police found the tape, and without a morsel of doubt, it was clear who the murderer was.

James was caught on tape, hitting Maria continuously in the doorway, followed by a struggle as he pushed her into the house.

A few minutes later, he was seen coming out of the house, carrying out what would appear to be a body bag, dripping with blood, and blood on his hands. As he opened the door, I could be seen lying on the floor, unconscious.

It was clear who must have committed the murder. I was in the clear.

In those few days, there was so much media frenzy.

Headlines blurted out all over the internet, broadsheets, and magazines.

The media loved the story.

It signalled the incompetence of the justice system at having almost convicted the wrong person, albeit that the trial had not set started.

The media saw this as a way of directing their preconceived motions, that the federal system did not care about justice- they just wanted a high conviction rate, and lawyers would do all they could to point fingers.

I tried not to get too entrenched in all the media fury. I had a new role to play, and that was the part of a mother.

I visited my baby daily, and by the end of the two months, she could go home. I was still living with Amanda and Christian at this point as I could not face going back to James's house.

My parents had returned to London after we christened my baby. Before they departed, we all sat in a room together and went through different names, but it was Christian who hit the nail on the coffin and came up with the beautiful name- Faith.

Through much adversity and hopelessness, we had kept positive, we had hoped for the best, we had Faith. So, in the same church where I had taken my vows to a dutiful and faithful wife, we had christened my child, Faith McCullum, opting to erase of links with the Foyler legacy.

Amanda and Christian were chosen as Godparents, much to Sarah and Harry's slight irritation, but as they were not able to fly out at such short notice, it made sense that it was Amanda and Christian.

Besides, I wanted little Faith to have two sets of Godparents, so it made sense that she would have Amanda and Christian in America, and then by default, Harry and Sarah would be her British Godparents.

———

James's trial was wrapped up very quickly, as the evidence was incontrovertible.

The jury came back with a unanimous verdict only after ten minutes of deliberating.

In the closing statement to the trial, the judge labeled James as a *'callous, vindictive degenerate,'* who was willing to allow his wife to stand trial for a murder which he had committed in cold blood.

The judge expressed that it was a pure act of lunacy, and if he had the power, he would see to it that James be executed. James was convicted of one count of second-degree murder and one count of perverting the course of justice and was sentenced to nineteen years in federal prison-to be eligible for parole, only after twelve years served.

Of course, he would never serve this. He turned out to be a man of his word after all, and after five years in prison, he committed suicide, after repeated reports of inmate violence and rape against him.

I felt a twinge of sadness when I received the news of his death.

Faith had never gotten to meet her father, and we barely ever told her stories of him, as I wanted to forget the hurt he put me through, he had hurt me, and so many others.

Everyone is free to choose, but no one is free from the consequences of their choice. He would forever remain a part of our lives, as his legacy would carry on if Faith was alive to keep it burning. Still, it wasn't to burn brightly but only retain a faint dimmer, to remind us that nothing in life is perfect, and that truth in its integrity, is not what it seems, but what it is.

Julia, my ex-colleague, was also sentenced to eighteen months in prison for giving a false alibi.

She served for seven months.

After James's sentencing, I immediately filed for a divorce.

James did not protest and was accommodating.

Under the laws of the state, I was entitled to half of everything James owned, and as his assets were not frozen, I ended up with a divorce settlement of a staggering, twelve million dollars, and the deed to the house we once shared, which I hired a team, to sell it off quickly.

The settlement was more than enough to see to it that Faith nor I would ever want for anything again.

On some level, he had paid his dues, but no amount of money could pay for the scars he had laid on me. I sent a cheque to Maria's family for a sum of two million dollars, as a small gesture of goodwill. I knew it wouldn't bring their daughter back, but I felt partly guilty for her death, and it was just my way of trying to ease their burden and let them know that I had acknowledged their plight and their suffering.

I received a letter from Maria's mother a few weeks after, which read -

> "No money can take away the pain of the death of a child, you should know- But I hear you, and I accept. You cannot be held accountable for the villain that your husband was. Next time open your eyes to what is in front of you. Don't play the victim, wake up to life, wake up to the truth. Gracias- Felicia Gonzalez"

A year after James was sent to prison, I wrote to him, what would be my final word and testament to him and our failed marriage.

Dear James,

It torments me to write to you after so much time. Much like you, I too have been imprisoned, not by any walls that could shackle me, but by my cowardliness, not to have been able to stand up for myself. I was a victim of your sickness. My memory of you is scarred by the torments and the visions I endure each night, as I close my eyes. I am angry that I ever loved you, and that deep down, some part of me perhaps, on some level still loves you, even after everything-but my hate for you, surpasses any love that I could ever feel now. You tried to break me, but I'm stronger now.

"All those women, Maria, her death, I still cannot come to terms with it all. But from tragedy, something good did happen, my sweet daughter, Faith. I don't have much else to say, but this will be the only letter I ever write to you, as I now erase you from my life, so that I can be happy. James, you brought love to my life in a twisted way, and then took it away. Still, I thank you nonetheless, as I wanted to find myself, and, because of you, I realise that I already knew who I was, I just needed something to remind me how great I already had it- before you.

Fiona.

After tying up all loose ends, I eventually returned home to England, after fourteen months from the date of my acquittal and I bought a three-bed house in Greenwich, London, just by the riverside.

I was a free woman, to do as I pleased, and my whole life still ahead of me. James had been a short but significant chapter in my life, he had been a lesson in life, and with his demise, something anew and wonderful could flourish from all the absurdity and anguish. I couldn't stay in Chicago, for after the trial was done and dusted, his infamy remained, and my face was still all over the local tabloids.

If I wanted to forget the whole debacle, to live freely, in a place where my child could grow up freely without having to face the sins of her father, then I would have to return home, to England, a haven, with the people I left, to welcome me back with open arms.

———

By the time I returned to England, Sarah was pregnant with her third child, she turned out to be a real homemaker, just as she had wanted. Her husband was reaching all corners of the globe with his work and was on the way to becoming a huge success.

I also met an amazing man, Phillip DuMont, ironically, while out browsing at a bookstore in Soho; but this time, I wasn't looking at the self-help books, more so, on books on travel and adventure.

Phillip was a tall, attractive, French, semi-wealthy businessman. He was a philanthropist at heart with an admiring humanitarian world view. He wanted to change the world and like many before him, wanted to end world poverty.

He believed that no child should go to bed hungry. I had never met a kinder and more compassionate soul. We dated, and he proposed after only five months. I told him about my past, and this just brought us closer.

I fell in love with him deeply, and a year later, by the time I was ready to walk down the aisle, I was already three months pregnant. My daughter, Faith, had just started to come into her own. She was walking and talking and would provide us with countless hours of entertainment.

Phillip adored her, and during dinner, one night had asked if he could adopt her after the wedding, a way of making our little family complete. I, overjoyed by this, agreed wholeheartedly and straight after the wedding, once all the formalities were completed, Faith was to become his daughter legally, and we could finally be able to put the past to bed and close the chapter on James, for good.

Christian and Amanda had been to visit me several times after I moved back to England, and Christian, Phillip, and Harry had become quite attached.

They became good friends and would often take trips abroad together. I loved spending girlie times with Sarah and Amanda, and perhaps it helped that Amanda was spending time amongst pregnant women because soon after this, she also fell pregnant.

It was as though the universe was clicking her fingers and cleaning up the mess that had occurred in the past.

There we were, on my wedding day, a second attempt at making it right. The ceremony was held in the summer, at a small decorated barn, overlooking a beautiful lake in the countryside.

We were blessed with beautiful weather, as we basked in the warmth of the summer's sun. There were only twenty guests in all, a small but intimate affair. I wore a simple cream silk gown that I had picked up at a department store in London, quite the contrast from my first wedding gown.

It was exquisite in its simplicity, and it made me glow, as pure happiness radiated from the top of my head to the tips of my toes. I walked down the aisle with my father, hand in hand, while Sarah and Amanda, my two pregnant bridesmaids, walked behind me, in a symphony, dressed in simple light peach gowns.

As we approached the alter, I couldn't help but appreciate how far I had come. There I was, stood next to Phillip, a dashing six-foot-three hunk of a man that was to be my husband.

On the other side of Phillip, stood Christian and Harry, his best men. I looked over at my father and saw that he had tears of joy in his eyes. My mother also looked over-joyed. This was all she had hoped for, a happy ending to all the calamity that we had endured.

After I had said my vows, this time, in my own words, my father leaned over and whispered how proud he was to be stood next to me.

This time, it felt different though, there were no falsities, no pretensions, and affectations, just love in its uncomplicated effortlessness.

This time, with the past truly behind me, it just felt right.

Epilogue

I was once beaten, I was once shy,
    And so I endured, and I withstood.
  Today I reclaim but I do indeed lament,
  For I have lived a life of sorrow, a life of regret, but I have also lived a life of joy.
  Each part of me once ripped to pieces, now makes me whole.
  I once breathed you in, and then exhaled the putrid dust of your flesh,
  Each morsel of me which you stole, now all returned home to nest.
  Today, I smiled as I woke,
  For today marked a new beginning, where once all I knew, was the end.

Acknowledgments

Writing a full-length novel was something that I never thought I could accomplish, but here it is, in black and white. I am very proud to have something that I can forever own, and that will remain for all of time.

This has been my lifelong passion, and seeing my name in print is such a remarkable feeling. There have been ups and downs and times of doubt, but through perseverance, my dream has finally become a reality. One real challenge through all of this was finding the time to write whilst juggling a full-time career, getting married and planning for the future, but it has been a truly remarkable experience, one that I would never change.

I would like to thank all those who contributed to inspiring me to keep on writing. A very special thanks to my husband, Douglas. D, for putting up with my incessant rants about the book and spending a large portion of our vacation time having to put up with me either writing or editing.

Thank you.

I am immensely grateful to the friend who gave me the idea for the initial concept of the book. Only through hearing some of her stories, was I able to create the framework of the book which focused on domestic violence. Many parts of the book were then fictionalized for a dramatic effect, but it was her initial story that led me to write this book- so a big thank you. I do hope you get to read this. You know who you are- R.H.

Thank you to Pippa. B, a dear friend, who was involved in the editing of the initial first few chapters and who gave me the confidence to continue writing the rest of the book. Your input was invaluable.

Thank you to my parents, for all they have done for me. Only through their sacrifices have I become the woman I am today, someone who loves to write and who sees possibility in all things.

Thank you Emily McDowell for allowing me to use your "Finding yourself quote" at the start of the book. The quote completely resonated with me and inspired me in so many ways.

And finally, a warm thanks to my publishing team at BNBS for believing in the book and working with me all the way to getting it to print, it was a long journey, but we got there in the end. I hope we get to work on many more books together.

About the Author

Lynda Ihenacho is an emerging writer of both fiction and Poetry. She has a degree in Business studies at the University of Roehampton, United Kingdom, and although coming from a finance background, with a full time career as a Treasurer, her main passions lie in writing and traveling.

She has lived in several cities of the world, from Lagos, to London, to Dubai in the United Arab Emirates, where she currently lives with her husband, son and their beloved and crazy Cocker Spaniel, Chloe.

A pure romantic at heart, she started her writing at the young age of thirteen, discovering her passion through poetry, where she could express herself through her writing on difficult and even sometimes personal matters of the heart.

Prior to writing her debut novel, most of her work could be found on her blog and website, where she showcased some of her poetry pieces and travel blogging. You can find out more about this on her website www. inmyquarter.com

Today, she is building a family, working on her next book and planning for her next big destination-maybe a Camper-van trip around Europe, or the simple life back home in the United Kingdom, who knows, its all about the adventure!

Printed in Great Britain
by Amazon

83420771R00169